Praise for the novels of

"Charish Reid is definitely an author to watch."
—*Love in Panels*

"Reid's latest romance is a perfectly shaken cocktail of grumpy and sunshine characters, delicious banter, and heat. Suggest to readers looking for contemporary romances that bring humor and heart to the happily-ever-afters of hardworking characters."
—*Library Journal* on *Mickey Chambers Shakes It Up*

"Reid skillfully navigates Diego's grief for his wife and guilt over finding new love and balances these heavier themes with Mickey's infectious lightheartedness. The resulting slow burning will-they, won't-they romance is sure to win fans."
—*Publishers Weekly* on *Mickey Chambers Shakes It Up*

"Like my favorite cocktails, Reid's witty & humorous take on grumpy sunshine is equal parts smooth and refreshing, with a healthy punch of spice—it's masterful and delicious."
—Taj McCoy, author of *Zora Books Her Happy Ever After*, on *Mickey Chambers Shakes It Up*

"My heart is happy after reading this book. Charish Reid writes character you can't help but fall in love with and stories you can't put down. *Mickey Chambers Shakes It Up* is funny and sexy with an emotional depth that packs a delicious punch. Consider this book the perfect cocktail—flavorful, comforting, and a lot of fun to consume."
—Denise Williams, author of *How to Fail at Flirting*, on *Mickey Chambers Shakes It Up*

"Readers will adore this addictive romance."
—*Publishers Weekly*, starred review, on *Hearts on Hold*

Also by Charish Reid

Canary Street Press

Mickey Chambers Shakes It Up

Carina Press

Hearts on Hold
The Write Escape

For additional books by Charish Reid,
visit her website, charishreid.com.

CHARISH REID

JEWEL ME TWICE

CANARY STREET PRESS

CANARY STREET PRESS™

Recycling programs for this product may not exist in your area.

ISBN-13: 978-1-335-00946-3

Jewel Me Twice

Canary Street Press
22 Adelaide St. West, 41st Floor
Toronto, Ontario M5H 4E3, Canada
CanaryStPress.com

Printed in U.S.A.

Black girls deserve diamonds.
We deserve the world, the sun and every possibility in between.
I don't know about you, but I'm ready to take them all.

1

I should be stealing something shiny...

But instead of doing what she loved, Celeste St. Pierre was busy running an antique furniture store in Manhattan. She glanced from the eighteenth-century Austrian grandfather clock to her assistant, Beatrice Hill, trying to catch the young woman's eye. They were hoping to close in the next five minutes, but two shoppers still perused the Chippendale bookshelves.

From what Celeste gathered, a husband and wife. He looked deeply uninterested in the shopping trip while she went on and on about the decorative wood carvings. Both appeared wealthy enough to afford several Chippendale pieces, so Celeste didn't want to shove them out the door too quickly.

"Well, if you like it so much, just go for it," the husband said, testily. His white mustache gave an agitated twitch as he surveyed the rest of the store. He, too, checked the time.

His wife could not be rushed into a decision. She pulled a pair of reading glasses from her black Chanel bag and peered at the shelves' description. "I just wonder if it will fit the upstairs study..."

Celeste had to intervene. If she couldn't get these customers moving, she and Beatrice wouldn't have enough time to go downstairs to their command center and prep for this evening's job. One way or another, she planned on attending Victor Sanderson's emerald reveal party. And while people were distracted by the treasure he discovered in the jungles of Colombia, she'd be in his study stealing a rare kokoshnik tiara.

"I see you're very interested in our Chippendale piece," she said, leaving the front counter. "You have a good eye."

The wife smiled brightly, stepping away from her husband. "My grandmother had something similar. A beautiful mahogany shelf that she used in her library. I used to spend hours in there reading and writing."

Celeste softened as she listened to the older woman. "So, you're already familiar with the style. I acquired this piece from Westland London about two years ago and you're the first person who's given it the attention it deserves."

The woman beamed, proud to know she had taste. "Is this also mahogany?"

"I'm afraid this is made from walnut. It's just as sturdy, though, and it has the same rococo embellishments you'd normally find of the time. Dare I say the upkeep is slightly easier."

"Do you have cleaning instructions?" the woman asked. "I'd hate to ruin something so lovely with carelessness."

"Of course," Celeste said with a smile. "My associate, Beatrice, can help you with those details, plus measurements and delivery. We can schedule a time to work with you at your earliest convenience."

"Agnes, if we don't leave now, we'll be late for the show," her husband interrupted.

"Hold your horses," Agnes said. When she turned back to Celeste, she rolled her eyes. "After forty-seven years, he should know better than to rush me."

"Do what you want. I'll be outside," her husband groused as he moved toward the exit.

Agnes waved her hand dismissively. "I'll take the shelf, my dear. Would you like me to pay now or after we talk details?"

At the sound of payment, Beatrice immediately got to typing. She would search for the certificate of authenticity and the necessary paperwork for measurements and delivery consultation.

It never ceased to amaze Celeste how quickly rich people spent money on a whim. The bookshelves were at least seventy thousand dollars, and Agnes was ready to pick it up because of nostalgia.

They got her squared away, made a follow-up appointment for a future delivery and sent her on her way faster than Celeste thought was possible. Once her customers were out the door, Beatrice quickly ran through the store and flipped the sign and locked the door.

"Are you ready?" she asked, dimming the showroom lights.

"Been ready," Celeste replied with a sigh. "Walk me through the plan again."

Together, they disappeared into the back office, closing another door behind them. The command center was safely hidden in the basement of their business. To reach it, Celeste needed to slide back a shelving unit in her office to reveal a secret stairwell.

As they jogged downstairs, Beatrice recited the plot for tonight's festivities. "The invitation list is about thirty-six associates. I've been surveilling the building and no new cameras have been installed since we delivered there three months ago. Just the elevator and balcony. While people are milling around the living room, dining room and kitchen, you'll need to get to the west wing of the penthouse where his study is."

"Yep," she said, flipping on the fluorescent lights of the basement revealing computers, camera monitors and walls that were lined with weaponry, tools and disguises. In the corner of the large space was a small gym where she kept fit with strength training and yoga. In her line of work, Celeste needed to be flexible enough to get into tight spaces and strong enough to fight her way out of them.

She walked behind a dressing partition and quickly disrobed. Tonight's gown was recently back from the dry cleaners and waiting on her. Beside it, a replica of the crown she planned to steal that evening.

"A Protex safe is located behind the oil painting of a generic hunting scene. I don't know what the four-digit code is, so you need to take your setting powder and brush for fingerprints. Although, I have a feeling it's his birthday," Beatrice said with a chuckle. "I'd bet the rest of my student loan repayment."

Celeste laughed. "I know that's right."

"Switch the real crown with the replica, wipe everything down and get the fuck outta there."

"Not immediately," Celeste said, letting the black silk gown cascade down her body. She adjusted her breasts and checked the height of the slit at her thigh. Scandalously high. "Leaving before Victor has revealed the emerald will look suspicious."

"If you say so…"

"I do. He invited Celeste St. Pierre, the antiquities dealer, not CeCe, the smash 'n grabber. I need to continue mingling with these rich white folks to make up for my six-minute absence from the party just in case the balcony footage catches anything." She stepped out from behind the dressing screen. "How do I look?"

Beatrice spun around in her desk chair. Her dark brown eyes widened until her brows reached her hairline. "Hot. Very hot. Maybe a little too hot?"

Celeste checked herself out in the gym mirrors. Yeah, maybe. But she didn't mind the attention. She grabbed the replica crown and fitted it over her short-cropped curls. "Can you help me with the head wrap?"

"Got it."

She sat down so that Beatrice could hide the crown with a black scarf. Her assistant jerked her head forward and then tugged it back as she wrapped tightly. Celeste hadn't felt this kind of discomfort since she was a little girl, sitting between her Granny Jo's knees, getting a comb yanked through her tender head. She feared that if she moved just a little, Beatrice would also pop her with a comb. "Damn, Bea, do you think it's tight enough? I'm gonna get a headache before I arrive."

"I don't want anything unraveling while you're there."

"You worry too much," Celeste gently chided.

"And you don't worry enough," Beatrice said, tucking the last bit of scarf at the nape of Celeste's neck. "Your car should be here in thirty minutes. Are you ready to go steal something shiny?"

Celeste gazed confidently into the mirror. "Ready, sis."

"We've got three adjuncts who can take on some of the Intro to Earth Sciences."

"How many classes?"

Papers shuffled. "Well, okay, it looks like it's just two."

"Check to see who's worked this semester. We'll distribute based on that."

"Do we know who has a preference? I heard Nicole has something lined up with Pace."

"Eh…put out some feelers. Do we know anything about the others?"

"Magnus? You've worked with Dave. Does he have any other prospects? Magnus?"

Magnus Larsson blinked out of his stupor and looked up at his colleagues. Around the long table, six professors stared at him as though he'd grown a second head. "I'm sorry, what?"

Dr. Robert Harding squinted at him in that weird Bob way he always did. Like his whole face scrunched up and his mouth puckered beneath his bushy beard. "Dave Jessops. Do you know if he *needs* classes for the fall?"

Magnus didn't know Dave from Adam. He only used the same classroom after the guy, but never really talked to him.

He assumed that he was like any other poor adjunct running from one institution to another just to keep up their hours. "I couldn't tell you, Bob. As the department chair, you might have to ask Dave himself?"

Robert squinted so hard that his face seemed to suck itself in.

Magnus looked down at his watch. It was already 5:30 p.m. He absolutely did not have time for this. Victor Sanderson was throwing a party tonight and Magnus had every intention to steal a Romanov crown hidden in the man's penthouse. Through whispering back channels, Magnus had monitored the movement of the piece and followed it to Sanderson nearly a year ago. He'd waited for the perfect opportunity to hit the man's home.

The emerald reveal was the perfect opportunity. Or as perfect as it was going to get for a man in his position. He worked alone now. And without a decent crew, Magnus had to stick with small jobs with small payouts. *This* job was supposed to be different. Reward would outweigh the risk, considering the amount of resources and effort he'd put into it.

This meeting…his colleagues. None of it mattered to Magnus.

Another day, he'd be happy to keep up the front of being a geology professor. But today, he was aching to stretch his legs and run like he had when he was younger.

"You know what, Bob?" he said, standing from his seat. "I've got a prior engagement that I need to see to. If you all will excuse me." He didn't wait on anyone to excuse him. He gathered his leather satchel and backed out of the room with a wave. "Take it easy, guys."

There was a spring in his step as he exited the room and eventually Newton University. When the golden sun hit his face, he perked up. He had about two hours to get back to his condo, change and get a car to a party located on the Upper West Side. There was a safe in Victor Sanderson's penthouse with his name on it. Inside that safe was a royal family crown that he *needed*.

As he crossed the street to the nearest subway station, he couldn't help but remember the crew he used to run with. His crew leader, Dr. Doris Grant, was an art historian with a flair for drama and a wicked sense of humor. She invited him to steal with her team about a decade ago.

Magnus fell back on his contingency plan because he couldn't play well with others. He split from the crew after a job had gone bad. Real bad. Dr. Grant couldn't convince him to stay once he failed in Stockholm. He'd failed to secure the bag and he'd failed to make his partner see reason and come away with him. He had come very close to confessing his feelings to her. But shit fell apart too fast for him to take that final step.

That was about five years ago.

Since then, Magnus learned how to work alone. He studied what jobs he could pull off on weekends and during holiday breaks. But things had slowed down considerably without his old crew. He needed this. He needed to feel alive again. It had been too long…

2

As Celeste took an empty elevator up to the Sanderson penthouse, she fretted with her head wrap and dress. She had to remind herself that all jobs started this way; her stomach would always flutter with excitement, adrenaline or nausea. But once she got to work, her brain took over and told her stomach to hush. It also helped to have Beatrice in her earpiece, listening to every quiet mutter as she picked locks and squeezed her body through tight spaces.

"You'll do well," Beatrice said, reciting the same mantra from the past two years. "You'll steal the fuck out of that crown."

"Thank you," she murmured softly as she stepped out of the elevator and into a brightly lit vestibule.

Time to perform and pilfer pockets.

Men with as much wealth and prestige as Victor Sanderson walked a thin line of either hiding it away in false modesty or displaying it with the same false modesty. The Sanderson fortune was as old as it was hefty. His heirs, and their heirs, would enjoy the same kind of luxury as Victor's robber-baron ancestors had. First, it was steel, then came the newspapers; now who knew what kind of diverse portfolio Sanderson possessed? On the rare occasions when he did display his wealth and prestige, it was a brilliant display of opulence that almost made Celeste forget who she was.

As she crossed the threshold of his home and walked amongst the thirty-or-so people, she reminded herself of her goal. She needed to rub shoulders with those who had supposedly *earned* their fortune, titans of industry and philanthropists who tossed checks to the poor kids from developing nations. Tonight, however, charity was not on anyone's mind.

They were all invited to look at a rock.

The Ring of Fire Emerald, as Victor called it, was discovered by his private excavation team. No doubt, a bunch of mercenaries who intimidated a local mining operation in Colombia. Celeste had very little interest in it but kept her eye on the shrouded display case resting on the main room's grand fireplace. Victor would let the drama build until revealing the stone at 10:00 p.m. Until then, she would pretend to be excited about the hype, mingle with other collectors and sample the sumptuous spread.

"Find Victor and chat with him," said Beatrice through the earpiece.

"Give me a minute," Celeste replied, keeping her face immobile.

"He's thirty paces ahead of you."

"Mmm-hmm."

Celeste quickly swiped a glass of champagne from a passing waiter and pushed herself farther into the throng of partygoers. This was a security nightmare for Victor and a delight for Celeste. She eyed the stairwell that she needed to make her way toward and bit back her smile. Nothing was roped off in this small museum, and people traipsed around the open area as though they belonged.

Of course, the guests had home training; they didn't intend to steal from their host. And Sanderson was among his people. Any whiff of security would dampen the illusion of trust. So the very real Picassos, Chagalls and Matisses hung without concern. These priceless works were meant to be looked at, not talked about. The wealthy shouldn't have to address the obvious.

Celeste took a quick sip of the crisp bubbly and held it in her dry mouth. She wouldn't drink any more for the rest of the evening, but she would hold the glass as she spoke to people. One rule to conning: never become as intoxicated as your mark; only give the appearance of indulging.

As she approached the small clump of guests surrounding Victor Sanderson, she noted two familiar faces. The first was the assistant director of the Museum of Natural History, Kevin Phillips. His barking laughter was loud and crass, making Victor flinch as he looked for a way to exit the conversation. The other person who stood out made Celeste swallow her mouthful of champagne hard.

"Jesus Christ, is that the Commissioner of Police?" Beatrice asked.

Celeste ignored her and trained her face into a serene smile before stepping up to the small group of men. "Mr. Sanderson," she announced, extending her hand past Commissioner Joseph Doyle.

Victor welcomed the distraction immediately. "Dr. St. Pierre," he said with a white-veneer grin. He took her hand and pulled her into the circle. "So good of you to come."

"Thank you for extending an invitation to me," she said with an easy smile. Doyle backed up to make room for her as she took her place beside Victor. "Congratulations on your latest acquisition. I hear you've found quite the gem."

Victor took her proximity as an invitation to rest his hand on her bare back. Celeste relaxed her muscles as she held on to her clutch and fluted glass. "Thank you. Though I'm afraid I cannot take credit for the discovery," he chuckled. "Research members will be here to explain the events."

"How fortunate for us," she murmured into her glass. His hand, once at the center of her back, dropped to just above the small of her back.

"Aren't you going to introduce us, Victor?" asked the assistant director. His glassy eyes roamed over Celeste's body without a shred of subtlety.

"Of course." Victor's hand dropped as he made introductions. "Kevin, this is Dr. Celeste St. Pierre, of St. Pierre Antiquities. I found a mid-eighteenth-century Queen Anne cabinet made of the most exquisite pearl inlay at her store. Celeste, this is Kevin Phillips, of the Museum of Natural History."

Celeste gave Phillips a quick and firm handshake, taking care not to stay in the man's grip longer than necessary. "Lovely to meet you, Mr. Phillips," she said.

"Please call me Kevin," he replied. "Surely, you're too young to be selling antiques. You can't be more than twenty-five!"

She gave a pleasant chuckle, touching her fingers to her neck. "You flatter me..."

"Jesus Christ..." Beatrice sighed.

Part of Celeste's job was navigating these spaces where men were especially cloying. She smiled coquettishly to gain their trust and make them more relaxed, but her internal sigh reflex was always activated when men like Phillips wore wedding rings and flirted shamelessly.

"And perhaps you already know Commissioner of Police, Joseph Doyle?" Victor interrupted.

She turned to the tall, broad man who stared at her with the same intense interest as Phillips. A small smile appeared beneath his thick mustache as his cold blue eyes took her in. "Nice to meet you, Commissioner Doyle."

He gave her one firm pump and a slight nod of his head. "Likewise, ma'am."

Good. A short and sweet introduction to law enforcement was just what Celeste needed. She knew that Beatrice was holding her breath in the command center. She took another tiny sip of her champagne before turning back to Sanderson. "That reminds me, you should be due for another wood finish waxing. Please call my office so I can send someone by."

"Or you could do it?" Victor said with a bright white smile. "I'm not sure I could trust such a valuable piece to just anyone."

"I can send someone by," she repeated, returning his smile. "Gentlemen, if you'll excuse me." She left before anyone could object and wandered over to the buffet station. She needed a breather before she got to work, and schmoozing with Victor and his pals was a major distraction. Beatrice told her as much.

"Eat one of those giant shrimps and look cool," her assistant said in a low voice.

Celeste looked down at the spread and rolled her eyes. "Easier said than done," she whispered.

"Look at all that waste…" Beatrice admonished. "There's more food here than most families from my neighborhood would see in a month."

"Mmm-hmm." Celeste helped herself to a small plate and immediately stuffed a prawn into her mouth. When she was a kid, and living with her Granny Jo, they were on a fixed income that didn't allow for this kind of food. She remembered a steady diet of rice and beans, some chicken if the sales were well-timed and, for a treat, homemade baked goods. Even though her grandmother provided as best as she could, Celeste was always hungry.

Now that money was no longer a worry, she still found herself hungry.

Her eye was always on the next big prize and tonight would be no different.

Magnus arrived to the party and posted up at the bar, waiting for a suitable time to make his move. He could say what he wanted about Victor Sanderson, but the man knew how to throw a party, and he knew what kind of liquor to serve. Magnus nursed two fingers of Lagavulin while he watched the mingling revelers waiting on the unveiling, eating and drinking their fill.

The penthouse luxury was a far cry from his condo in Astoria, but none of it impressed him too much. When you really got down to it, Sanderson was also a thief. He had just worked within the bounds of what was considered lawful. A descendant of a robber baron was hardly clean.

A flash of black from the corner of his eye caught his attention. A Black woman several yards away, engaged in a conversation, made him take notice. She was the only woman of color in the room, making her very noticeable. With her back to him, she spoke in hushed tones. Her hands were like small birds, fluttering around and never settling at her sides. Magnus was not the only one watching her intently; the men and women who surrounded her were rapt. They smiled and nodded as she spoke, laughing occasionally. Whoever she was, she captivated her audience.

He was tempted to leave his perch and get a closer look, but that would mean engaging with people. Magnus settled with watching from afar. His eyes trailed down her body, starting with her long neck, which was free of jewelry. When she stopped speaking, he noticed as she twisted her neck to listen to the woman beside her. Magnus caught a glimpse of her profile and noted the black-rimmed glasses that covered her face. The low lights of Sanderson's home complemented her brown skin, making it shine like bronze. And so much of that skin was exposed in her backless black gown. Her spine was straight with a natural confidence that affected the tilt of her imperious chin. The rest of her gown began again just above her bottom and hung elegantly to the floor.

Was that her thigh peeking from the slit of her dress? He craned his neck to get a better look and was delighted to discover her graceful leg stretching against the black fabric. Magnus took another drink to extinguish the rising fire in his belly. He was here to steal a crown. He would not let his dick lead him into interactions he wasn't prepared for. But then she laughed. It was a deep, full-bodied chuckle that made her throw her head back and touch her chest with a fluttering hand.

The sound made Magnus's blood run cold.

He could recognize that laugh anywhere. It had been five years since he'd heard it, but he knew those uniquely warm notes that dripped like honey. They fell in a beautiful cadence that struck him directly in the chest, forcing him to grip his glass tighter as he stared on. Celeste St. Pierre. It couldn't be… Yet, he knew better than to go against his memories of her body, her laugh, the way she angled her head when she spoke. The hand gestures made sense now. Only Celeste spoke like that. As if she were constantly conducting surrounding people. The way she had pulled the strings of his heart years ago.

She spoke to the group for a moment longer before she pointed to something in the distance. She excused herself and walked a leisurely path toward a painting that hung near the stairwell. Magnus watched as she admired the Marc Chagall print. She took her time, leaning forward to take a closer inspection. The black turban she wore tilted to the side as she examined the bottom of the print. When she straightened up, she looked over her shoulder at the rest of the partygoers. Magnus froze as her gaze scanned the scene behind her. She didn't make eye contact with him, but he did see her face better. His heart sank when he realized it truly was Celeste.

He let his gaze wander around the space of Victor's living room and saw that Sanderson was engaged in a conversation with an older gentleman in NYPD dress blues. He snuck a covert glance in Celeste's direction while the men stood not but three meters from her. She gave one last look at her surroundings and quietly made her way up the stairs. As far as he could tell, no one noticed her disappearing act but him.

Celeste wasn't here for the free food and drink; she was working. Possibly the same job as he was. Five years ago, when they worked together, they were highly competitive. They tried to one-up each other until they lost focus on the actual prize. It didn't surprise him that they had finally overlapped in jobs. If he had the resources to find out about Sanderson's Romanov crown, Celeste would know about it, too.

In the five minutes he stood there thinking, Celeste had probably done the deed and was on her way out.

There was no security, no noticeable cameras trained on the stairway. These were perfect conditions for a thief like Celeste. He'd worked with her long enough to know how she completed a job. She charmed the pants off anyone she encountered. Her disarming smile and sincere laughter made people flock to her, while he usually stood off to the side and cased the joint. It was his attention to detail that made it possible for them to breach security systems. He found the vulnerable spots and exploited them, while Celeste made the grab. Who was she working with now? What alias was she going by?

He finished his scotch with one last gulp and followed her. After five years of not seeing her, Magnus had to know what trouble she was up to. His curiosity and her lure were too powerful to resist. He moved through the partygoers, trying his best to appear relaxed. He, too, stopped at the Marc Chagall painting and spent a suitable amount of time staring at it. Again, the wealthy people were in a world of their own and he was on the outside. No one would notice his disappearance, either.

As he ascended the darkened stairwell, he took care not to announce his presence with a heavy footfall. He passed the many open doors of the wide hallway before coming upon a closed door. Light shone from the crack at the bottom, letting him know that someone may be inside. Ahead, there was another stairway, leading to another floor. He looked up at the loft and rooms above him and assumed they were only bedrooms.

Magnus was certain he had the correct door but waited before entering. He held his ear to the oak surface and listened for any movement on the other side. There was a small scratching sound. And then a creaking noise.

When he opened the door, he found her.

Her back was to him again as she stood beside a grand dark-stained bookcase that must have spanned the far wall by twelve feet. Magnus's eyes darted around the room, searching for evidence of a break-in, but found nothing disturbed. Celeste was hanging a painting on the far wall, beside a massive oak bookshelf, and apparently missed the sound of him opening the door. Had she lost her edge or had she gotten sloppy?

A thrill shot through his body as he watched her furtive movements. He wondered how he would approach her after five years. What he would say to the woman he came uncomfortably close to loving. Magnus stepped forward and closed the door behind him.

3

As soon as she entered the room and closed the door behind her, Celeste ripped the wrap from her head and flung it around her shoulders.

"Starting the clock," Beatrice said.

"Give me four minutes."

Her assistant sighed in her ear. "I wish I could be in the field with you. I could have been in the hallways keeping an eye on things."

Celeste rolled her eyes as she quickly removed the painting.

This wasn't the first time Beatrice started this conversation. Each time Celeste was confronted with the reality that they couldn't pull off bigger jobs, she had to shut it down. She pulled a compact of loose setting powder from her purse and dipped her brush into it.

"I don't mean any harm, Bea, but you're not old enough to be in the field. It's very dangerous," Celeste whispered, fanning the brush against the digital keypad. Powder settled into the fingerprint smudges of four numbers: 1-3-5-0.

"I'm old enough to correctly assume this Boomer used his birthday for the code," Beatrice muttered. "According to purchase paperwork, he was born on January sixteenth, 1953. I told ya."

Celeste couldn't help but grin at the girl's surly attitude as she tapped out 0-1-5-3. "That's why you're so valuable in my ear."

The safe emitted an electronic beep of confirmation, allowing her to use her headscarf to pull the handle open. Stacks of money, important paperwork, boxes of jewels… She'd skip all of that in favor of the plum-colored velvet bag on the top shelf. She extracted the bag and pulled the kokoshnik crown from its protective sheath.

"Two minutes, forty-seven seconds. You were younger than I was when you first got started."

"That's true," Celeste admitted as she quickly examined the weight of twenty-five drop pearls and 144 diamonds carefully cradled in bands of platinum. It felt like stolen riches all right. Victor Sanderson came by this nineteenth-century piece the same way he got all his other treasures: paying the right people to steal on his behalf.

After she switched the real thing for her replica, she carefully placed the bag back on the top shelf and closed the safe with her scarf. Next, she efficiently wiped down the keypad, erasing any trace of her makeup.

"Get to wrapping," Beatrice said. "You've a minute and sixteen seconds. So, what's the difference?"

"What?" Celeste frowned while holding the tiara in place as she rewrapped her head. It wouldn't look as good as what Beatrice had managed, but no one at the party would notice.

"What's the difference between us?"

"I worked with a team of professionals," she explained.

"Don't you miss it?" the young woman asked. "Wouldn't you rather have a crew to help you?"

"No, ma'am," Celeste said. "Trust me when I say you don't want a smaller cut of the profits. You don't want to keep an eye on all the moving parts of the bigger jobs." She gave her wrap one last pat before picking up the oil painting. "And if one person fucks up, the whole team is up shit's creek without a paddle."

"Fair… Seems a little lonely, though."

She smiled. "I'm not lonely when I have you."

If she could help it, Beatrice would remain safe in the command center and not be swinging from fire escapes like she'd been at twenty-six. Unlike Celeste, the girl still had a family who cared about what happened to her. She was forty-one now, and the days for big jobs were probably long gone. It was time to be sensible.

The soft *snick* of a door closing made Celeste freeze in place.

"Well, this is awkward," said a man's voice. It was deep, barely above a whisper and frighteningly familiar. Jesus Christ, she could practically hear the smirk in his voice as she stood still.

"Wait, who was that?" Beatrice asked, her voice tense.

Celeste closed her eyes as her body chilled and blood roared in her ears. It couldn't be him. Not after all these years; not here. She adjusted the bottom corner of the painting before turning around.

"Up," the man said. His command was abrupt. "Hands where I can see them."

She let out a bitter laugh as she stared straight ahead. "You're a little late, my friend."

The air in the room shifted as the man's footsteps moved quietly against Victor's Turkish rug. Within seconds, she could feel the heat from his body standing directly behind her. After all these years, a dozen tumultuous emotions spiraled through her body. Mostly embarrassment and anger.

"Better late than never," he murmured. His warm breath tickled her ear, sending a shiver down her neck. "What makes you think I wouldn't just take it from you?"

Before she willed her body not to respond to his proximity, the man took it upon himself to run both hands along the sides of her torso. Starting with the sides of her breasts, down her ribs and settling on her hips. Celeste inhaled sharply as one large calloused hand slid down her bare thigh where the slit in her dress left her exposed.

"Who is it?" Beatrice asked, panicking at the helm. "Are you okay?"

"Because you used to play fair," Celeste said in a clear and steady voice.

The hand paused in its brisk pat down. "I used to do a lot of things, Celeste."

She'd had enough of this dance and turned to confront her past. Being face-to-face with the man she left five years ago shouldn't have shaken Celeste to the core, but she was...shook. Magnus Larsson, her former partner and lover, had barely changed during that separation. Forty-four looked good on him. His strong jaw was still clenched, muscles twitching and flexing just below the skin. His eyes were still bluer than icy Baltic waters, still narrowed in that annoying accusatory manner. Only a few small lines etched the corners, but they still pinned her with a steely stare that was meant to make her squirm.

Not today.

"This is the reason we work alone, Bea. Meet Magnus Larsson, my old partner."

He tilted his head, spotting the small mic in her ear, and grinned. "Is someone eavesdropping on us?"

"Do you want me to call a bomb threat?" Bea asked.

"Not necessary," Celeste said, giving Magnus a sweet smile. "I'm getting out of here the old-fashioned way."

Goddamn, she looked good.

Seeing her, touching her, stirred something within Magnus that he was certain he'd buried five years ago. He doubted they had the time, but he still took a moment to examine the woman standing before him. Time had barely touched Celeste's nut-brown skin, which now glowed from the soft light of the desk lamp. She'd always had a wide smile, so tiny wrinkles arched from the corners of her eyes. Her expressive brow had created one or two lines across her forehead. But she was the same dark-eyed mystery from their younger years. Except for the glasses, which he now recognized aided whoever was in her ear.

"I'll just take these," he said, quickly removing her glasses before placing them in the breast pocket of his jacket. She jerked her head back and opened her mouth to protest. "You've never needed glasses, Celeste, and you don't need them tonight. Plus, I don't want to be watched by your mysterious friend."

Celeste reached for his pocket, but he caught her by the wrists. Now, as their hands were joined between their bodies, he gently pushed her back toward the wall. She followed his footsteps. "Magnus."

"You can't be hiding anything under that dress," he mused as his gaze traveled down her body. "Your purse is far too small…" His eyes darted back to her head wrap.

Of course… The crown was hiding under her elaborate head wrap. "Undo the wrap, Celeste."

"No," she hissed. "I got here before you. You know the rules."

Yes, those *were* the rules, and believe it or not, there was honor among thieves. Magnus just didn't feel gracious tonight. However, before he could argue, he heard the unmistakable voice of Victor Sanderson on the other side of the door. Celeste heard it, too. They exchanged panicked expressions before springing into action.

He yanked the chain of the small Tiffany lamp on the desk, immersing them in darkness while Celeste darted across the room, behind the long drapes of the bay windows. Magnus joined her seconds later, climbing up onto the bumped-out window seat beside her, just as the door opened and the soft glow of the overhead light illuminated the room. Sounds from the party below filtered in as Victor and another person walked into the room.

Well, this is just perfect.

Here he was, late to the prize and crouched behind a curtain next to the woman who'd bested him. They faced each other, frozen on the balls of their feet, barely breathing as they listened to the intruder.

"You know I could have sent this along to the museum treasurer," Victor said with a chuckle. Judging by the distance of his voice, Magnus presumed he was at the desk near his secret safe. Where they had stood seconds before.

"Oh, you know me, Vic," said another man. It sounded like Kevin Phillips. "I don't mind collecting on behalf of the institution. It's eighty percent of an assistant director's job these days."

"Make sure this goes to some educational program or something," Sanderson said, ripping paper. "I've heard some of your trustees grumbling about how the emerald should be donated to a museum. Theirs, no doubt."

"Vanessa?" Phillips asked. The sound of ice tinkled as it rattled against glass. "Don't worry about her. She's a bitch whose days are numbered."

The two men laughed it up before there was a pause. Magnus rolled his eyes upward, desperate for these assholes to just leave already. "Is that the cabinet?"

"It is."

Footsteps upon the carpet. Magnus and Celeste exchanged tense glances as the men approached the window. Every muscle in his body was taut like a bear trap.

"It's nice enough," Phillips said with appreciation. "Seems like an impulse purchase if you ask me."

"You saw her, right?" Sanderson chuckled.

"Jesus, Vic. A body like that might convince me to buy more than a cabinet."

"Do me a favor and hold on to that check tighter."

The footsteps finally receded away from them. "What was her name?"

"Celeste St. Pierre," Sanderson purred. The overhead light flicked off as he closed the door.

They were once again alone, in the darkness. Magnus willingly let his body relax, despite feeling anger toward the men's comments about Celeste. Eventually he settled himself onto his stiff knees. Both let out respective sighs of relief but neither moved from their positions behind the curtain. Only the city lights from below illuminated their faces.

Celeste bit her lip as she stared at him. He read conflict in her expression. This night wasn't going as planned for her and she seemed unsure of her next move. The microexpression could have gone unnoticed by anyone else, but Magnus knew her face well. Some of the frost surrounding his heart shook loose as he watched her dark eyes dart to his mouth.

Everything about this night had gone to shit, but the reckless thrill of almost getting caught with Celeste grabbed him by the collar and dragged him right back to the past. In Lisbon, they'd almost gotten caught in the archival basement. By the time they got back to their safe house, they couldn't keep their hands off each other. He remembered whispering absolute filth in her ear as he fucked her in the doorway of that dingy flat.

Without thinking it through, Magnus caught her mouth and pushed forward with insistence. Celeste let out a shocked squeak but melted against his lips within seconds. He let out a low moan against her open mouth and teased her with his tongue. A shiver of pleasure ran through his body as Celeste returned his kiss with urgency. Her tongue plunging without shame and her teeth nipping at his lower lip without grace.

It was a wicked kiss, stolen without thought, and he felt justified in taking it from her. If she won the night, he'd at least have this: the forbidden taste of her lips against his. He could have the thrill once more. Unfortunately, it didn't last long enough. Celeste's head snapped up as she touched her ear. "No," she whispered.

Magnus breathed hard after their kiss, convinced he'd drowned in her. "What?"

"I know," she snapped. "I'm getting out now."

She wasn't speaking to him.

Magnus cleared his throat and climbed down from the window seat before leaving the safety of the curtain. Celeste soon followed him, adjusting her dress and patting her head wrap. In the darkness, the room was oddly quiet.

"Get out of here," he said in a tired voice.

Her body tensed at the sound. "I'm sorry."

An apology? From Celeste? A lot of good that did after what she put him through. He wouldn't fall for honeyed words tonight. "For what?" He reached into his jacket pocket and retrieved her glasses. "You're queen for the day, my darling. Enjoy fencing what's left of the Romanov legacy."

Celeste walked up to him, plucked the glasses from his fingers and placed them on her face before walking away. He couldn't see her face clearly, but he heard the smile in her tone when she spoke. "Until next time, my dear."

He grinned despite his crushed feelings. "Another kiss for the road?"

Once at the door, she let light spill into the room before she glanced over her shoulder. "The first one's always free, Mags, even you know that."

And then she slipped out of his life for a second time.

He stood in Victor Sanderson's office, empty-handed but full of turmoil as his ex-lover outsmarted him and left him aching for more. Served him right. He could never trust the woman, and this was a well-timed reminder that working alone should have been his initial route in life.

But God help him, Celeste St. Pierre still had him in her grips.

4

"Hurry it up, CeCe," Magnus muttered in her earpiece. "We're running out of time."

This entire plan was flying right off the rails in front of her eyes, but she was going to make it off Princess Astrid's balcony with some royal jewels. Except the pouring rain made it difficult to get a decent grip on the rope attached to her grappling hook. She looked down, but in the dark it was hard to see how far she hung above the cobblestone pavement.

Raindrops splattered her face through her ski mask, essentially waterboarding her, as she glanced up at the precarious hook. "I'm coming," she muttered. "The power is out. No one from the building can see me."

"For now," Lawrence said. "The front desk is going to alert security if they haven't already. Santiago, stand by."

"I'm not leaving," said their getaway driver. He was in a small motorboat this time, waiting in the river down below. "But the water is getting choppy, CeCe, step it up."

"I'm coming," Celeste said with more force. With the velvet jewelry box tucked under her arm, she shimmied down the rope as fast as she could without shifting the hook above her. She was getting closer to the ground but needed to move past three more balconies. In the darkness, she landed in front of one patio window just as a flash of light pierced the night. The white beam caught her off guard with its bright-ness, causing her to flinch. Someone with a flashlight illuminated her.

"She's been spotted," Magnus said.

"Hold on," she whispered, sliding down the rope. This would have to be a sharper descent than she wanted, but it was better than getting shot by security. She blew out a shaky breath before tightening her el-bows at her sides and loosening her grip.

One balcony, two…three…

"Oof!" she grunted as her feet made impact with pavement. "Fuuuuck." Pain shot through her ankle as she sank to her knees.

"CeCe." A new voice came over the airwaves, low and urgent. Doris. "Do you have the package?"

With her hands gripping the wet cobblestones, she breathed through the sharp pain before answering. "Yes, ma'am."

"Good."

"Are you okay though?" Magnus asked sharply. "That drop was too fast."

She couldn't respond to his panicked question because she was al-most afraid to test her legs. At the very least, she sprained her ankle. Her mind scrambled as she tried to ignore the throbbing in her left foot.

"She's fine," Doris said. "Get up, CeCe."

That's all she needed to hear. She was getting out of there with the package. The team was counting on her. Doris was counting on her. Celeste carefully drew herself up from the ground. She took a hold of the rope and lassoed the hook from the balcony above. By the grace of God, its metal latch landed a couple feet from where she stood.

"For Christ's sake, what are you doing?" Magnus asked in a fright-ened voice.

Celeste quickly wound the rope as she hobbled toward the embank-ment across the street. "I don't want authorities to collect more evidence than they need." Waiting eight feet below the concrete edge, she spotted Santiago and Magnus approaching her in the boat. But there was no metal ladder for her to climb down and no safe way to jump into the small inflatable vessel. "I'm going to toss you the box."

"Wait a second," Santiago said as he steered the boat. "I can't drop anchor, so you need to get it right."

"Hurry up," she hissed. When they were close enough and she saw Magnus standing, arms outstretched, she said a little prayer and tossed a 6.7 million-dollar jewelry box in the darkness.

"Shit!" Magnus cursed.

Celeste didn't have to guess what happened because seconds later, a soft splash could be heard over the pouring rain. Her heart dropped as time stood still.

"What's happening?" Doris asked. Her voice sounded hushed this time as if she already knew the answer.

Blood pounded in her ears as Magnus muttered the same curse.

Desperation was the only thing that got Celeste moving. They had not come all the way to Stockholm, broken into a royal member's condo and stolen nineteenth-century jewels to fail this hard. "I'm going in," she said, and foolishly jumped into the river.

Cold water rushed up her body and blackness enveloped her. The last thing she heard before her earpiece died was Magnus shouting, "God, noooo!"

Celeste awoke with a violent start, grasping at air and tangled in her silk sheets. Sweat-covered and chest heaving, she looked frantically around her surroundings before willing herself to breathe slower. Slipper satin-white walls, teak dressers from Thailand, cherrywood floors and her bed. She was in her bed. Five years after the bungled heist she had the misfortune of participating in.

The morning after meeting the man who ruined that night.

Magnus Larsson hadn't been in her dreams for years. She let out a halted breath as she ran her hands through her short curly hair but touched sharp metal and stones instead. Celeste patted around her head, realizing she'd slept in the tiara she stole last night, and let out a relieved laugh. The sound echoed in her bedroom, reminding her she was alive and had beaten Magnus.

Alcohol was the only reason she thought it was a good idea

to sleep in a diamond-and-pearl tiara instead of a satin bonnet. When she and Beatrice returned to her Harlem brownstone last night, Celeste thought it prudent the young woman spend the night instead of making her way back home to Williamsburg. So they broke out the champagne to celebrate and settle their nerves. One round turned to two. Two rounds turned to two bottles.

Once Celeste's blood pressure seemed to return to normal, she crawled out of bed and padded to her bathroom. In the large mirror, a puffy face with red eyes squinted back at her. A kid like Beatrice could probably bounce back from champagne hangovers, but not Celeste. Regardless of her rumpled appearance, the crown *did* look divine.

She eyed it with a grin, beating back the sadness of having to break it up. She hated the idea of destroying the platinum frame, but knew it was for the best. If her usual fencer, Dieter, couldn't find the appropriate buyer, he would refuse to move it while still intact.

It was time to move on. That was what Doris had taught her...

Laurels are just leafy crowns; why in the hell would I want to rest on them? Girl, you better rest when you're dead. Ain't rest for the wicked anyhow.

Celeste couldn't help her chuckle as she quickly brushed her teeth and washed the remainder of the makeup from her eyes. Dr. Doris Grant's phrases often popped into her mind when she worked, constant reminders to stay vigilant. The woman had taught her for nearly twenty years to be the thief she is today. If she were still speaking to Doris, the old woman would have scolded the way she handled herself last night. Soon, she thought back to her Stockholm dream.

She had to assume seeing Magnus triggered the memories. She hadn't had dreams of nearly drowning in at least three years. Back then, she frequently woke up breathing hard and frantic for light. The story never moved past the point of her jumping into the cold black water. She never dreamed of Magnus pulling her into the boat, waking up to his angry expression. Just when she thought she'd put him, that job and even Doris in her past, everything came rushing back into Victor Sanderson's penthouse like cold brackish water down her throat.

Ding-dong!

The front doorbell blared through her recollections, making her flinch. Celeste hurried back into her bedroom to the monitor on her nightstand. She pressed the touch screen, revealing the surveillance image of her front stoop. A young bike messenger stood outside her door, lank brown hair hanging from his helmet and a bored expression on his face.

She pressed the speaker function. "Yes?"

"Parcel for…" He looked down at a yellow manila folder. "CeCe St. Pierre? I need a signature."

Celeste's heart stuttered in her chest. "Coming."

A million clashing thoughts ran through her mind as she made her way downstairs. She met a disheveled Beatrice on the ground floor, who appeared to have found a blanket and slept on the couch instead of a guest room. "Who is that?" she grumbled from the couch.

"Bike messenger," she called over her shoulder.

When she opened the front door, the guy looked up from his phone. "Hey," she breathed.

He frowned as he stared at the top of her head. "Pretty fancy for the morning, huh?"

Shit.

She was still wearing the damned tiara…

Celeste let out a good-natured laugh as she took the manila envelope. "It's never too early in the morning for a tea party with the kids! Signature?"

"Uh, yeah, right." He produced an electric signing pad that she quickly scrawled on. "Have a good one."

"You, too!" she said, closing the door on him.

"Whadja get?" Beatrice called out from the living room.

Celeste's shoulders sagged as she pushed away from the door. "I don't know. You want some coffee?"

"Yes, and a gallon of water."

"Coming up," she murmured, walking to the kitchen. Her hands shook as she tore open the top of the envelope. CeCe wasn't a name respectable people called her. When attending auction appraisals, she was called Dr. St. Pierre. Celeste, if people thought they were familiar. CeCe was from another time.

She slipped a beautiful oxblood-red envelope from the package, heavy with quality cardstock and bright gold embossed script: *CeCe...*

Celeste didn't want to open it, already aware of its weight. Somehow, she knew its contents would herald terrible news. But her hands moved without her brain's permission, fingers carefully separating the folds and confronting a vellum sheath of paper. She recognized the script immediately; its dramatic loops and reckless dashes crawled along the page.

Celeste:

If you're reading this letter, then I am quite dead, my dear.

Dead, but not resting. That was never an option.

When the dying still possess regrets, we only have one option: perform beyond the grave with elaborate machinations that delight and annoy the living. I might have regrets, my dear, but I also have surprises. And you...have no time nor tears to waste. Come to my home, meet with Lawrence. He'll give you the details of my delightful machinations.

Sincerely, Dr. Doris Grant

P.S. I know I've told a number of fanciful tales in the past, but I am really, truly and honestly quite dead.

Celeste closed her eyes and laid the letter on her granite countertop. The urge to slump over and rest her warm cheek against the cold surface was strong. Instead, a noise bubbled in her chest and escaped her throat, piercing the silence of the kitchen. The sound of laughter shocked her, but she couldn't stop the reflex.

"Oh, God," she whispered through giggles. "Oh, my God."

She couldn't trace which emotion set off the laughter. She felt anxious, profound sadness and shock, but all of it was wrapped in so much absurdity, Celeste didn't know how else to react.

"What's so funny?" Beatrice asked from the kitchen entrance. The young woman scratched at the scalp beneath her box braids as she yawned.

"My mentor is dead," Celeste said, wiping tears from her eyes. Another hysterical peal of laughter escaped her as she nodded to the red letter. "She sent a letter telling me she's dead."

Beatrice's face fell as she looked from the letter to Celeste. "What? Who's your mentor? When did she die? Is there a funeral?"

Celeste shook her head while pulling a canister of coffee from the cabinet. "Highly doubtful," she scoffed. "She'll most likely be cremated."

Her assistant approached her the way someone might approach a wounded animal, warily. "Are you okay?"

"Ooh, girl…okay? I don't know about all that," Celeste said, dumping several spoonfuls of grounds into her machine. "Between Magnus and this? Check the fridge for creamer. I haven't been to the store in a minute. In fact, I don't even know how old this coffee is."

"Celeste."

She looked up to find Beatrice standing right beside her, hands hovering as if she wasn't sure if she should make physical contact. "What?"

"Do you want a hug? Do you need to cry?" she asked.

Celeste woodenly wrapped an arm around the girl and patted her back with an efficiency that probably shocked Beatrice. "No tears, honey." She turned the coffeemaker on and moved away to find clean mugs. "That much was in the letter. Doris says I don't need tears for this occasion."

5

Sweat poured down Magnus's face as his sneakers pounded relentlessly against his treadmill. Two miles ago, a familiar ache returned to his right knee. He was ignoring it while huffing through his punishing run. He woke up that morning at his customary 6:00 a.m. and couldn't think of a better way to ease his frustration.

Another jeweled treasure slipped right through his fingers last night.

It brought him right back to that night in Stockholm when Celeste flung millions of dollars of diamonds at him in the dark. The box bumped his fingers, and he grasped its corners as quickly as he could but when he heard the splash, it was over. Magnus remembered feeling his body go numb with the knowledge that they'd fucked up. Why the hell did Celeste throw that box? Why hadn't she just waited until the damn boat was right under her before dropping it down?

Because she's reckless.

Even last night, she could have been caught by anyone. Celeste was *lucky* that Magnus snuck up on her. She should have combed the room longer, really cased the place like he had when they worked together. He usually covered the details that she missed. Had they met eyes during Sanderson's party, they could have... *Could have what?* Magnus sighed as he jammed the button on his treadmill. His speed slowed until he ultimately stopped to slump over the rails. He couldn't even imagine the disastrous confrontation of meeting her gaze in the middle of that party.

Good God, she looked amazing. And if he was more honest with himself, that was a large part of his frustrations. To see Celeste St. Pierre at that party, looking as beautiful as the day he'd met her, made him ache with desire and anger. Their urgent kiss in Sanderson's office, the way her full lips moved against his... It relit a fire in his chest that he'd worked hard to extinguish years ago. The work he'd put in to forgetting her was suddenly unraveled and lying in a heap at his feet.

As he stepped off the treadmill, he collapsed on his couch and faced the large windows of his Red Hook loft. He closed his eyes and let the sun illuminate his face as he remembered the feel of Celeste's bare skin beneath his hands. So soft and familiar.

"Stop it," he muttered.

Try as he might, he couldn't shake the sensations from last night.

He should be beating himself up instead of imagining Celeste's body. Magnus should have known better than to let his guard down at a party of that magnitude. She still lived in the city, most likely in Harlem. Last time he checked, she was still running that front of an antique store in Manhattan. Until last night, he had long believed that New York City was large enough for them to keep avoiding each other. Now he realized how foolish he'd been.

As a person with dual citizenship, Magnus could have put the United States in his rearview mirror and returned to Sweden years ago. But he had no family to return to and nothing to occupy his time. He was a bit lonely here, but at least teaching kept him busy. While he graded papers, oversaw lab studies and met with students, no one would suspect that he was researching his next mark. Newton University didn't have a clue.

Vbb vbb…

Magnus glanced at the coffee table where his phone vibrated. Michelle.

She was a lovely woman, a principal dancer with the New York City Ballet. When she wasn't busy with rehearsals, she'd call him on a Saturday night for a quickie. He didn't mind being a casual fling for the young woman, but today he wanted to stay home and lick his wounds, get drunk and think about Celeste. Magnus wasn't a complete ass, though, so he picked up the phone and tapped out an apologetic lie about grading finals. He tossed the phone on his couch before Michelle could reply.

Buzz, buzzzz…

His face screwed up with annoyance. *Now what?* As he pushed himself from the couch and trotted downstairs, he searched his mind for any expected orders and came up empty. On his doorstep, a young woman held out a yellow envelope while steadying her bicycle against her hip.

"Magnus Larsson?" she asked, her eyes flitting between his sweaty chest and his face.

"Present."

Her face reddened. "I need a signature."

They exchanged signature for parcel before Magnus closed the door on her. He stood in his vestibule and ripped the package apart to get to another barrier. A beautiful red envelope with his name in gold. He frowned.

When he reached the contents of the red envelope, his frown deepened. Certain words and phrases stood out, but he barely believed their meaning. He read and reread the line *I am really, truly and honestly quite dead* until his eyes blurred in confusion. None of this made any sense. Doris was old, but she wasn't that old. She couldn't seriously be dead. Not now. Not when

Celeste St. Pierre had suddenly been thrown back into his life. Though he didn't run with the old crew any longer, he still kept contact with her. But how long had it been?

Magnus stumbled through his foyer, loosely clutching the letter, wondering if it had truly been a year since his last email to Dr. Grant. It was brief, but he'd written to thank her for the Sanderson tip. He blew out a sigh. Had she known that Celeste was after the same mark? No, no. Doris was messy, but she wouldn't purposefully let her two best thieves land in the same predicament.

And then Magnus laughed.

"Of course she would," he said, shaking his head.

And now she was dead.

When he met Dr. Doris Grant at the Museum Association of New York, in Syracuse, he hadn't expected anything more than a research trip he could write off as professional development. He liked attending conferences to keep abreast of any museum knowledge that might help in the future. Apparently, Grant did the same. She intrigued him immediately when she sat beside him at the Marriott Hotel bar. All it took was a knowing smile and he quickly fell into her web.

"You don't look like the type who usually comes to these things," she said after ordering two fingers of Old Grand-Dad's whiskey, neat. He remembered how odd the order seemed compared to the classy woman next to him. She wore a smart navy blue pantsuit with gold embellishments and a gold shawl. Her jewelry was understated: pearl earrings and necklace against deep brown skin. Her gray hair was swept up in a delicate gold comb.

He smiled back. "Now I'm fascinated to know what my type looks like."

"Oh, you know…" she said, absently tapping her coaster with a bloodred fingernail. "Handsome and aloof, cocksure while casing the space. I don't see that amongst other academics."

"What do you think I'm casing?"

She shrugged her narrow shoulders and took a dainty sip of her whiskey. "I doubt there's anything of interest here in Syracuse, but if you ever find yourself in need of a challenge, you should give me a call, Dr. Larsson."

Magnus took the card she slid across the bar. Dr. Doris Grant, Professor Emeritus, Stony Brook University SUNY. Awareness pricked him hard, making the hairs on the back of his neck rise. He hadn't been wearing his name tag at the bar.

"From one professional to another," she continued, gingerly getting down from her bar stool, "I've had my eye on you."

Magnus stood with her. "Have you?"

With both feet on the floor, the elderly woman stood at least two feet shorter than him, but looked up at him with a cheeky grin that immediately disarmed him. "And a gentleman, too," she said. "You'll do just fine for my crew, Magnus. Give me a call when you get back to the city. We'll get you out of that classroom."

Thus began their professional relationship.

Apparently, it had come to an end with this letter. He read through it again, this time carefully dissecting the message. She spoke of regrets and machinations; the latter sounded like Doris down to a T, but he couldn't imagine what kind of regrets the woman would have. He was certain she'd led a storied life, amassed wealth from all four corners of the globe and still managed to keep her teaching reputation intact.

His mind went back to Celeste and wondered if she knew about Dr. Grant's passing. How was she holding up? If he felt numbed by the news, *she* would be absolutely crushed. Magnus had joined the crew well into his solo-thieving career while Doris had trained Celeste at an early age. Dr. Grant had approached her in college when she was still a student. Thieving was all Celeste knew, which made Doris more of a mother figure than a teacher.

One thing was for certain: if he wanted to learn more, he'd have to go to her home where Lawrence would receive him. If Lawrence was handling her estate, surely he'd have the answers Magnus needed. The old gang back together? He didn't suspect that it would happen in his lifetime, but Magnus felt an odd thrill knowing that he might see the crew again.

6

"My, my, my…" purred a dark voice.

Celeste and Beatrice's Uber let them out a block away from Dr. Grant's town house when Celeste heard a familiar voice up the sidewalk. A few yards away, the sun was setting on a tall, lean figure wearing a charcoal-gray three-piece suit and what she assumed was a feline smile. Her heart immediately lifted.

"Who is that?" Beatrice whispered as they approached the man.

"Santiago Peña, The Wheels."

"Is he dangerous?" she asked in a lower voice.

"Your pockets are safe," Celeste chuckled. "Keep an eye on your panties, though. He's quite the charmer."

"What are you saying about me, CeCe?" Santiago asked as they stopped in front of Dr. Grant's stoop. He was as devilishly handsome as he was several years ago, with the same dark hair buzzed close to the scalp and Van Dyke beard. He'd always been fastidious about his appearance.

"Your ears burning, Santi?" she teased.

His languid posture was catlike and dangerous as he sized the women up. His focus lingered on Beatrice a beat longer before answering. "You look good, mana. Who is your friend?"

"Beatrice, but my friends call me Bea," her assistant said, sticking her hand out for a shake.

In true Santiago fashion, his eyes flickered with intense interest before taking her hand and kissing her knuckles. "Then consider me a friend, Bonita Bea. It's lovely to meet you." Beatrice bit her lip to keep from grinning, which wasn't a shocker.

Santiago had a way with women that had never influenced Celeste. She fought hard not to roll her eyes at the man she'd always considered her kid brother. "Slow your roll, Santi."

He straightened away from Beatrice and glanced up at Doris's front door. "So. This is the end, huh. Mother is gone."

Celeste's stomach flipped at the mention of death. "What did you think about the letter?"

"Playfully macabre. You think Mags got one?"

She sighed. "I'm almost positive he has. I'm not sure if I'm ready to see him again."

"It's been a long time, mana," Santiago murmured. "I wonder where he is. Will he show?"

Beatrice and Celeste exchanged a meaningful look before Celeste spoke. "I'm willing to bet he'll be here. He still lives in the city."

"We saw him last night," Beatrice added before pressing her lips together tightly. "Sorry."

"And what a sight it was," said a man's voice behind her.

Santiago's dark brown eyes brightened as he glanced over Celeste's shoulder. "Mags!"

Oh, Lord... It took a lot of effort for her to turn around to face this man again. But Celeste was going to be mature as fuck because today was not about Magnus or even her. They were here to recognize the passing of a great woman. A woman who taught Celeste everything she knew about thieving.

Magnus stood over her, wearing jeans and a T-shirt, hands in his pockets. His blond hair was wet, probably from a recent shower. This time he wasn't smirking; he wore a somber expression as he studied her face. They shared a brief connection before he broke eye contact, and a smile lit his face. He shook hands with Santiago and sank into a brotherly hug. Celeste looked at the two and immediately felt like an outsider. When the crew disbanded, neither Santiago, nor Lawrence, nor Doris took sides, and Celeste didn't ask them to. The problems between her and Magnus were simply that. It still stung to see the men pick up where they left off.

"We're all here, plus an extra," Magnus said upon releasing Santiago. He raised a brow at Beatrice. "I'm assuming you were in her ear last night?"

Beatrice offered the same friendly handshake. "I was. I'm Beatrice."

Magnus was not nearly as effusive as Santiago but greeted her politely. "How old are you, Beatrice? Has CeCe told you how dangerous this line of work is?"

Irritation tore through Celeste as she interpreted his scolding. Thieving was indeed a dangerous business and she'd done an excellent job of keeping Beatrice out of the field. "It starts immediately, doesn't it?" Celeste asked. "We come back together and you're back to running things."

"I'm twenty-six," Beatrice said with a smirk. "And we've been doing well over the last few years. In fact, we did extremely well last night up against you."

Magnus fell quiet as he glanced between the two women. Internally, Celeste was proud of her little protégé.

"Last night?" Santiago intoned. "It sounds like our little family reunion started early…"

"Maybe we should see Lawrence," Celeste said, starting up the stairs.

"Yes, let's get this over with," Magnus mumbled, following her.

She stood at the door with a burning face, realizing that he was directly beside her. His closeness and the heat of that June evening made their proximity more intimate than it should have been. His cologne and soap wafted too close to her, an old and familiar memory scent that reminded her of his body and how entwined they used to be. Celeste rang the doorbell and waited for Lawrence, hoping he'd rescue her from her thoughts.

"You did extremely well, Dr. St. Pierre," he whispered, stiffly.

His warm breath caressed her ear, sending a tingle across her skin and raising the hairs on the back of her neck. It took everything in her power not to close her eyes and sink against his chest. "I know it's killing you to admit that," she muttered instead.

He grunted in reply.

She didn't like how her body reacted to his nearness. As if her tightened nipples had forgotten about the past; as if Magnus Larsson *wasn't* the most annoying, pretentious asshole in all five boroughs. A steady thrumming between her thighs grew stronger at the thought of their kiss last night…

The door flew open, revealing an older gentleman wearing a sad smile. Since Celeste had last seen him, a few more wrinkles creased Lawrence Cole's deep brown skin, and his tight curly hair had far more salt than pepper. "Hello, kids," he said in a warm gravelly voice. "Nice to have you back."

Tears immediately pricked her eyes. Of course, to someone who was in their sixties, the rest of the crew would look and act like *kids*. Lawrence had always been a serene father figure for her. He tried to offer as much wisdom as he could in the face of Dr. Grant's ostentatious ambitions. Part of her wondered if she had spent more time listening to him, would she be in this position without her old crew.

No, that would let Magnus skate by without blame.

She crossed the threshold and gave him a fierce hug. "It's nice to see you, too," she whispered.

Doris greeted them in her library.

Her remains sat on a great oak desk in a black marble urn.

Her chosen resting place was small but incredibly sophisticated. It was difficult for Magnus to tear his eyes from the vessel, but he managed to snag a glance at Celeste, whose eyes were misty with emotion. Beatrice sat beside her, holding her hand, while whispering something inaudible.

He wondered if he should have offered her condolences when he saw her on the sidewalk. She was dressed casually that evening, wearing joggers and a denim jacket, nothing like the audacious gown she wore last night. Her hair was much shorter than he remembered. A mop of curls tapered into a fade down the sides and back of her head, revealing the sharpness of her jaw and chin. Anger and panic had flashed across her face when their eyes met and he chickened out to greet Santiago instead.

And now he could tell she was trying her damnedest to hold back her grief. Like the rest of them, Celeste had plenty of experience with loss. Santiago's father, a former associate of Dr. Grant's, died in prison when Santiago was eighteen. Magnus's parents were killed in a car accident while traveling through Northern Sweden. He didn't know Beatrice's story, but he wondered if the girl was in the same piss-poor shape as the rest of them. The orphans that Doris gathered.

Santiago was the only one to pour himself a cup of tea before sitting in a high-back chair. Magnus claimed a chair for himself and waited to hear Lawrence out. He hadn't realized how much he missed the old man until he saw his tired expression at the front door. He looked good, though. Healthy enough for Magnus to not worry. When they all worked together, Lawrence oversaw most of their gadgetry and supplies. If they needed night-vision goggles or lock-pick kits, it was his responsibility to test them out for effectiveness. As far as Magnus knew, Doris had worked with the man well before any of them ever knew her. It didn't surprise him that she entrusted Lawrence with her estate.

Lawrence walked behind the desk and sat down with Doris on his right. Only the gentle clatter of Santiago's spoon against his teacup broke through the heavy silence of the room. Lawrence took a moment to stare at the marble urn before taking a deep breath. When he spoke, his voice shook.

"The funeral home delivered her this morning. I suspect around the time you all received your letters." He paused, took off his wire-rimmed glasses. "She passed on Tuesday after about a year of breast cancer treatments. Doris never liked going to the doctor, but she complained about some pain in her chest, under her arm. She had a hard time breathing and so on. By the time I begged her to go to the doctor..." He trailed off, looking down at his hands for a beat. "Anyhow, when they caught it, they called it...uh, secondary breast cancer. Stage four, I think. It got into her lungs.

"We worked at it, though. Shoot, what's the point of having all this money if you can't fight? That's what I told her. She worked at it. Gave it her best. But, uh, you know..." He shrugged his narrow shoulders. "There's only so much you can do."

"When did she stop treatment?" Celeste asked, her voice flat and her face blank.

Lawrence looked up sharply as though he forgot they were in the room. "Oh, uh, about two months ago."

Magnus let out a breath through his nose and closed his eyes. A whole year of living with this. The obvious question that hung in the air was why didn't they say anything? Had he known, he would have—

Would have what? Flown to her doorstep after years of self-imposed exile? He was the first crew member to leave. She'd asked him not to, but the thought of working beside Celeste after that night in Stockholm scared him off bad. After fishing her out of a river, he issued her an ultimatum. He was sick of Celeste taking unnecessary risks for Doris, and that jewelry set was one of them. Once he hauled her onto the boat, he'd cupped his hands over her ashen face and chattering jaw and shouted, "Aren't you done yet?"

Celeste had made it clear she wasn't.

And rather than see the woman he cared for jeopardize her life again, he left them all behind. Including Doris. And now look at her. Ashes in a beautiful jar, added to her priceless stolen artwork and jewels.

"How did she seem?" Magnus heard himself ask. Numbness settled over his body as he stared at Celeste, willing her to break first. Perhaps if she could show a bit of emotion, he might let himself feel something.

Celeste looked back at him. Her full lips set in a straight line, but her eyes swam with unshed tears. She wasn't going to blink.

"Hopeful," Lawrence said. "She was relieved to know there was an end and giddy to know there'd be a beginning."

"I'm sorry?" Santiago asked, setting his cup down.

"Well, that's the thing about Doris. She had to do everything on her own terms. Especially dying. That's where y'all come in."

They looked around the room at each other in confusion. "Does this have something to do with the letters we received?" Magnus asked. "Her invitation wasn't just a death notification."

"No," Lawrence said, pulling open a drawer beside him. From it, he extracted a medium-size wooden box. "Her invitation was to something much larger. Before I get into that, I'd like to know if you promise to hear everything I have to say before devolving into a shouting match." His gaze flickered between Magnus and Celeste with a fatherly warning.

"I'm not here to shout," Magnus said defensively. "Talk to her."

Celeste rolled her eyes and sucked her teeth. "*I* don't have anything to shout about."

"And are we sure Miss Beatrice needs to be here for this?" Lawrence asked.

"Let her stay," Santiago said with a shrug. "If this is what I suspect it is, we'll need all the help we can get."

"She stays," Celeste agreed. "We've worked together for a few years now. She's a crew member by proxy."

The young woman tucked her braids behind her ear and looked around the room before thanking them. Magnus didn't have an opinion one way or another. He was more interested in the business at hand.

Lawrence pulled a silver chain from his neck and used a key to unlock his box. The first thing he retrieved was a letter. "I oughta start off by saying that you're going to have a lot of questions. I know about as much as Doris allowed me to know. She planned the details and the goals so that I could gather you here. What comes next will be a surprise for all of us. That's how she wanted it."

And what Doris wanted, she usually got.

7

"'My darling little thieves…

"'Please do not mark my passing with too many tears. I was born, I burned a bright trail and now I fade to make way for you. There's always another treasure to reach for and I hope you'll do my reaching. My final wish, that is if you hardheaded fools can work together, is a hunt for the next treasure.'"

Lawrence paused to run his hand over his lips and shake his head. "Oh, brother…"

Celeste could tell what Doris was gearing up to ask and her stomach fluttered wildly as she imagined the possibilities. "Please keep going," she quietly pleaded.

Lawrence sighed. "'My stubborn Celeste, arrogant Magnus, sly Santiago and constant Lawrence… I'm asking you to unite one final time for my last heist. Beyond the grave, I'd like to correct mistakes I made when I was alive, and I think this should be the ticket. There will be different stages, multiple marks, leading to one true goal. I pray that you excuse one another's weaknesses and take solace in one another's strengths. If you're to accomplish this feat, you'll need each other more than you ever believed. I had Lawrence, but who do you all have?

"'Celeste, I beg you read my short collection of journal entries. I've written about myself from the time I was a young woman, all the way to my death, and I've taken the bits of myself you will need to learn about *yourself*. Magnus, it's time for you to see outside of your narrow window and join something larger than yourself. You're not getting any younger and I worry that Nordic veneer will never melt enough to let someone in. My dear Santi, you're perfect as you are, don't ever change—'" Lawrence cut off with a snort.

Celeste couldn't help her laughter, but Doris had a way of slipping levity into any uncomfortable occasion. Soon, the entire room fell into a fit of giggles while Santiago flashed them a smug grin. "We all know I was Mother's favorite," he said above the noise.

"Ah, hush up," Lawrence chuckled. "You were just the baby of the group."

"I wasn't called hardheaded or an icy Scandinavian," Santiago retorted.

"I don't think she said I was an icy Scandinavian," Magnus said, rolling his eyes.

"All right now, everybody calm down and let me finish this."

Once the room settled down, Celeste smiled and redirected her attention to Lawrence. The promise of a last heist hung in the balance, and she wanted to hear more.

"'Lawrence, give them the tools, be patient and guide them as best as you can. What they will need to get started is in the box I have left for you. More will be offered at a later stage. Thank you for being my steadfast and most trusted companion throughout the years.

"'Now, on to the first clue to their first location. Peter promised her home but when he died, she couldn't imagine a hearth without him. Not even the god of the seas could lure her back to the flowers and fountains. That kind of love is nestled deep, but it's also quite fragile. If ever you were to take hold of it, be gentle lest you crack its surface. But go with a bold voice. Sing a joyous song that's loud enough to drive the bear back to his iron cave.'" He flipped the letter, glancing at the backside before taking off his glasses. "That appears to be it."

She didn't know what she was expecting, but Celeste certainly needed more than that. They all sat there for a moment, perplexed and quiet.

Finally, Santiago scowled. "I don't get it. Give us a hint, Lawrence."

"Son, I don't know what she's talking about. This is my first time reading the letter."

"Is she talking about a place or an object? Or both?" Beatrice asked, pulling out her phone. "There was a bear…is it folklore or something?"

"Possibly," Celeste murmured. Good God, she hated riddles and Doris knew that. Why would she want to make it even harder on them? She glanced at Magnus, whose eyes seemed fixed on the urn beside Lawrence. It didn't appear that he was thinking hard. It looked like he was seething behind his narrowed eyes.

"Wait," Magnus said. "Are all of you just going to skip over the part where a dead woman just assigned us to go on a scavenger hunt?" He stood up and began pacing the room. "Forget the clue for a second and let's get back to the fact that we haven't seen each other in years and now she's asking, no, demanding, that we move on with a joke or two?" He stopped at the desk and picked up the urn, testing its weight in his hands. "Why are you doing this to us?" he whispered to it.

Everyone sat in stunned silence.

Except for Celeste, who frowned in annoyance. "Did you know her at all? This is who Doris was. Were you expecting a traditional funeral where we'd all stand over an open grave weeping and wailing?"

"I don't know what I expected," he snapped. "Certainly not this."

"What do you need to rehash to make this day acceptable?" Celeste said, walking toward him. She could feel her heart rate rise and her hands shake in anger as she approached him. "Do you finally want to talk about Stockholm?"

He scoffed. "Do you?"

"I jumped in the water because you dropped the damn box," Celeste said, her voice rising to an uncomfortable shrillness she had tried to avoid.

Magnus set Dr. Grant's remains down with a heavy *thunk* before wheeling on her. "A boat on the river was not my original plan and you know it," he said, pointing his finger at her face. "But you didn't listen to me. You were obsessed in doing her bidding until you couldn't keep a rational plan."

"Get your finger out of my face," she said in a steadier voice.

His blue eyes flickered to his hand before lowering it. "Do you finally want to acknowledge why you ended up scaling down an apartment building in the middle of the night?"

"Your plan was going to take much longer and we didn't have the time."

"Reckless," he growled.

"Chicken shit," she countered.

"How can I talk to her?" Magnus thundered, looking around the room. "How am I expected to work with a woman who doesn't give a damn about her safety or anyone else's?"

Celeste gasped and recoiled from him as though she'd been hit. *His* words were far more hurtful than her calling him a chicken shit. She had only endangered her life that night, no one else's. Since then, she'd taken every care to make sure Beatrice never had to see action.

"Lawrence, were you finished reading things?" Santiago asked in a bored tone. "Because I think they've devolved into shouting."

"Now, listen, you two," Lawrence said, rising from the desk. "It's all a package deal. She made it clear that it's all of you or no one. The scavenger hunt, as you put it, is going to be hard enough with four of us. It'll be damn near impossible if it's just three."

"So, I'm being coerced into participating in this insanity?"

"How dare you make this about you!" Celeste shouted. "Are you even remotely curious about what Doris left us? Are you just going to shut it down like you shut everything else down?"

"I can take his place!" Beatrice volunteered.

"Can it, Bea!"

"Have you changed yet?" Magnus asked.

"Have you pulled the stick out of your ass yet?"

"You know," Santiago interrupted. "You two worked well enough together when you were fucking. Why don't you try that again?"

Celeste's mouth fell open as her face grew hot.

Magnus scrubbed his hands down his face and gave a frustrated growl. "If she can't even listen, I can't do this." He stepped away from her and strode out of the library.

"That's it, just run away when it gets difficult!" Celeste called out, chasing after him. He cut a fiery path throughout the ground floor of Doris's home like a tidy tornado, full of fury and focus. But she didn't want him to leave with the last word hanging over her head. She *wasn't* reckless, she was creative, she thought on her feet. Celeste could manipulate any plan to suit the same goal. It didn't matter about the means; she always found her end. "You want to shout at someone for not listening, why don't you do it in a mirror, Mags? You've never wanted to listen to me. You always dismissed my ideas!"

Right before he got to the front door, he stopped abruptly, dropped his head and let out a tired sigh. "That's not entirely true. Against my better judgment, I took a backseat to some of your most outlandish ideas. And at one time, it seemed worth it. But near the end? We were fools to go to Stockholm."

Anger flared through her as she searched for a retort. "But—"

"Doris is dead, Celeste. Can I just sit with that for a minute?"

She paused midstep as a chill ran through her body. Every time she heard the words *Doris* and *dead*, her brain froze in fear and guilt. Her mentor had been dying, and she hadn't even known. She had visited this house at least once a month, until Doris began waving her away in February. Celeste took to calling her a bit more, but their conversations were short and to the point. When Doris gave a ragged cough, she dismissed it as a cold or a long bout of pneumonia, assuring Celeste that she was seeing a doctor.

And now Doris was dead.

"You're right," she breathed. "She is…"

He turned around. "And last night was the first time I'd seen you in five years."

She nodded.

"It's a lot, don't you think?" he asked, letting his eyes rove over her.

Celeste suddenly felt naked under his stare and Santiago's words came back to her. They used to fuck. They used to be good together. She hated the way her thoughts ricocheted from grief to embarrassment. "It is."

"Just give me a minute to get my shit together. My semester is nearly over, and I need to sort that out before I can think about…any of this. Maybe we can talk on Wednesday?"

She scrunched her nose. "You're still teaching?"

Magnus shrugged. "Doris always told us to keep a day job, a good front. I like teaching."

"Makes sense. You love lecturing people," Celeste said without thinking.

His dry laughter almost shamed her. There was no reason to be so reactionary toward a man who was suggesting a truce. "Santi really got under your skin, didn't he?"

She crossed her arms over her chest. "Excuse me?"

He pushed away from the door and made a languid path toward her. She inhaled sharply when he stopped just before her. At this distance, she was able to see the blond-and-silver whiskers sprouting on his jaw, the strong column of his neck where the muscles made a barely perceptible twitch. "He reminded you of our not-so-subtle dalliances," Magnus said in a low voice.

Celeste shrugged. "And?"

Before she realized what he was doing, Celeste felt his warm fingers dip under her chin and pull her gaze upward. "When we weren't arguing with each other, we spent a lot of time pleasuring one another."

Her face was on fire and her mouth went dry. "So what?" she croaked.

His eyes landed on her mouth as he lightly brushed her bottom lip with his thumb. "What did you feel when I kissed you in Sanderson's office?"

Thrill, excitement, fear...desire. She had kissed him back with the same ardent energy he gave until Beatrice told her to hurry up. His lips moved just as expertly as they had years before and it shocked her how quickly she found herself back in her stride. But Celeste would be damned before she told Magnus Larsson that. "Nothing," she said, shaking her head.

His hand slipped away, leaving her bereft of his intimate touch. "I know enough about you to say that's a lie," he murmured, drawing even closer to her. Soon, she'd be lost in the deep blue of his eyes. "The Celeste I knew felt everything. That's why she snaps and bites," he whispered in her ear. "I've always been able to read your face, the blush that creeps up your chest and the way your nipples tighten when you stand too close to me... After Wednesday, I can gladly lecture you about the rest of your body, Dr. St. Pierre."

She drew her head back sharply and looked him in the eye but couldn't bring herself to speak. It had been a long time since someone had dragged her like this, and she didn't know how to respond. Luckily, Magnus leaned back on his heels with a tired smile. Only then did she feel safe enough to take her next breath. "Get home safe, Mags."

"Sleep tight, CeCe," he replied as he walked away.

She watched him exit Doris's home without another word.

Celeste stood in the hall, frozen in shock, dreading what Wednesday would bring.

8

July 20, 1965

Dear Diary:

Remember Buena Vista Hotel? Daddy worked so hard as a porter before gaining enough favor with his boss to get me a housekeeping job. Ooh, the way he stayed on to me about keeping my eyes down, working fast and "don't let these white folks catch you slipping." Well, I got caught, but I wasn't slipping. Mrs. Parsons, I'll never forget her name, said I took a diamond brooch from her room when I cleaned it last. I didn't, but she wouldn't listen. Lord, the way she hollered at me while I searched. Made me empty out my pockets, my apron. We never found anything, but Mr. Kelly fired me anyway. Daddy was so disappointed...

They called that sad little place in Biloxi "The American Riviera." Ha ha! What a joke. Now that I'm in Nice, I ain't never going back to Mississippi. In fact, the entire French Riviera is lovely, nothing like the South. Looking out my hotel room and seeing the blue Mediterranean Sea is proof of that. I'm not here to change the sheets or clean the toilets. Some French boy comes up here to deliver me room service. The porters are all white and they take my bags! Boy, if Daddy could see all of this, he'd be tickled.

Sebastian says if I enjoy this, wait till we get to Monaco. I'm absolutely sick with excitement. Lord knows how I'll be able to leave him and go back to school after this! But I might be able to take more trips like this after my senior year. Art History is getting a whole lot more involved, and I need to start thinking about my thesis. I wonder if Sebastian will wait for me to finish school, and then graduate school. I think I love him, but some days I'm not sure... Maybe I love the jewels and the sunshine more. He's so handsome and such a gentleman and very, very rich. He's bought me a few pieces, sayin' I need to look like the kind of girl he'd have on his arm. He told me I can keep the pearl necklace, but I'm not sure. Lord knows if I want anything in this world, I gotta take it for myself.

Like the emerald earrings that are now hidden in my hatbox. I took them from a jewelry counter with a little sleight of hand. You should have seen Sebastian's face when we left out of that store. He kissed my neck and called me naughty. But he also said I was meant to have them. Shoot, I already knew that!

Celeste set Doris's journal on her office desk and absently listened to the conversation between Beatrice and a customer in the storeroom.

"We'll attend our next auction in about two weeks," her assistant said. "If you're more interested in the Queen Anne design, I would wait. I don't want you to invest in something you won't be happy with."

"Mmm... I think I'd still like to look around, though," replied a woman. "Where does this mirror come from?"

Celeste tuned them out, thinking about the passage she'd just read. Doris never spoke about her early life, and much of her thieving career was shrouded in mystery. As a born and bred Harlem girl, Celeste had heard the differences in Doris's accent when the old woman didn't think anyone was paying attention. She mostly spoke like a haughty New Englander, but when she was tired or snappish, a Southern twang would jump out. She would have never guessed Biloxi, Mississippi, though.

Anger burned her cheeks when she read the portion about Doris being accused of theft. The embarrassment and fear that she must have experienced while just trying to do her job must have felt defeating. *You can see it in their eyes, can't you? You can see them assuming the worst. They think they already know you…* That was how Doris had spoken to her when she explained what working for her would entail. A young Celeste sat in her art professor's office, feeling alone on a large, mostly white college campus. It seemed that Doris could sense her frustration and it didn't take long for Celeste to open up about her background.

Before she knew what she was doing, she had confided the struggle of being raised by her grandmother, Josephine, after her mother died giving birth to her. They didn't know who Celeste's father was, so it was just the two of them against the world. That was until Granny Jo fell ill and died when Celeste was just sixteen.

When she became a ward of the state, she understood that no one would rescue her. She learned fast that life wasn't kind to women who didn't have resources. The only thing Granny Jo left her was a little mattress money that she almost didn't find when DCFS made her pack up. It was at the Harrison Home for the Youth where teenage Celeste learned to fight, cuss and steal, while protecting her grandmother's small fortune.

She struggled through her last year of high school but made it out well enough to attend Queensborough Community College on a needs-based scholarship. As far as studies went, Celeste didn't know what she wanted to do until she transferred to Stony Brook University and met Dr. Grant. In the stuffy Long Island culture, where she didn't fit in, she found another Black woman who reminded her of Granny Jo; sturdy and bold, but with a touch of elegance. Dr. Grant arrived to class every Tuesday and Thursday dressed in pressed pantsuits and a different jeweled brooch. The way she dressed herself matched the confident way she carried herself. Celeste was desperate for just a piece of poise.

Even now, at forty-one, she still had days filled with doubt...

Perhaps that was why Dr. Grant's entry surprised her. Celeste hadn't anticipated the giddiness and uncertainty. Her youth shined through the passage as she described living it up in the French Riviera. When she wrote about Sebastian. Celeste had never experienced such girlish fun in her life, not even when she, herself, had visited Monaco. And as far as men went, she doubted anyone had made her feel as excited as Doris's mystery man. Well, perhaps just one man had lit a fire in her belly...

Around his twentieth final exam, Magnus had made his decision.

By the time he entered grades, he'd added a condition to that decision.

When he stood outside St. Pierre Antiquities, he'd all but kicked himself and checked his watch for the next train back to Astoria. It was too late. Today was Wednesday. He was free from his academic obligations and ready to see his former partner again. A crystallized image of her expectant eyes and parted lips took up shop in his head and plagued him for most of the day. Some of his students had Celeste's mouth to thank for his lenient grading. Was she ready to see him?

He pushed his way into the store before he could fully consider the question. A small bell tinkled above him as he stepped inside. Immediately, he spotted the young woman from the other night, Beatrice. In the daylight, she looked as young as one of his graduate students, just not quite as cynical yet. Her bright smile greeted him from behind a counter, as he moved through the large showroom.

Talk about fronts… Celeste hid in plain sight with all this antique furniture. He didn't have the eye for it like she did but could tell the pieces were quite valuable. Magnus couldn't help but stop short before a massive mahogany china cabinet with flourished inlay and intricate carving detail. Did Celeste steal or bid for most of her inventory?

"Looking for anything in particular?" Beatrice asked, suddenly standing beside him. He jumped slightly before putting his hands behind his back, fearful of breaking something valuable near him.

"I'm not in the market for anything right now," he murmured as he peered down at the girl. She was slightly taller than her boss, a lot lankier. Beatrice appeared quite different from the casual denim shorts and T-shirt he met her in while at Dr. Grant's house. Today she wore a sleeveless white blouse and gray slacks and swept her braids into a tight bun atop her head. "Where do you get your inventory?" he asked lightly, returning his gaze to the china cabinet.

"That's a trade secret," she said in an innocent voice. "That's like asking 'who's your fencer?'"

He chuckled at her little retort. Echoes of a secretive Doris shined through her words… Celeste was teaching her well. "Excuse *me*."

"So, you and Celeste…"

Magnus glanced at Beatrice to see her looking him up and down. "Yes?"

She scrunched up her nose and shook her head. "I don't see it."

"Don't see what?"

The young woman shrugged. "You just seem a little too IKEA-straight for her. Celeste is from around the way, a Harlem girl who knows how to scrap."

He rolled his eyes. "Believe me, I remember all too well."

She frowned when she got to the top of his head. "Does your hair move?"

Magnus self-consciously reached for his hair. "It shouldn't," he muttered while running his fingers along the perfectly laid strands held together by a Danish wax he specially ordered. "Is your scrappy boss in, or are you holding down the fort?"

Beatrice nodded over her shoulder. "She's in the back going over invoices. You need me to grab her?"

"Please," he said with a tight smile.

Before turning away, Beatrice put her fists on her hips and narrowed her eyes on him. "Are you back with the crew?"

He had to admire the girl's boldness as he bit back a wider grin. She was definitely a toned-down version of Celeste, a lot less aloof and a lot more guileless. "I don't seem to remember a Beatrice in our crew. You're taking attendance now?"

She pinned him with one last look, with eyes full of mirth, before walking away. "Celeste, you have a customer," she called out.

Magnus straightened up when Celeste's head poked out from the back offices. He smoothed his crisp white button-down against his belly and tried to train his face to something more placid. When she locked eyes with him, he tensed immediately like she'd trapped his balls in a vise with a simple gaze.

"It's Wednesday already?" she said, stepping into the show-room. She dressed in all black like a cat burglar: turtleneck, tight leather leggings, ankles boots. Her short black curls were glossed and falling against her brow. A pair of simple pearl earrings studded each ear, adding a small touch of softness to her overall look.

Beatrice busied herself behind the counter but kept a watch-ful eye on her boss and Magnus. He ignored her surveillance and focused on the woman approaching him. "I said I'd reach out."

"How are you doing?" she asked, stopping at a heavy oak writing desk. She tapped her nails against the surface while searching his gaze.

"I'm well," he replied. "You?"

Celeste nodded.

He couldn't get a good read on her nod, but assumed it was her way of saying she'd handle shit on her own time. "I'd like to take you somewhere for the afternoon."

She folded her arms across her chest. "Where?"

"Against my better judgment, I've made an appointment with the fine jewel counter of Bergdorf Goodman. If we leave now, we can arrive flushed, out of breath and looking like an engaged couple who lost track of time." He looked down at his watch.

"You want to do the Ball and Chain *with me*?" Celeste asked, her eyes widening in surprise.

"It's a good way to see if we can work together."

She seemed to turn the idea over in her mind as she stared at him. He hoped to God he wasn't making a mistake. The driving force of the Ball and Chain was their chemistry. They needed to appear in love: cosseted affection, adoring glances, the occasional familiar caress. They'd only done it once before, back when they were in the throes of a relationship. He remembered pulling off the score without a hitch and marveling at how well they played off each other.

But that was nearly six years ago.

They did *not* have the same fondness for one another these days. Celeste liked a challenge, though. And even if they had to work together, she still enjoyed friendly competition. In her head, she was probably devising ways to appear more in love with him than he her.

"Let me grab my purse," Celeste finally said. "Bea, can you watch the store?"

"Where are you going?" the young woman asked.

"Ring shopping."

Magnus exchanged a tiny smile with Beatrice. She raised a brow as Celeste disappeared into the back. "I still don't see it."

He liked the girl. Her sunny disposition could be a welcome addition to the group. But her words nagged at him. If she couldn't see the attraction between him and Celeste, there was a good chance the salespeople at Bergdorf Goodman wouldn't, either.

He needed to fix that immediately.

9

When Doris introduced Magnus Larsson to the crew, Celeste disliked him immediately.

She could tell he came from money, though she couldn't be sure how much. He just carried himself with an air of sophistication that she couldn't trust. She later learned that his parents had died and left him a small fortune, which he spent on an American education. He earned his degrees like she had but hadn't needed to steal to pay for them. Magnus stole because he felt like it.

And that was how he set himself apart from everyone else in the crew. Santiago was a bit of a loner because his father and older brother had been sent away for grand theft auto. Lawrence, a lifelong bachelor, was the last of his family and had partnered with Doris sometime in the seventies. Even young Beatrice, who grew up on Staten Island, had only her father and a mountain of debt from studying at Pace University. Magnus had experienced loss, but he never knew what going without looked like.

She held his privilege against him until she saw him work. When Magnus was on his game, he was a marvel to watch. Charm and finesse weren't things he had to learn like Celeste had. They were simply ingrained in him. If Celeste was more honest with herself, she'd admit that she envied his savoir faire. Deep down, she knew how invaluable a thief like Magnus was to their little crew. People asked fewer questions when he was in their presence.

She hoped today would work like it had in the past. When they exited their car at the Fifth Avenue store, Celeste blew out a nervous breath as she looked up at the building.

"You're fine," Magnus said, sensing her energy.

"I know," she said with a little more tart than was necessary.

On the sidewalk, while people were rushing around them, Magnus took her hand and brought it to his chest. "Hey… whatever is going on in your head, move it aside until we get back here. You can go back to hating me later."

Celeste frowned as she stared at her hands pressed to his starched shirt. "I don't hate you, Mags," she said. Did he really believe that? Was she behaving as though she did? *Yeesh…probably.*

He stroked the back of her hand with his thumb and stared into her eyes. "You don't have to be my friend. You just have to be my lover."

The urge to clench her thighs and roll her eyes was strong but she resisted both with a darting glance at his mouth. "Just for today, right?"

"Of course," he said, taking her by the back of her neck, his fingers smoothing against the fade at her nape. "Perhaps we should practice a kiss before going in?"

He was leaning toward her, very slowly and deliberately, as though they had all the time in the world to be dawdling out there on the busy sidewalk. "I know how to act, Mags," she said in a low voice.

"But do you know how to feel?" he asked, glancing from her lips to her eyes. "Are you scared?"

Celeste rolled her eyes that time. "Boy, ain't nobody scared of you."

"Then kiss me now. Kiss me like I'm the man you're meant to marry in the autumn. Our colors will be burgundy and gold. We'll have potted mums at a barn reception somewhere upstate."

She couldn't help the bubble of laughter that tickled the back of her throat. He sounded ridiculous, but his imagination was a delightful distraction from the fear she felt. In truth, Celeste *was* scared. She was afraid of performing with him and afraid that she might not have control of this little test.

"There's that laugh…" he murmured before pressing his lips to hers. It happened so slowly that she could have stopped him. She could have ducked her head and kept laughing at his corny attempt to be romantic. But she relaxed under his mouth for the second time in days. Aching for the familiarity just as much as the lust that tore through her body. She didn't hate him, but she hated what Magnus Larsson did to her.

She matched his kiss, moving her lips against his, tasting him. He nipped at her and sighed with what sounded like… contentment? Her mind couldn't shut up. Was he kissing her delicately because they needed to appear in love or was he enjoying himself? And what the hell was she doing?

Celeste pulled her head away, nearly out of breath. She scraped her nails along his shirt and felt his heart quicken. "I think I remember what it's like to feel something with you," she panted.

"Do you?" he breathed.

She nodded. "What are our names today?" she asked, giving herself some space. Magnus was always better at planning the theatrics.

He adjusted his collar before running his hands down the front of his shirt. "I settled with Joshua Matthews and Claire Adams for us," he said with a cough.

"Eww," she said as he took her hand and walked them to

the entrance. "That feels like a Montauk wedding I don't want to attend."

"Yeah… Claire does sound like a bridezilla, doesn't she?"

The good thing about Bergdorf was that the jewelry department was located on the first floor. No need to worry about a slow escalator or busy elevator in the event something went wrong. And Celeste would make sure that nothing went wrong. The Ball and Chain depended on an amorous act to distract the victim. She'd hang up whatever irritation she had for Magnus and pretend to love her fiancé.

It started with leaning into his hard body and wrapping her arm around his waist. He joined in by slinging an arm across her shoulders and whispering in her ear. "You smell delicious. Do you still wear Romance?"

"You remember my perfume?"

"I had an intimate relationship with it," he replied coolly.

She ignored that. "There are two badges walking the first floor, our three o'clock and ten o'clock."

He nodded.

As they made a leisurely path toward the jewelry department, Celeste prepared herself for the first person they'd interact with. A white woman with shoulder-length brown hair and dressed smartly in a light pink pantsuit smiled brightly at them.

"How are you doing today?" she asked in a well-practiced tone.

"Well, I'm hoping that you have an appointment for Joshua Matthews and his fiancée, Claire Adams," Magnus said, looking lovingly into Celeste's eyes rather than at the saleswoman. She had no choice but to return his amorous gaze, bite her lip and pretend to swoon.

"Of course, Mr. Matthews! My name is Janet and I'll be helping you with this momentous occasion." She immediately ushered them away from the regular foot traffic and deeper into her department. As far as Celeste could tell, Janet was the only person working the counter. "If you'll just wait a moment, I can show you the items I've picked out according to the carat specifications and ring size you gave us. He explained you'd have an intimate engagement party and that you'd want to surprise your loved ones *together*."

"Thank you for fitting us in for this," she said.

Janet chuckled, retrieving three velvet cases from beneath the counter. "It's not a problem. I just hope you're pleased with the selection. Mr. Matthews was very specific."

"He's very rigorous when it comes to these things," Celeste said, joining in the laughter. "Babe, I can't believe you did all this."

"Anything for my love," he said, watching the store while Janet busied herself.

When the saleswoman opened the boxes, Celeste gasped. "Darling, what have you picked out for me?"

"Only the best," he said, caressing her jaw with his fingertips.

Oh, boy... She arched up into his touch and almost melted from the warmth of it.

"How did you two meet?" Janet asked with that dreamy look that people get when they witness love. Celeste tried not to react with too much relief.

Magnus leaned his elbows against the counter. "We met in a medieval town just outside Rome. Viterbo. I got lost looking for a restaurant when I saw her at a little café near Palazzo dei Papi... She was just sitting there looking like a dream." Magnus turned to her. "The sun was shining on your face as you wrote in your notebook, and you let your gelato melt in the heat. You said you were trying to capture the moment, but I was, too."

Janet sighed while Celeste tried to hide her shock. For a moment, Magnus's blue eyes softened while regarding her and she felt the lie he was feeding Janet. The best she could do was build on it. She turned to the saleswoman and laughed. "He came to my table, exhausted and sweating."

"I can only imagine," Janet said.

"He just needed a gallon of water and a spot in the shade."

"You were my oasis," Magnus said.

"And I didn't think I'd fall in love with you," she said in a breathless voice.

"I can't imagine spending my life with anyone else," he whispered, taking her hands in his.

Her heart leaped up into her throat as her body warmed in his grasp. If they didn't get to the stealing, she'd soon lose the plot and fall into the story too deeply. She giggled nervously to break the thick tension in the tiny room. "Well, Janet, I think it's time to see what Josh picked out?"

To her surprise, Janet appeared to be close to tears. "Oh, of course! Excuse me. I just love hearing how couples meet. And in Italy of all places…it's just so romantic."

Celeste ran her fingers across the edge of the first box and sighed. "These are all so beautiful, babe… I don't know how I could possibly pick one."

"I'd love for you to stick to one for today," he said with a chuckle.

Three cases of seven rings. Twenty-one rings for Janet to potentially lose track of. She rolled her eyes in feigned annoyance and spotted two domed security cameras above them. One above the cash register and the other positioned right above them. Janet was cautious, but Celeste was sneakier. She had learned this ring counter lift from Doris.

"I don't want to go home!" screamed a nearby child. "I want to see the toys."

The three of them looked upon the red-faced child who was gearing up for a massive tantrum. The boy's mother also went red with embarrassment as people passed by. One security guard watched the boy intently. *God bless the petulant child…* Celeste quickly plucked a ring from the first box. A simple circle cut diamond affixed to a white gold band. It was probably the least expensive piece on the counter. "What do you think?" she asked Magnus.

He frowned. "It's a little simple, don't you think?" But he wove an arm around her back and tapped his finger a single time against her spine.

"Are you sure?" she asked, feeling for his tapping finger.

He nodded and pressed once more. It was his signal. One tap for yes, two taps for no. Magnus wanted her to take *this* ring. "Janet has picked out some lovely rings. Don't get hung up on anything yet."

"I don't wanna gooooo!" the child cried, now sinking to the floor.

"Oliver, get up this instant," his mother hissed.

Janet was already distracted. "Someone's having a bad day..." she huffed as she faced them again. "Oh, yes, Ms. Adams. Please examine everything before deciding. You only get one chance at your perfect engagement ring."

"I suppose you're right," she said, slipping the ring from her finger. Celeste placed it back in its spot and began the classic game of cups and balls. One by one, she tried on rings, making comments as she went. Magnus offered feedback, marveling over her hand and giving effusive comments. Meanwhile, Janet's attention volleyed between young Oliver, who was now laid out in the middle of the floor, and Celeste's hands.

"Would you like one of those?" Magnus asked, nodding toward the screaming kid.

"Not that one," she joked. "But maybe..."

Truthfully, Celeste didn't have any desire to have children. And while that wasn't necessarily Oliver's fault, he certainly solidified that choice. At forty-one, she was still living a life for herself.

"I hope our daughter has your beauty, intellect and humor." Magnus planted a kiss on her forehead for every attribute. His finger was still on her back, giving her a double tap that meant "no." She was relieved because, for a moment, he almost looked serious.

"If she has your charm, I don't know what we'll do with her," she said, playing along.

"Oh, my God, he's actually turning red," Janet muttered as she stared at Oliver. "Is she going to do anything? Is this some kind of gentle parenting tactic from TikTok?"

Celeste was so thankful for the screaming child that she wanted to gather him up in her arms and kiss his little tear-streaked face. Janet hadn't paid any mind to their little lover's conversation, how many rings Celeste had tried on, or that the first ring had slipped into the hem of her turtleneck sleeve. The sharp diamond scratched against her wrist every time she extended her hand toward Magnus. On the last examination of a ten-carat emerald-and-diamond set sitting atop a platinum band, he pulled the piece from her sleeve and tucked it into the groove of his palm.

"My love, this is the one," he announced as he slipped his hand into his blazer pocket. His other hand held hers tightly, stroking the giant gem on her ring finger. "Surely, you can see it."

"I love it, but it's a little flashy."

Magnus closed the first two velvet boxes with a swift snap, to distract from the blank spot of the first case. She made sure to take one from the very edge to make it less noticeable. He pulled her close and whispered in her hair, outside of Janet's notice, "I'd love to see you in this ring and nothing else, in my bed, tonight."

Celeste gasped at his words and drew back sharply. He sounded serious!

"Janet," Magnus said, presenting her hand. "I think we've found the one."

What was he doing?

Celeste watched on in amazement as he whipped out a credit card and slapped it on the glass counter. Even more surprised that the name on it was Joshua Matthews. The saleswoman appeared more excited than she felt upon seeing one of their most expensive rings spoken for.

Celeste's jaw dropped. This wasn't how the cups and balls game worked. They were supposed to play until a distraction forced them to make a quick exit. Oliver was providing that distraction, so why on Earth was Magnus going through the act of paying for something?

Time seemed to speed up *and* slow down as her partner moved on without her. She accepted Janet's congratulations and watched her put away the discarded rings. At some point Oliver was dragged away; his wailing receded into the distance while Celeste smiled and nodded at their saleswoman. The cabochon emerald-and-diamond ring, retailing at a hundred thousand dollars, was wrapped and bagged before she could understand what was happening.

She thanked Janet for her time and was walked out of Bergdorf Goodman in a loving embrace with her *fiancé* before she could signal some kind of "what the fuck are you doing?" When they made it to the sidewalk, beneath the waning sunlight, Celeste's jaw was clenched in anger.

"What was that?" she asked as Magnus led her down Fifth Avenue. Their steps were fast, and his grip was tight.

"A little insurance never hurt anyone," Magnus said when they crossed the street.

This is what she *hadn't* missed about her thieving partner.

The lack of communication when they worked together.

The way she was on one page, and he was in a whole other book.

10

At the end of the day, he couldn't trust that the little boy screaming at the top of his lungs was a good enough diversion. He didn't trust that Janet could be fooled into believing that she had twenty-one rings when she only had twenty.

Magnus ultimately couldn't trust in himself.

He'd treated Celeste as though she was the only shining star in his black night, and surely Janet had seen that. He'd played the Ball and Chain with too much gusto. And when he saw a familiar warmth in Celeste's eyes, felt it in her touch, he reared back like a nervous horse. It felt *too* believable. In that moment, he felt like a ballroom dancer who forgot how to dance. He felt clumsy and unsure about his next steps. He was certain he'd stumble over his partner because he hadn't had a partner in so long.

So he fell back on practicality and slipped the original ring back in its case while the child caught Celeste's attention. He then purchased an emerald ring he didn't need. An engagement ring that wouldn't unite a damn thing. Even as he held on to her, he could feel Celeste's body tense.

They walked wordlessly until they were at least two blocks away, on Seventh Avenue. She whirled on him and shot him an accusatory glare. "What happened?"

"It got too hot," he said. "I changed directions and decided to go straight."

Celeste's jaw dropped as her eyes roved over his body. "You left the original ring, didn't you?" She took it a step further and began going through his jacket pockets. Her hands swiped across his chest, then to his pants pocket... She was frisking him right there on the street. "You for real bought an emerald ring? Jesus Christ, Mags. Why would you do that?"

Because it felt too real and I panicked.

"Buying this ring is nothing," he said defensively. He could feel his face heating under her glowering stare. "If I want, I'll fence it. It's not that big of a deal, Celeste."

"*That* wasn't the goal!"

Magnus took her by the shoulders to stop her from spinning out. "We did accomplish the goal. You stole the ring, Janet didn't notice and we probably would have gotten away with it."

Celeste shook herself free and marched toward the street.

"Where are you going?"

"Back to my store," she said, hailing a cab.

Magnus blew out an exasperated sigh and followed her. He suddenly did not feel like a man in his forties, accomplished and self-assured. After his third meeting with Celeste, he was now back in his adolescence. Young, silly and mildly horny at the sight of her. As they waited for a yellow cab to pull up to the curb, he stood behind Celeste and watched her shoulders drop.

"What?" he asked. He remembered she had made that gesture when she finally released all the air in her body and was ready to give up.

"Give me a minute," she said in a tired voice. Once the cab pulled up, Magnus stepped around her to open the door. She slid inside without a word, and he followed her. They didn't speak for the first block, but he kept catching glances at her, wondering how angry she was. They sat a respectable distance apart and their thighs didn't touch, but he felt the heat radiate off her body just the same. "You got the twisties, huh?"

"The what?"

Celeste kept her eyes on the back of their driver's headrest. "It happens to gymnasts while they're in midair. Their brain kind of shorts out and they lose control of their routine while they're flying. They don't remember which way to twist."

Oh... Magnus bit the inside of his cheek. He didn't like being found out. All his insecurities were supposed to be nailed down, caged up and hidden from women like Celeste. "I guess," he grumbled, glancing out his window to avoid her.

She sighed. "Well, it's really fucking dangerous if you don't communicate it to the person you're working with. We both end up falling down and busting our asses."

"It won't happen again," he said immediately.

"It happens to all of us," she shot back. "But you're supposed to say something."

Magnus gritted his teeth. "Was it the twisties when you jumped into a river in Stockholm?"

When their eyes met, Celeste's gaze burned into his. He matched her intensity because she didn't get to walk away from this blameless. Not again. She shook her head and let out a huff before facing the window. "I can't believe I pretended to be in love with you," she muttered.

"It didn't look like a hardship from my end."

"I don't think we can work together," she said.

No, he didn't think they could, either. Except this time, he was the one who'd been reckless. After all these years of stewing over Celeste's antics, he had behaved in the same way. He had made a big show of inviting her on this outing only to fuck it up. They hadn't gotten caught but he'd still managed to fuck it up.

Doris would have been disappointed with his performance.

The thought struck him as worrisome. Did Dr. Grant's opinion of him still matter? After all these years, and after her death? On a very deep level, yes. Her last observations of his attitude had bothered him. Nordic veneer…narrow window? The itch to prove a dead woman wrong had also bothered him. That was the whole reason he'd even shown up at Celeste's shop.

Magnus rubbed his sweating hands on his pants before speaking. "I can come back…" He gripped his knee and muttered the last part. "Different."

Celeste turned to face him. "Different? That doesn't sound like you at all."

"According to Doris, we could both stand to be a little different," he argued.

She narrowed her eyes on him. "So, you *were* listening to the letter?"

He fought not to roll his eyes.

"If you're serious, pack a go bag and meet me at Doris's house tonight."

He raised a brow at her demand. "Tonight? Are we inviting anyone else?"

"No," she said, turning her face to the window. "I'd like for us to have some kind of united front before we meet with Bea and Santi. If we're going to do this right, we need to convince them we can be in the same room without wanting to fuck each other up."

Interesting choice of words…

"It's going to take a lot of convincing for Beatrice to buy us," he said, gesturing between them.

Celeste scoffed. "She's a smart girl."

Magnus rolled his eyes. "And Lawrence?"

"We need to be there for him. He's suffered a huge loss."

He studied her as she continued to face the city. The Dior bag that she hung on to was of little significance to her as she kept picking at the loose threads. Her shoulders may have relaxed, but she only managed to transfer her nervous energy elsewhere.

He wanted to ask her: *But what about you? Who's there for you?* He kept his mouth shut instead. He didn't want to fight Celeste for her feelings. Her mind was a near impossible safe to crack.

"We can be there," he finally said.

"Have any clues as to the first location on our hunt?"

Impressive sidestep, Dr. St. Pierre... He shook his head. "I didn't give any thought to it."

"Really? Besides teaching, what have you been thinking about for the past two days?"

Nope, it's not going to be that easy. If she was going to keep her true thoughts behind a massive vault, he wasn't going to volunteer ammo for her to use the next time they went at each other's throats. He chose to lie instead. He examined his manicured nails and said, "I occupied my time with a friend. She helped keep my mind busy."

Instead of jealousy, Celeste shot him a grin. "A female friend?"

"She's a ballerina," Magnus offered easily. In truth, he hadn't seen Michelle in over a week. "You might be familiar with her work. She's the principal dancer with the ballet."

"Michelle Waterson?" Celeste laughed. "I saw her a couple months ago in the *All Balanchine*. She's fantastic. You're dating her?"

Magnus suddenly lost his footing. This wasn't the reaction he had expected. "I don't know if what we're doing is dating. Also, you don't have to sound so surprised."

Her laughter grew louder. "I'm surprised because she's a random name to throw out there, not because she's too good for you. Although, she is quite stunning..."

"She's a lovely woman," Magnus muttered.

"Very flexible, too, I bet," Celeste teased.

As much as he wanted to hear Celeste's husky laugh, a sound that loosened the knots around his heart, he wasn't sure if he wanted to keep up the ballerina banter with her. "Yeah, well, I don't see the relationship working out."

Celeste rested her elbow on her knee and her pointy chin on her fist. "No? Getting too old to keep up with her, Mags? Worried about her long line of dance partners?"

"Don't doubt my stamina. I can still run circles around you," he said, flicking an invisible speck of lint from his pants. "And besides, I'm not the jealous type."

Her grin widened. "So, what is it?"

He sighed. "If I'm on schedule for a score, I don't have time to think of anything else. As long as you and I work together, you'll have all my attention, whether you like it or not."

Celeste's brows lifted as her smile fell away. "Oh."

Now she was on shaky ground. Magnus relaxed in his seat as they traveled another block. If he read her right, she was searching for her next retort. Either engage him in a petty battle or let the ballerina go. He was almost ashamed for even bringing Michelle's name into the conversation.

"No distractions," she murmured.

"No distractions."

"You know I don't hate you, right?" she said, switching directions again.

This time, Magnus looked at her sharply. "Okay?"

"I still think you're an arrogant prick who's too wealthy to be doing this. You tend to hijack plans when they don't work for *you*. But I don't hate you. Oh, this is our stop."

He couldn't help the chuckle that escaped his throat as the cab pulled up along the curb. "An arrogant prick…"

She shrugged, reaching into her purse to pay. "Calling it like I see it."

"I've got it," he said, pulling a couple bills from his wallet.

"Thanks, man," said their driver.

Celeste shook her head and climbed from the cab. "See? You buy me an engagement ring and then pay for my ride."

"It's not your engagement ring and a gentleman pays for a lady's ride."

No, he didn't need to steal. Yes, he had family wealth that

brought him to America with ease. Magnus hadn't struggled and it was unlikely he ever would. Those were the facts.

"Oh, so I'm a lady?" Celeste asked in a singsong voice when she reached the sidewalk.

You used to be my lady.

"Last time I checked."

"And you're definitely fencing the ring?" she asked, placing her hand on the door of her establishment.

"I'm not giving it to you, Celeste."

She shrugged. "I don't want it."

"Then you don't have to worry." The ring was safely tucked away in his jacket pocket, waiting for Keith, his fencer. If he called him up tonight, he could have a meeting tomorrow morning. Easy peasy.

"Who's your guy?" she asked.

"Doris always taught us it was in poor taste to talk about fencers."

This brought a smile to her face. It shined bright with genuine pleasure at the mention of Doris. Magnus locked that knowledge away in his brain to save for another day. Or maybe later this evening.

"I'll see you tonight, then? How about nine?"

Magnus nodded. "Sure."

She waited a beat before disappearing inside, leaving him on the sidewalk. The ring sat heavy like lead in his pocket. He absently thumbed the small velvet box and thought of everything that Celeste said. His mind kept landing on *arrogant prick*. It wasn't clear how successful their Ball and Chain job went. Even less clear on how their cab ride went.

He bought an engagement ring.

He tried to provoke her with another woman.

Magnus didn't know how to interact with Celeste. It felt a lot easier several years ago, back when Dr. Grant forced them… to work together. He chuckled to himself as he walked toward the subway. *Dammit, Doris.*

11

"Now, look at this…" Lawrence said with a raised brow as he let Celeste in. "And with a go bag. Where do you think you're headed, little lady?"

Celeste hugged his neck as she stepped inside. "I'm here to check in on you and investigate the Doris mystery. Unless… you have answers you're not telling us?"

The old man rubbed her back. "I told you. I only know as much as you kids."

She hitched her backpack on her shoulder while tossing her go bag at the stairwell. "Magnus is stopping by, too."

Lawrence's eyes widened. "Well, maybe I should go ahead and put the tea on."

"Hold off on that. I'll pour myself some whiskey instead."

"Back to the library, then."

They went back to the library, where Celeste served herself while Lawrence sat himself in a comfy chair. "So how have you been holding up?"

Celeste took her first sip, let it burn a fiery path down her throat before shrugging. "I'm all right."

"You wanna talk about it?"

She didn't want to talk about Doris being dead, not when she was so full of life. "Tell me about how you met."

He ran his hand over the tight springy curls of his hair and rolled his eyes to the ceiling.

"I met her in 1977. I was fresh from the South. Didn't know what the hell I was doing up here. I was young, gay and running around like I was gonna live forever. If you can believe it, I met Doris at Studio 54."

She grinned as she took another sip. "Nuh-uh."

"Yes, ma'am. I had made some friends who lived five to an apartment in the East Village. Billy was a go-go dancer who had an invite and he let me tag along. They were hell-bent on me shedding this country shell. I was a little scared at first, but when we got there, I shed Menifee, Arkansas, all right..." He trailed off with a sad chuckle. "Boy, I was finally at home. I met her at the bar. She was surveying the scene all catlike and mysterious. It didn't take long before I found myself talking to her. We talked about the South, the arts, the state of Black folks back then. She was my best friend. The light of my life. I was charmed by her."

"She has a way of doing that," Celeste said, resting her head against the back of her chair.

"Doing what?"

She shrugged. "Pulling you in like a flame pulls a moth. She's really the light."

Lawrence fixed his jaw and pursed his lips before replying carefully, "Doris found people when they needed her. She helped. But not without a price."

Celeste peered at the old man with curiosity. "What do you mean?"

The doorbell interrupted them. "That must be our friend Magnus," he said, pulling himself from his chair. "Save him some whiskey, won't you?"

She placed her glass on a nearby table and frowned as Lawrence left the room. What did he mean by that? He made Doris sound like a spider trapping him in her web. Had he not benefited from her teachings like the rest of them? When Celeste had no one else in her corner, she had Dr. Grant. It didn't sound like Lawrence to be this critical. And so soon after her death.

She heard masculine voices echoing from the entrance, filtering toward the library. Magnus's laughter and Lawrence chiding him. Had she time, she would have talked to Lawrence about the Ball and Chain debacle from earlier in the day. To Celeste, they couldn't have had better conditions: a busy store, a screaming child and a distracted saleswoman. And above all, they worked well together...for a moment, at least. They riffed with each other with an ease that Celeste hadn't expected.

She'd had fun with Magnus until he went off in his own direction.

Celeste had almost pinned him down in the cab ride back to the store. He was very close to admitting that he might not know what he's doing at every twist and turn. But he said he could be different. Against her better judgment, she'd have to trust him.

Speaking of the Nordic devil... He appeared around the corner, dressed in a pair of gray tweed slacks and a black polo shirt. His hair hadn't moved from its stiff blond coif from that afternoon. "Hello again, Celeste."

"Magnus," she replied with a nod.

"I'm gonna leave you kids to the mystery," Lawrence said, checking his watch. "I've got a show and dinner with a friend. I'll be out fairly late."

They both gasped in half-shock and half-teasing. "You've got a date?" Magnus asked.

"Who's this friend?" Celeste pressed.

Lawrence gave them a dismissive wave. "Contrary to what you might think, I got a life outside of this big old house."

Magnus leaned against the door frame with crossed arms.

A grin stretched over his handsome face. "Don't do anything I wouldn't do."

Celeste let out an unladylike snort.

"Y'all help yourself to the kitchen," Lawrence said, patting Magnus on the back. "Spare rooms are already made up. Don't wait up."

"You're not leaving money for pizza?" Celeste protested.

"Good night!" the old man said over his shoulder. "And behave yourselves."

"Scout's honor," Magnus said, staring at her. His eyes twinkled with mirth from across the room. They sent a prick of awareness through her body that made her sit up straighter. Like she needed to be on guard. He pushed himself farther into the room and took Lawrence's seat. He seemed to carry himself with the confidence he didn't have earlier.

"You want anything to drink?" she asked politely.

He shook his head. "Better not," he said. "Don't let me stop you, though."

"You're not."

"Are you ready to figure out this riddle?"

She scrunched her face as she got up and took her backpack to the desk. "I hate riddles. And Doris knew that. I don't know why she couldn't just tell us where to go and what to find." She rifled through the box that Lawrence had presented to them and found the letter.

"Have you ever known her to say what was on her mind?" Magnus asked, crossing his legs. "She lived her entire life like a riddle. Why would things be different now?"

She was getting the sneaking suspicion that everyone knew something about Doris that she didn't. First Lawrence, and his offhanded comment, and now Magnus was calling her secretive. What was wrong with a woman who liked to keep secrets? Not every little thought or feeling needed to be shouted from the rooftops. "Do you need to hear the clue again?"

"Lemme get my pen," he said, reaching for his go bag. When he pulled out a legal pad and pen, she chuckled. "What?"

"You didn't bring a laptop?"

Magnus flipped to a free page in his notepad. "Don't need one."

"Fair enough. 'Peter promised her home but when he died, she couldn't imagine a hearth without him. Not even the god of the seas could lure her back to the flowers and fountains. That kind of love is nestled deep, but it's also quite fragile. If ever you were to take hold of it, be gentle lest you crack its surface. But go with a bold voice. Sing a joyous song that's loud enough to drive the bear back to his iron cave.'" She sat down at the desk and looked up from the paper she had just read from. "Anything?"

Magnus gazed thoughtfully into the distance with the tip of his pen on his bottom lip. He looked very scholarly...and quite attractive. "Give me a minute."

Celeste had to shake her head from the image of him in a classroom setting, leisurely pacing throughout the aisles and lecturing his students. For some reason, that did it for her, and she needed to shut that shit down to think about more important things.

"Well, it's got to be Russia," she said after about fifteen minutes of silence. The library was totally quiet save her typing and his scratchy note-taking. Even the suddenness of her voice startled her.

Magnus's head snapped up. "Yeah...but probably not." He flipped through his notes and read them aloud. "While it's likely she's talking about Peter the Great, his building a home for Catherine isn't exactly news. I wonder if she's referring to an egg when she says 'nestled deep' and 'fragile'... Possibly a Fabergé egg? And of course, there's the bear in the iron cave."

"All of which sounds like Russia to me," Celeste said, finishing her whiskey. She decided against pouring another. She was feeling loose as it was. If she was going to be alone with Magnus, she needed to keep her head on a swivel. The more time she spent with him, the more she began to doubt her own firm stance of never touching him again.

Pretending to be a man's fiancée did things to a woman's stomach. Even after she returned to her store, she couldn't stop the butterflies from going wild. They were fluttering dangerously close to her nether regions despite her annoyance with him. He had kissed her a couple times that day, and it was difficult to shut those memories off when they shared a stuffy little library in a house where they were impossibly alone.

"Unless..." Magnus murmured, tapping his pen to his lip. "I stand corrected. I do need a computer." He stood up and crossed the room in several long strides. "Can you pull up a map of the countries surrounding Russia?"

Before she could answer, he was standing over her with one hand beside her laptop and the other resting on the back of her chair. Boxing her in a warm, albeit hands-off embrace. He didn't need to touch her for Celeste to feel her chest tighten and her thighs clench. As steady as she could, she brought up a world map and zoomed in on Eastern Europe.

"Mongolia, Finland, China, Latvia..."

"It's a lot," Celeste finished. "Fourteen nations, including the former Soviet Union countries."

His heavy sigh blew warm breath against her ear and sent a shiver down her neck. "Right, never mind." Magnus read the letter next to her once again, under his breath while she fought the urge to rest the back of her head against his chest. "'Sing a joyous song that's loud enough to drive the bear back to his iron cave.' That part. That's why I don't think she's sending us to Russia."

"Well, I sure as hell don't want to be in Moscow right now.

Or St. Petersburg, for that matter. Remember the job we pulled in Kazan?"

Magnus chuckled. "In February…it was hell."

"Poor Santi got his snowmobile stuck in a drift."

"Lawrence didn't say much but that was how you could tell he was pissed."

Celeste laughed with him. "The quieter Lawrence gets, take a couple steps back."

"Kazan was exhilarating, though…" Magnus murmured.

He was right. Despite the oppressive weather and a watchful regime, she felt so alive while stealing beside him. Occasionally, Doris gave them charitable jobs to complete. A Ukrainian collector led them to Kazan for what amounted to a rescue mission for his family's long-lost Taras Shevchenko painting. The planning took a couple months, but it went off without too many hitches.

The first thing Celeste remembered was the cold, but then her thoughts quickly went to the part where Magnus heated her up. Outside, in the alleyway of a bar, he took her by the hips and pushed her against the wall. He kissed her deeply, high on celebration and adrenaline. She'd stared into his dark, dilated blue eyes long enough to lose herself. Of all the memories from that job, how on Earth did she get there?

"Joyous song…" she muttered. "What joyous song?"

"How do you sing Russia back to their side of the border?" Magnus asked.

Celeste shrugged. "I have no idea."

"Just google singing and collapse of the Soviet Union?"

She turned in her seat to look at him. "What?"

Magnus was right in her face. Just an inch or so away. "Just try."

Celeste quickly turned around to escape his mouth. "Fine." She typed his keywords and they both glanced through the results.

"There." He jabbed at her screen. "Click that."

She clicked the article about Estonia's thirty-year anniversary of the Singing Revolution. As she scanned the article, everything fell into place. Good Lord, he was right. The home that Peter built for Catherine was in Estonia's capital, Tallinn. Those same people took to the outdoor amphitheater and literally sang the Russians out of the Baltic region. "Fuck," she whispered.

Magnus straightened away and gave a single loud clap. "Fuck yeah!"

"That's it, isn't it?" she said excitedly. "We're going to Tallinn?"

"I think so?" he said, planting his fists on his hips. "I mean, I can't think of another place where the people sang the bear back in the cave. Peter built the palace, Kadriorg? It was for her. I'm pretty sure it was some kind of vacation home. If I remember correctly, she didn't want to stay there after his death, and it went into disrepair."

"No, it sounds about right," Celeste said, standing from the desk. "I think we figured it out!"

Without thinking they embraced.

She wrapped her arms around his neck and squeezed him tight. With the excitement of their discovery very much in the front of her mind, she neglected to think about the implications of such a familiar hug. It didn't occur to her until they lingered, interlocked, for a moment longer than they should have. Magnus released her first. She stumbled back a few steps, feeling embarrassed by the brief show of emotion.

"We did it," Magnus breathed, running his hands through his hair, leaving it less coiffed. "Have you ever been to Tallinn?"

She shook her head, returning to her laptop. "No, I haven't. I don't know shit about Estonia," she chuckled.

"I can't wait to show you the Old Town," he said, sitting on the edge of the desk. "It's really nice...and old."

She glanced at him as she sent an encrypted message to

Santiago, Beatrice and Lawrence. We're going to Estonia, get prepped. "Similar to Old Town in Stockholm?"

"Yes, but Tallinn is better," he admitted. "My parents took me on the ferry between Estonia and Finland and I remember having a really nice time."

His broad smile lit up the dim library in a way Celeste hadn't seen in years. He looked genuinely happy when he spoke of his parents. When they'd had a more intimate relationship, Magnus rarely spoke of them, and she had never pushed him. "I look forward to it," she said.

"Tallinn?"

Celeste grinned. "The hunt."

This made him laugh. She felt surprisingly relieved to hear the sound he made when he let his guard down. It loosened something up in her chest, too. "Well, I'm going to find a room and get settled in for the night." He paused to rub the back of his neck. "Do you know where you're going to sleep?"

"I do," she said. She sure as hell wasn't going to tell him.

Magnus rolled his eyes as he took up his notepad and walked away. "All right, CeCe…"

12

After sorting out Doris's mystery clue, Celeste headed straight to the kitchen to root around in the refrigerator. Lawrence had made a baked ziti perfect for nibbling on. Magnus's footsteps thudded just above her on the second floor. She'd make certain to find a room on the third floor. The more space they had between them, the safer they'd be.

When he returned to the kitchen, he wore a black tank top and gray pajama pants. His hair was damp from a recent shower. "What's for dinner?" he asked in a tired voice that sounded slightly slurred.

Celeste got up from the kitchen island and scraped the remainder of her plate into the garbage. "Leftover baked ziti. Want some?"

He leaned against the counter and stared at the casserole pan. "I better not. I just took my pill."

"Lawrence got back to me," she said. "Apparently, Doris has a safe house in Tallinn. Maybe we'll post up there and see what other clues we can find."

Magnus nodded absently as he leaned against the counter. He appeared intoxicated even though she knew he hadn't had anything to drink. Not while they were working together. She peered at him as he stood there looking vacant as fuck.

"Mags? Are you okay?" she asked, running water over her dish.

His head swung around to face her; his eyes were flat and glassy. "I took an Ambien," he slurred in a confused voice. "They don't really work on a full stomach, I don't think?"

Celeste quickly set aside her plate and she took him by the shoulders. "A sleeping pill?" she asked.

Magnus nodded, trying to keep his eyes open.

"How long have you had trouble falling asleep?" she asked, holding him by both arms. He looked like he was close to falling over.

"A couple years," he said, weaving toward her open arms.

She frowned as she searched his eyes for some kind of awareness. "Stress?"

He nodded. "Did you know that I'm actually too rich to be teaching? Yet I'm still doing all this dumb shit for my department. I like teaching and my students are lovely… They're good kids really. Some of them are annoying grade grubbers, but that's just the name of the game these days, isn't it? I just don't remember being that ambitious when I was their age."

She tried to nod along to what he was saying but he was confusingly incoherent.

"And then there's the loneliness," he said. "Michelle is nice, but I don't think it'll work. I don't think I'll ever be honest with her about what I do." He chuckled to himself. "Honestly, there aren't many people like us. People who understand what we do. I think I'm lonely because I liked having you in my bed, and you haven't been there for years. What is it? Five years?"

Celeste's heart almost ceased to function.

What was he rambling about? They hadn't seen each other, much less shared a bed, in five years—like he said—why would he admit that to her? Because he wasn't himself. Her straitlaced Magnus was just high. On what was essentially truth serum.

Celeste tried her best not to laugh at the whole situation.

"I'm going to get you to bed, then," she said, pulling one of his muscular arms over her shoulder. "Watch your step."

"You watch *yourself*, CeCe," he muttered.

She raised a brow as she led him to the stairway. He'd murmured it as he nuzzled her neck, kissing the space behind her ear. "Why would I need to watch myself, Mags?" she asked, grinning.

"Because I have you in my arms again," he said. With most of his weight leaning on her, she tried to steer him up the stairs as fast as humanly possible. "Your hair smells like fruit," he breathed. She could feel his face pressed against the top of her head. "I like your hair like this. It's short and cool…like a cool assassin or something."

"You're going to have to help me out here, Mags. You're kind of heavy," she said through gritted teeth. They were halfway up to the first landing, not too far from the bedroom she'd heard him walking around in.

"You're strong," he said simply. "You're the strongest woman I've ever met. Not many people have had to overcome what you've lived. Have I told you how proud we are of you? CeCe gets a gold star. High marks."

"Thank you," she said, laughing. He was much nicer under the influence. She had to pause when they reached the top and took a short breather.

"Sleep with me tonight," he said. It certainly wasn't a question.

Celeste looked up at him; his hooded eyes stared back, as he gave her a lopsided grin. "Why?"

"Because I want you."

Oh, boy… He didn't know what he was saying. After he tried to bait her with the ballerina earlier in the day, Celeste figured he was full of shit. But now it sounded like he was full of something else. *Eww, not unrequited feelings…*

"I think you want sleep," she said, pushing him toward his bedroom.

"I want you," he repeated.

When she sat him on his bed, she pulled away to look him over. He sat up on his own but was a little wobbly as he shot her the same sleepy grin. "I want to snuggle with you. You smell nice," he said with a yawn.

Should I stay to snuggle? She could slip out of the room before he woke up the next morning. Celeste shook her head. No, it wasn't a good idea to indulge him in this state. She didn't want their relationship to get muddled any more than it needed to be. On the other hand, she didn't know when she'd get another opportunity to know exactly what was on Magnus Larsson's mind.

"Go to bed, Mags," she said, pushing his shoulders to the mattress.

He went down easily but patted the space beside him. "Stay for a little while, CeCe. I don't bite."

"I was never worried about your bite."

"Ugh…you still like a good fight, don't you?" he groaned, putting an arm over his eyes.

"It's hard to let shit go," she admitted with a sigh.

"You hold grudges."

She rolled her eyes up to the ceiling. "Oh, shut up."

"Come over here and make me," he said with another yawn. Part of him must not have cared that she was still there, because he absently stuck his hand down the front of his pants and adjusted himself. The reminder of his dick made her stomach dip and her heart skip a beat.

She needed to get the hell out of there.

Celeste jerked the blankets from beneath his heavy body and attempted to cover him.

"Where are you going?" Magnus mumbled.

She turned out the light and hurried to the door. "I'm going to clean the kitchen and go to bed," she said in a quiet voice. "Get some sleep, Mags."

Celeste didn't wait on his reply as she quickly put herself on the other side of his door. She leaned against the hardwood and let out a sigh of relief. She didn't need to see him like this tonight. A vulnerable Magnus wasn't useful to her while they worked. She only needed him to get back to prime stealing condition.

The world moved around them like a long, shuddering breath, building slowly and releasing in a staggering pleasure that made his toes curl and back arch from the bed. Magnus looked into Celeste's dark eyes while he grabbed a generous handful of ass and pulled her onto his dick. Her intense gaze pinned him straight to the mattress as she circled her hips above him.

"Come back to me," he heard himself say.

A smile grew on her lips as she shook her head. "I don't think you can catch me," she whispered.

Her teasing words made his breath catch in his throat. They felt like a bucket of ice water thrown in his face. Magnus's hands fell away from her body as she continued to rock against him.

"Sink, Magnus…" she said. "Stay in the deep."

Black waves lapped over his body. Cold rain tickled his skin. Darkness closed in on the outer edges of his sight and soon he could no longer feel the plush pressure of Celeste's curves wrapped around him. She, and light, disappeared until he sank into the bottom of some nameless space.

He was willing to hit the bottom, but a nagging thought kept him buoyed.

I can't let go.

In the next instant, he found himself under bright flickering lights. A new sterile environment where the floors squeaked under white sneakers. Nurses and doctors scurried about in confusion while he sat in a hard-shelled chair staring at his hands. The hands of a fourteen-year-old.

Swedish speakers were nearby, their voices hushed and somber.

"Does he have anywhere to go tonight?"

"He has an uncle living in Örebro."

"We cannot let him go."

Magnus couldn't open his mouth to tell the speakers that he could indeed hear them. He wanted them to know that he was in the hallway. He was there, but loneliness hung on his young body like an itchy woolen blanket, forcing him deeper into his chair.

Darkness was swiftly returning but this time, Magnus couldn't bear to be enveloped by its coldness. He fought, thrashing against the tide, desperate to push the scratchy blanket aside. He'd reach the surface if he tried. If his tired arms were strong enough, he'd see the light.

The muffled shouts pulled Celeste from her online reading about Tallinn, Estonia. The loud thump against the floor got her out of bed and running downstairs to Magnus's second-floor bedroom.

She didn't know much about Ambien's side effects, but she could assume that was what ailed him. Celeste didn't even bother knocking; instead, she entered his room and turned on a lamp beside his bed.

She found a bleary-eyed Magnus climbing from the floor. "Hey," he murmured.

"Are you okay?" she asked, scrambling across the bed to help him up. "Did you have a bad dream?"

Magnus frowned while squinting at the light on the nightstand. "I don't know..."

If he couldn't remember crying out and flailing in his bed, he could still be high, Celeste reasoned. She suddenly felt unsure about leaving him for a second time. "Let's get back in bed, Magnus."

He complied quietly and she settled beside him. "Are you staying?" he asked in a soft voice.

Celeste turned the light off and climbed under the covers. "I might as well," she grumbled. "You can't be trusted to sleep by yourself. Hey—" she protested as he dragged her into his embrace. "No one said anything about spooning."

"I'm cuddling you."

She'd forgotten what cuddling with Magnus felt like and was quickly reminded of how much she had enjoyed his strength. His long legs wrapped around hers as the heat from his body pulsed against her back. His arm snaked around her belly and held her in a loose, but secure, grasp that made her feel surprisingly safe.

"Are you comfortable?" he asked.

Celeste laughed at the ridiculous question.

"I miss that sound."

His words, however fleeting they were, made her heart stumble over itself. A lump formed in her throat as she attempted to engage him. "You miss my laugh?"

"Sounds like rain smells. Fresh and full of life," he murmured into her hair. "Completely guileless."

Celeste tested him for the sake of her vanity. "Magnus, do you think I'm— Am I still attractive to you?" It had been five years after all. She was now in her early forties and hadn't had a proper boyfriend in years.

He groaned and pulled her closer. His hips rocked forward, grinding against her butt in response. "Beautiful. Most beautiful woman at the party," Magnus said, nuzzling her neck. His evening whiskers scratched against her skin, sending a fresh wave of heat down her back.

She continued testing… "Do you still think I'm annoying?" she asked, grinning in the dark.

"Oh, God, yes. So fucking annoying," he said, running his palm down her bare arm. She felt his hand stop on her waist, his fingers rubbing against the bottom of her tummy. She wasn't sure if it was voluntary or not, but his hips rocked forward again, lightly nudging her backside. "You're a hardheaded woman who never stops."

She nodded because it was true. "And it bothers you?"

His lips pressed against the dip along her neck. "Mmm. Not all the time," he said. "Sometimes it's sexy."

Celeste shifted in his arms to face him. She pressed both hands against his cheeks and searched for his eyes in the dark. "Are we really going to work together again? For Doris?"

His hands were still busy beneath the covers, pulling her hips closer to his. "I didn't want to," he whispered. "But yeah, I will."

"Why?"

"Because I don't want you to get hurt," he murmured. "I have to go with you to keep you safe. From yourself mostly. Jesus, you take some careless risks sometimes. I used to wonder why, but the more I got to know Doris, I guess I could see it."

How long would he be like this before clamming right up and shielding her from his genuine feelings? "You don't have to do this."

"You're a liar," he said as his hand traveled down her ass and gripped her thigh. He hitched her leg over his waist, connecting them at the hips. Something hard and hot pressed against the apex of her thighs. She knew she should pull away from him, but it had been *a while*. "You want me to stay with you. Just say it," he breathed.

As truthful as he was being, Celeste couldn't bring herself to return the favor. She was slightly distracted by his hard dick throbbing between her thighs. "I don't want you to do something that will make you feel uncomfortable."

Magnus chuckled sleepily. "Kiss me."

"What?" They were already quietly grinding privates beneath a blanket, but kissing seemed like a bridge too far.

"Kiss me for real," he said. "Like we did in Victor's party."

"Are you sure?" Celeste asked, trying to peer at him in the dark.

"Mmm-hmm."

She stroked his cheek and waited a second before moving

closer to his face. Finally, she found the courage to lean forward to give him a quick brush on the lips.

Magnus caught her mouth and pushed with insistence. Celeste melted against his lips. He let out a low moan against her open mouth and teased her with his tongue. A shiver of pleasure ran down her spine as Magnus's kiss grew deeper.

Celeste suddenly found herself on her back, her hands pinned to either side of her head, slowly drinking in his wicked kiss. She pushed her hips beneath him; each cursory brush her clit made against his straining cock sent a jolt of electric pleasure throughout her body. Her nipples tightened against his chest, but she couldn't touch him. Not with her hands pressed against the mattress. She hadn't been held down like this in ages, nor had she felt the forbidden arousal of fucking an ex. There was a special kind of thrill in falling back in step with the man whom she'd left.

When he finally left her lips and pushed down her body, he let out a harsh breath as his tongue dipped into the valley between her breasts. "My sexy CeCe," he murmured against her skin.

And with that, Celeste's eyes sprang open. Jesus Christ, she had to put a stop to this. "Magnus, stop," she whispered.

"Why?" he asked.

Celeste hooked her leg around his waist and used her body to push him onto his back. It was easier than she thought it would be, which proved why they shouldn't be doing this. "Because I want you to remember in the morning," she said, perched on top of him. "If I finally let you fuck me, I don't want you to forget."

He chuckled in the dark. "As if I could forget… I remember the last time very clearly."

Celeste wasn't finished testing him. "Do you?"

"We were making love when we probably should have been planning the B&E at the princess's condo," he murmured, his voice seeming to grow tired. "That was the night I thought I almost had you, CeCe. But you slipped from my fingers..."

Celeste rolled off him and returned to her side of the bed without saying a word. What could she say? His words sounded like a confession she didn't want to hear. Sleeping with him was slightly easier than learning he harbored something for her that neither of them could understand. If she addressed these confessions, she might have to be introspective.

Her least favorite activity.

No, they didn't have time for that shit.

"Stay with me?" he asked.

She hitched the blanket over her shoulder. "Yes, but no touching."

"You're no fun," he said softly.

"We're not supposed to have fun," she said in her sternest voice, even though she was now wet and aching for him. Not Magnus. Just his body. "Just go to sleep," she whispered.

Magnus grunted something, but his body went still. Celeste listened for more incoherent nonsense, but he'd gone quiet. Soon, his soft snores filled the room. She closed her eyes and sighed.

Please don't remember this tomorrow...

13

Magnus wrenched himself upward with a powerful gasp and found himself back in the light. In an unfamiliar bed, trapped in an even more unfamiliar room. He looked around wildly to see a familiar, albeit shocked, face.

Celeste sat beside him, knees up to her chest and resting against the plush headboard. She wore sleeping clothes: a tank top, shorts and a satin bonnet on her head. She slowly placed the book she had been reading on the covers and searched his face with a concerned gaze.

"Are you okay?" she asked.

"What are you doing in here?"

Celeste scoffed as she returned to her book. "Okay, weirdo. You're the one who begged me to tuck you into bed. I only came back in here because it sounded like you had a nightmare last night."

"Nightmare?" What in the hell was she talking about? He hadn't begged her to stay in his room, had he? He flopped back onto his sweat-soaked pillow with a sigh. He couldn't remember anything, not even a nightmare. "The Ambien."

"The Ambien," she intoned, flipping to the next page. "How long you been on that stuff?"

"On and off for the last two years."

"Has Michelle experienced a doped-up Magnus?" The humor in her voice made him glance over. It sent a chill down his spine as he thought of an answer. He didn't know why her teasing tone did that to him. Celeste peeked over her book, waiting for his reply. "Sorry," she said. "It's none of my business."

"I've never taken it and gone to bed with someone. I have no idea how I act on it." He tried to keep panic from creeping into his voice. "Did I do anything embarrassing?"

Celeste shrugged. "You're very chatty when you're high. You desperately needed someone to cuddle with, we kissed until I put an end to it, you called me the most beautiful woman in the world."

Magnus's eyes widened as he stared at her. "I didn't."

"Okay, well, you said I was the most beautiful woman at Victor Sanderson's party."

He closed his eyes as his face went up in flames. He hadn't lied, but Jesus Christ, why would he tell her such a thing? "We kissed?"

"Mmm-hmm."

"Did I try to…" He trailed off, afraid to finish that sentence.

"You were actually kind of sweet," Celeste offered. "A bit clingy. Don't worry about it."

Easy for her to say. Magnus was fully worried now. "You kissed me back?"

"I probably shouldn't have… You weren't really in control of the situation. And from what I remember, you really like control in the bedroom."

An exasperated laugh escaped him. He couldn't believe he was in this position, left wondering how bad things were, and her describing how it had been even worse than he could imagine. But her jokes made the situation slightly better. "You liked it, too," he returned.

Another page flipped. "I don't remember all that," she murmured.

Magnus shifted on his side and raised himself onto his elbow. "No, you liked arguing with me in front of the crew just so I could get you home and spank you."

She scoffed, but didn't reply.

He suddenly had the urge to run his fingers down the length of her shin just to feel how soft her skin was. It was a crying shame he couldn't remember the feeling of it from last night. His dreams would have to be enough to sustain him until—

Christ, until what?

Just because they'd found themselves in bed with one another, didn't mean it would happen again. This was just a bizarre fluke.

"You're staring at me," Celeste said to the page she wasn't reading.

"I'm still waking up," he lied.

"We're not going to fuck any time too soon," she warned. "So, you can get that thought out of your head."

"I wasn't thinking about fucking you," he lied again.

"Or spanking?"

Her suspicious expression made him laugh despite his defenses. "Fuck you, CeCe..."

"Not in this lifetime."

"What did it feel like?" he asked before thinking.

"What did what feel like?"

Before Magnus could change his mind, he plowed forward foolishly. "What did our make-out session feel like? I obviously can't remember."

The small pause before she shrugged was barely perceptible, but he saw the conflict on her face in the shape of a tiny wrinkle in her brow and a twitch near her mouth. "It wasn't a big deal."

Liar.

Celeste had to work hard to suppress the microexpressions he'd picked up. He saw them all and read them like they were pages in a diary. Even though she was having fun at his expense, Magnus decided to let her have this one. He threw back the blanket and slipped out of bed. "Crew meeting today?" he asked, padding to the en suite bathroom.

"At 10:00 a.m.," she replied without looking up.

"I'm assuming we'll keep this to ourselves?"

A small smile slipped from Celeste's mask. "Of course."

"I'll be honest with you. I'd never heard of Estonia before you texted me last night," Santiago said, pouring himself another cup of coffee. This morning, he dressed down a bit, going for a gray twill dress shirt and charcoal slacks. Magnus felt a little slovenly sitting beside him dressed in an undershirt and pajama bottoms.

"Americans tend to skip over that part of Europe," Magnus replied, trying to shake himself of his Ambien hangover. Now that he was working, that would have to be the last time he'd take it. He'd need to be on his toes and keep his head in the game.

The crew, as it was, gathered in the kitchen going over what little plan they had. No one had commented on the fact that he and Celeste spent the night at Dr. Grant's home, and he wouldn't give them the ammo. For her part, Celeste had kept their strange evening to herself.

"Mags has already been," Celeste said, standing at the stove, helping Lawrence make breakfast. "Though I can't imagine what the hell we need from Tallinn."

"Doris has a safe house in the city. She hung out there in the eighties and nineties. Whew... I'll tell you what, the fall of the Soviet Union was a helluva time. All the corruption and confusion made it easy for a thief to get lost for a while," Lawrence said with a chuckle. "I'll get us there and we'll figure out the next step."

"Sounds good to me," Beatrice said, quickly shoveling scrambled eggs into her mouth. While sitting between them at the kitchen island, Magnus noticed how closely Santiago watched the woman and how oblivious she was to his attention. If he didn't know better, he'd call Santi...smitten? Which was strange because Santiago didn't get hung up on any woman. "Are you going to eat that?" Beatrice asked Magnus, pointing her fork at the toast on his plate.

"Have at it," he said, pushing the plate toward her.

"So, we're heading out when?" she asked.

"As soon as possible," Magnus said, rising from the breakfast nook. "Celeste?"

"Affirmative," she said, popping a piece of bacon into her mouth. "Santi? Got a way for us to get there?"

Santiago was their logistics and transportation man whose fast driving got them out of more than one jam in the past. He took a contemplative sip of his coffee while staring at Beatrice.

Magnus snapped his fingers under the man's nose. "Santi?"

He blinked and ran his hand over the top of his buzzed head. "We'll take the Gulfstream," he murmured. "I can hire a crew for this evening if you don't mind a red-eye."

"That soon?" Beatrice asked, pausing her meal.

"The sooner, the better," Celeste said. "Update the store's website with a message for our customers. Tell your dad we're headed to Europe for an emergency auction trip."

Beatrice cleared her throat and put a scrap of toast down. "I mean, I just assumed that we needed to train or something. Like in the movies?"

Everyone in the kitchen laughed.

"What's your skill?" Magnus asked the girl.

Her brown skin darkened with blush. "I usually take care of tech for Celeste."

"Then you're our tech person," he said. "You have all the training you'll ever need. We won't know what we're prepping for until we get to Tallinn. For now, get all the tools you'll need for a month of travel."

"A month?" Beatrice blanched.

He now worried that the young woman wasn't up to the task of being with this crew. Magnus glanced at Celeste, waiting for her to reassure Beatrice, but she continued eating alongside Lawrence.

"Pack with practicality," Santiago said with a grin. "It's a Gulfstream, not a 747. I suspect this job won't take longer than a week if we're smart about it."

"*Always* overpack your tools. Bring your laptops, backup drives and whatever else tech people need." Magnus waved his hand dismissively. Hacking stuff wasn't his area of expertise.

"Okay, Grandpa," Celeste said, teasing a smile back on her young protégé's face. Beatrice polished off her breakfast before springing from her chair. As she walked to the sink to wash her plate, Magnus watched Santiago's eyes follow her with intense interest. He could tell he'd have to get out in front of this. The last thing the team needed was their getaway driver asleep at the wheel.

And then Magnus wondered if calling Santiago out might be hypocritical after a night of begging Celeste to sleep with him.

Once the women had their heads together, he could hear Celeste talking softly. She playfully nudged the girl's shoulder. "You wanted this, right?" she said. "To hang out with the big kids?"

The girl shrugged her narrow shoulders. "Of course... I just thought we'd have a little time to get ourselves situated."

Celeste rubbed her back. "No time like now."

"Does Beatrice have a change of ID?" Magnus asked.

"I've got her covered," Celeste said. "My forger was able to hook her up last year."

"Okay, so we've got a location," Santiago said. "Is there anything in the clues that could suggest a mark?"

"There's mention of Kadriorg Palace," Magnus said. "Which is incorporated in the city's museum system."

"Anything in there worth stealing?" Santiago asked.

Magnus shrugged. "Depends on who you ask. As far as palace museums go, it's not very exciting. There's a permanent exhibition of Dutch and Italian art, but I could think of better marks."

Santiago nodded thoughtfully.

Lawrence sighed. "Knowing Doris, it could be anything. CeCe, you find anything interesting in her diary yet?"

Celeste wiped her hands on a dish towel before leaning against the kitchen sink. "I was reading it this morning, but I got interrupted," she said, smirking at Magnus.

Ahh, so that's what she was reading in bed… The tips of his ears burned in embarrassment.

"I'm still in her early years, though," Celeste continued. "If I can get some peace and quiet, I can keep reading on the plane."

Magnus fought the urge to roll his eyes. For a moment, he ignored her snarky quip and surveyed his team. After an unbelievable turn of events, he had returned to his crew. Well, not exactly *his* crew… Lawrence was older and without Doris, even more reserved. He wondered if the old man still had it in him to get into some trouble. Santiago still looked like he was in good shape; light on his feet and slippery as ever.

Beatrice was a concern. He'd never worked with her or seen her in action. But if she and Celeste bested him at Victor Sanderson's emerald party, there was hope. Hell, if she was being mentored by Celeste in the same way Doris mentored *them*… Beatrice would become a cutthroat thief in no time.

14

December 13, 1972

Dear Diary:

It's already been hard to keep coming back home. Every journey back to Biloxi threatens to tear up each new piece of me I've created. When I'm in New York, I'm Dr. Grant, the self-assured woman who speaks before a classroom about neoclassicism. But when I come home, I'm met with suspicion. The fast girl who knows too much. The Grants are proud of my education and ability to get out of the swamp, but there's an undercurrent of distrust.

And Auntie Belinda leads the charge, lobbing quiet, innocent accusations. "Girl, you don't need to wear those shoes down here. Lord knows you don't want to dirty 'em up in this mud..." Or my favorite: "I didn't know teaching got you diamond earrings like that..." Her siblings and my cousins will laugh to relieve the tension of me showing up, bearing gifts from Europe. My heart falls into my stomach every time and I dig my fingernails into my palms to keep from crying.

But Daddy was always there to tell her off. "Oh, Lindy,

hush up now. Dorrie has always liked shiny things. And when you're a smart cookie like her, you can buy anything you want." Auntie Belinda would quiet down for a minute, but the way she stared at me said she knew better. She could have never guessed what I did for Cartier earrings, but she knew it wasn't just because I'm a smart cookie.

I don't know if they realize it, but this is the last time I'll come back to Mississippi. My only reason to return was buried in the Beauvoir Memorial Cemetery today. My daddy now rests with Mama. I guess I was too late. If I had stolen my first painting ten years ago, I could have made Daddy retire earlier. He could have enjoyed the house I just bought him for a few more years. Instead, he chose to stay where he was. Worked his way up from porter to concierge…and then just stayed there until he had a heart attack.

Everyone was at the funeral, and it was overwhelming. Even Cousin Willy managed to get back from Vietnam just in time. He looks like a shell of himself. Not that his mother really noticed. While Auntie Belinda was hollering and crying for the Lord to take her, I saw Willy slip from the pews and leave the church. And even though I was sitting in the front pew, I followed him. He jerked loose the necktie of his dress greens and headed for the full parking lot. "Where you headed, William?" His brown face shined with perspiration even though it's winter. I think I saw relief in his eyes, though.

"I needed a smoke."

Well, so did I.

We sat in his car, where he rolled some reefer. I did my best but kept coughing. Willy is a professional, though. I guess you have to be with four years in the jungle. "I'm sorry for your loss," he finally told me. I thanked him and told him the same because it had to be true. You don't get to leave Saigon without losing something. He took a deep, shuddering breath and nodded. I might have been the first person to tell him something like that. "I'm

*glad I saw you today because I ain't about to come back here if
I can help it."*

I smiled with tears in my eyes. "Me neither."

"Where you headed?"

*I told him I was going back to New York and staying, that he
was free to visit me anytime he wanted. He said he'd get around
to it when he got settled in Los Angeles. "You gonna be okay?"*

*By then, a nice fuzzy feeling came over my body and my chest
didn't feel quite as tight. "Shiiiiit... I will be."*

*We laughed. And it was the best laugh I'd felt in Biloxi in
the longest time. I hate that it was at my daddy's funeral, but he
knows I love him. I just don't like the place I come from. If I had
my way, I'd be running every damn day. My feet would never
get tired. I took Willy's hand and squeezed his fingers. "And
you will be, too," I told him.*

Celeste folded the corner of the page over and drew a deep
breath. She sat in the back of the Gulfstream jet where it was a
bit quiet. They had been in the sky for about four hours before
she asked their steward to pour her a bourbon. Celeste had barely
touched it as she read through Doris's entries. Apparently, her
mentor and Sebastian were spending quite a bit of time together
outside of her studies. Frankly, Celeste was surprised by how
little was written about her time at Spelman and then Columbia.
But she remembered that these entries were curated for a reason.

This passage of her life, when her father died, quietly broke
Celeste's heart. Doris had obviously felt alienated from her
family, no doubt keeping a large part of her life secret. Celeste
didn't have any experience with that. As the last of her family, she didn't have to lie to those ones she loved. She rubbed
her temples before finally taking her first sip of bourbon. The
sweet burn stung her throat and warmed her belly.

"Are you going to get any sleep?"

Her head shot up to find Santiago standing in the aisle. He

was out of his suit jacket and shoes, looking a bit more comfortable than usual. "I'm not sure." As far she could tell, the
others were taking advantage of the red-eye flight. "Sit with
me for a minute," she said, patting an open space on the couch.

He joined her, took the glass of bourbon from her and helped
himself to a sip. "Reading Doris's diary?"

Celeste drew her legs to her chest and snuggled against Santiago. They fell into a quiet sharing of whiskey, passing it back
and forth. "You ever think about why Doris chose us to help
her steal?"

Santiago tipped his head back and closed his eyes. "What
do you mean?"

She wasn't sure what she was asking, but a thought scratched
at the back of her mind after reading that passage. "Was it because we didn't have family?"

"My dad was incarcerated before he died," he corrected.
"And Rafael will hopefully get out in a year or two."

"Sure, but your dad and brother were part of the criminal
underworld. You'd never have to lie to them about what you
do. Beatrice is the only one who has a straight relative. Her dad
has no idea what we do." Celeste faced Santiago and took another sip of whiskey. "Do you think it's a bad idea to drag Bea
around the globe for this? Will this mess her up?"

Santiago's dark brows furrowed. "Her enthusiasm for this
job doesn't seem to match your concerns."

"Probably not. She's been begging for bigger jobs…"

He waved a hand, dismissing her. "She's a big girl. She'll
figure out something to tell her father."

"Hmm…maybe you're right. I've met him, really nice guy.
He came to the store one day to meet me. He was so proud of
his daughter when he saw her work." She remembered how
he walked around the store, afraid to touch anything. He was
a short, hefty man, the opposite of his tall, willowy daughter.
But they shared the same bright grin and dark, smiling eyes.

"Nice guy?" Santiago asked, stroking his mustache. "Did he seem overly protective?"

Celeste rolled her eyes. "Are you serious? You can't really be sniffing around my assistant, Santi."

His eyes flitted to the front of the jet where Beatrice slept. "Don't be crude, mana. I'm not sniffing, I'm observing," he said with a low purr. "She's a fascinating woman who I'm very interested in…"

"This is where I give you the obligatory 'if you hurt her, I'll stick your nuts in a vise and crank' speech. Beatrice is my ward."

"You should know me well enough to know how hot that sounds," he teased. "Now I'm imagining kissing your innocent ward."

Celeste slapped his arm. "Shut up."

"I'm making love to your ward," he whispered.

She jerked his ear. "I swear to God, I will end you, Santi."

He hissed as he tried to fight her off. "Fucking hell, CeCe!"

"She's not one of your conquests," Celeste whispered.

"Bea is not a conquest. Like I said, I'm very interested in her. She's a beautiful chatterbox whose mind is like a computer. I *like* her, you loba loca." When he straightened away from her, he smoothed down his dress shirt and took her drink back.

"You just met her."

"Have you never heard of instant attraction?" he asked, raising a brow.

"You're too old for her," Celeste countered.

"Ouch. You know how to cut a thirty-four-year-old very deep. Do you abuse Magnus like this?"

"Magnus deserves his abuse, too," she muttered.

"For real, though, how long are you two going to be at each other's throats? The Stockholm job wasn't his fault and it wasn't your fault. If anything, Doris sent us out with half a plan that you two tried to cobble together. It was probably doomed from the start."

"Magnus literally fumbled the bag," Celeste said. "I tossed the jewels into the boat and he couldn't catch them."

"Then you tossed yourself in the water and he had to catch you," Santiago added. "Apparently, saving *you*...was slightly more important than the job?"

"If he had let me swim—"

"In the pitch-black water? While it was raining? The river current was not in our favor that night. I had a rough time keeping the boat under control as it was."

Anger coiled inside her chest as she listened to Santiago's excuses for their collective failure. She absolutely did not need to remember that Magnus saved her. The fact that she needed to be snatched before being swept out to the Baltic Sea was so fucking embarrassing.

"This is why you left him, and then us?"

That wasn't exactly how she remembered it. After he fished her out of the river, they'd lost whatever magic they had. They no longer trusted one another to make decisions, to catch one another when they fell. "Things had changed," she murmured. "I'm sure you guys saw it."

Santiago nodded. "We did."

"She never said anything, but I got the sense I'd let Doris down. She always talked about separating business from personal feelings. Magnus and I clearly didn't do that and look where we ended up." It was the first time Celeste had admitted the thought aloud and immediately felt guilty. She looked to her friend to gauge his expression.

He rolled his eyes and chuckled softly. "Doris couldn't possibly be disappointed in the woman she trained to become her. Like I said, she sent us on a fool's errand. We did the best we could under the circumstances. She may have been on the radio that night, but Doris wasn't fully *there*. Didn't you notice something was off in Tangier?"

She didn't exactly remember it like that. Acquiring the Grecian horse statue in Tangier was stressful, but it was also thrill-ing, and they managed to pull it off. She couldn't remember Doris being distracted when she looked back. Only excitement.

Celeste sighed, not entirely believing Santiago. "So, how's the club going?"

"I'm hurt that you haven't stopped by," he said, pulling a face.

Santiago's club, El Carnicero, was a business front for the il-legal chop shop he ran. The nightclub was in the Meatpacking District, not too far from where she lived. While Celeste had visited a couple times, with the intention of seeing Santiago, she always chickened out at the last second. She felt like she'd let him down, too. Soon, it just became easier to stay away. "I'm sorry, Santi."

"You're carrying a lot of something, amor. You need to fig-ure out what it is and let it go. It shouldn't have taken Doris's death to bring us back together."

She nodded, finishing off the whiskey. "You're right."

Santiago gasped. "I'm right? Did my CeCe say that *I* am right?"

This pulled a grin from Celeste. "A broken clock can be right twice a day."

"So, the gang is back together and you're going to play nice, right?"

She stared at him with a blank expression. Now, why did she have to play nice? After spending the past twenty-four hours with him, it was evident that Magnus was just as confusing as she remembered. "It's all business from here on out."

"Was it business last night?" Santiago asked innocently.

"God, you're the worst."

Her friend chuckled. "He told me that you two pulled a Ball and Chain at a jewelry counter."

"Did he?"

"How did it go?" Santiago asked.

"Well enough."

He eyed her closely, but let it slide. She was grateful that he chose not to interrogate her. "Thank you for the drink. I think I'm going to close my eyes before we land. You better get some rest, too."

"I will," she said, placing her empty glass on the table beside her.

He stood, stretched his lean limbs and flashed her a feral grin. "We're on the hunt again. How exciting is that?"

This was one thing she could agree with Santiago on. Celeste was ecstatic with the possibility of getting into criminal mischief. "The night before Christmas exciting."

15

Everything was moving too smoothly for Magnus's liking.

He knew better than to question Santiago's logistical abilities, but it still surprised him when a Tallinn Airport concierge guided the crew from the Gulfstream, through customs and then to two black SUVs prepared to transport them to Dr. Grant's safe house, located in the Pirita district along Tallinn Bay.

Their fraudulent identities held up in security.

Their luggage was passed through without a problem.

The pleasant drive to the safe house only took twenty minutes...

Yeah, this was too smooth. Not that he *wanted* the other shoe to drop, but if it had to, he'd love for it to happen early in their journey. Magnus shared a car with Santiago and Lawrence, unable to enjoy the bright blue view of the bay from the highway. He didn't remember being this pessimistic during their international jobs. Cautious maybe, but not full-on anxious about fucking up.

He wondered how Celeste was handling herself as she traveled with Beatrice in the other car. Was she just as nervous? She seemed poised while they moved swiftly through the airport. But she routinely excelled at preventing people from seeing her sweat. Perhaps she had to keep her own nerves in check for the sake of her young assistant.

"Beautiful, isn't it?" Lawrence intoned from beside him.

"Yeah," Magnus said, watching the scenery pass them by. He could tell that Pirita was the wealthy part of Tallinn. The mansions were spread out throughout the heavily wooded area, a stark difference from the brutalist apartment blocks in the city center. This natural setting promised seclusion for them to do their planning. "I can't believe I'm here."

"You look a little nervous."

Magnus pulled at the collar of his dress shirt. Even though he wanted to look presentable while traveling, he wished he had worn something a little more comfortable. He couldn't wait to get somewhere and settle down. "Not nervous," he lied. "You're sure you don't know what's waiting on us here?"

The wrinkles of Lawrence's brown skin deepened as he smiled broadly. "Son, you're going to have to take my word when I tell you I don't know what that woman had planned." He shook his head and chuckled. "All I know is that we're probably in for a wild ride."

Magnus sighed. "This is ridiculous."

"That's Doris for you."

He glanced at Lawrence and saw that the old man was much more relaxed than he felt in that moment. "Has Celeste said anything to you?" he asked in a low voice.

"About…"

Magnus shrugged. "How does she feel about things? Anything about Doris? This job?"

"Oh, you know CeCe. She keeps her cards close to the vest."

In the rush to get to Tallinn, Magnus hadn't had a chance to spend any one-on-one time with Celeste. They'd all gone their separate ways, prepared for the journey, only to meet at JFK. "The journal she's reading. She hasn't talked to me about its contents. Do you think Dr. Grant left her clues about the job in it?"

"That's a good question," Lawrence said, pulling at his earlobe. "Doris wrote in a diary nearly every day of her life. Or at least for as long as I've known her. What I gave CeCe is just a compilation of entries. I didn't read it, though."

"You mean to tell me Dr. Grant just gave you these things, these tasks, and you blindly trusted her?" Magnus asked, scoffing. "You weren't tempted to read the journal yourself?"

Lawrence scoffed right back. "I trusted *my* partner. What would I have gained from digging in business that didn't concern me? I kept enough of her secrets. Sometimes you need to let a person keep something for themselves."

Magnus pulled at his collar again, slightly more agitated this time. "I trust Celeste," he protested weakly.

"Y'all are doing a good job of being civil to one another, but I don't believe you trust each other. I reckon things wouldn't have fallen apart so spectacularly after the Stockholm affair if you had."

The calmness with which Lawrence spoke jarred Magnus into sitting up straighter. He didn't perceive judgment from the older gentleman, only his usual form of straight talk. Lawrence's tone forced Magnus to reflect on the idea of trust. Who had he last trusted? What had it felt like to let someone else take the reins?

Unfortunately, the jewelry counter immediately came to mind. He'd left Celeste hanging in the wind while he changed plans to suit his own comfort. While part of him felt guilty for keeping her uncertain, another pettier part of him liked being in control of the job. He enjoyed knowing that she couldn't access all his secrets, just as he couldn't fully reach beyond her well-trained facade.

Jesus…how helpful could that be?

Did they truly know each other? Beyond the intimacy they shared? She let him into her bed, they knew each other's bodies, but amid the work they did with one another, had they really understood each other? Their romance was more or less a workplace tangle and falling into bed with his coworker was a lot easier than it should have been. It was a fun affair, exploring the world, stealing and then exploring her body before the adrenaline wore off.

His one-dimensional view of her was simple. She was an orphan, like he was…check. There was their common interest. Outside of that, he knew that she had a rough upbringing through the foster system, but she never talked about it. According to her, that was then and there was no use in crying over being alone. So he never broached the topic. Magnus also knew her mind worked faster than his. Celeste seemed to think like a fast-spreading web, extending possibilities and contingencies to problems he wasn't even aware of.

But had there been anything deeper to their relationship?

Magnus stared at the rapidly passing trees outside his window until he saw only a green blur.

Yes, there had been. He'd trusted her with enough of his heart that he had almost told her he loved her. It was the night before the Stockholm job. She had convinced him that they needed a break instead of casing the princess's condo again. She asked him to hold her…a request she rarely made. Celeste was exhausted from their months of working, each job more intense than the last. All it took was a quiet evening with the woman who knew him better than most for him to realize that he may have loved her.

Perhaps it was the softness in her eyes when she looked up at him… Or when Celeste kissed him gently on the cheek, something broke within him. The gesture hadn't been sexual. Instead, it felt like an expression of intimacy he desperately needed. It had been too long since someone had embraced him with tenderness.

And he hadn't said anything.

Even after they'd made the sweetest love that evening. Magnus never admitted that he had probably fallen in love with her somewhere between Rome and London. Instead, he asked her if she'd ever given any thought to leaving Doris's breakneck quest for fortune in favor of something safer. Between the two of them, they could handle just about anything. Dr. Grant had trained them well enough that they could work for themselves.

Celeste had balked at the suggestion.

Even after saving her life, she wouldn't choose him.

"We're here," Santiago said from the front seat.

Through the dense forest stood a secure gate. As their vehicle drew close, Lawrence unclipped his seat belt and exited the car. Magnus, Santiago and their driver watched him amble to a keypad, take a cursory glance around him and enter a code before the steel gates slid open.

"Still works," he called out.

"Thank God," Santiago said, grinning at Magnus. "Because this is where my expertise ends."

When Lawrence returned to the SUV, both vehicles passed through the threshold and continued down a winding road toward the property. Tall hedgerows lined the well-paved path, not revealing the full grandeur of the Scandinavian estate until they were nearly on top of it.

"Jesuchristo..." Santiago murmured. "She owned this in the eighties?"

"It didn't always look like this," Lawrence said with a chuckle. "She had worked on building it up since the eighties."

"How many of these properties did Doris have?" Magnus whispered, mindful of their driver.

Lawrence also glanced at their driver before replying, "A few..."

Magnus couldn't have been surprised, given Dr. Grant's secretive nature, but this estate was not what he expected out of a safe house. "Okay, then."

"Listen, son," Lawrence said, placing a hand on Magnus's

knee. "I know I've scolded you about getting along with CeCe, but I need you to start this job with a little more confidence. A little more swagger. I got a feeling we're gonna need it more than ever. Ya hear me?"

Magnus took a deep breath and nodded. "Yeah."

"Not all the fussin' and fightin' you do with Celeste is bad for the job. I don't know what it is about you two, but bickering seems to fuel you both toward the common goal."

He could have told Lawrence what had made their arguments so worthwhile at the end of the day but kept his mouth shut instead.

"I'm saying this as your family," the older gentleman continued. "As a man who knows you pretty well."

Magnus was moved to place his hand over Lawrence's in solidarity. Family? They had always called themselves a crew of criminals, but he'd never felt as though he was a part of a family unit. Hearing the words of Doris's most trusted friend made him feel different. "Hey, of course. I get it."

As they rounded the circular drive, drawing closer to the front double doors of the estate, Lawrence gave his knee one last squeeze before unclipping his seat belt. "More now than ever, dear Magnus, we're gonna need that Nordic charm. The show starts now."

"Nordic charm," Magnus snorted. "I've been told that my people are lacking in that area."

"Well, luckily, you're Swedish-American. You're welcome."

This pulled a laugh out of Magnus and loosened his tight nerves. Lawrence was right. The show was on, and he needed to play his part. Confident, cold and arrogant if need be. And when it came to Celeste, a little sexual bravado might be helpful. It would be safer to tease and flirt with her than to make another mistake.

16

"I expected a little more than this," Santiago said.

Lawrence chuckled. "Honestly, me, too."

"At least we know we're in the right place," Beatrice said in an uncertain tone.

As they stood at the front door of the Tallinn safe house, Celeste couldn't help but feel a shudder of grief as she gazed upon the same kind of red envelope that had been delivered to them several days ago. "Let's take it inside," she said, glancing over her shoulder at the two black SUVs in the driveway. "Where we aren't being watched."

"They're leaving now…" Santiago murmured from behind dark sunglasses. "From here on out, I'll take care of transportation."

"Vehicles are in the west side of the compound," Lawrence said, unlocking the front door with another keypad. "I think you'll find something you'll like."

Magnus peeled the envelope from the door as they entered the mansion. Inside, a large foyer with cherrywood floors, white walls, a table with the largest bouquet of silk flowers Celeste had ever seen. Pink and blue hydrangeas were Doris's favorite, and they greeted the crew like a sunny smile. Another pang of sadness hit her as she drifted farther into the home.

The first floor was flooded with natural light, plush white furniture in the living room, leading to a paver patio. To her right, a massive kitchen. To the left, there was a small library. At least, smaller than Dr. Grant's library in the US. She couldn't wait to explore the rest of the house and the grounds.

"There are four bedrooms, two on the first floor, two on the second. All of them have one bed. Doris's personal office is upstairs, her library is right there," Lawrence said, gesturing beside the group. "The vault is in the basement, along with her training room and my workshop. I don't know if any changes have been made since I was last here, but I'm prepared for a surprise or two."

Four bedrooms. Celeste let that fact tumble in her mind while she watched Magnus turn the envelope over. Perhaps she should get used to sharing quarters with him. If they had any hope of getting the team back in working order, they would need to put their heads together and provide that show of a united front.

Of course, sleeping in the same bed as Magnus was not as awful as she imagined it to be. Celeste would never tell him to his face, but cuddling with him at Dr. Grant's house was comforting. When he admitted that his bed had been lonely for the past few years, she understood his sentiments.

"Maybe we can split up and take a rest after we've read this," Magnus said. "I'd love to know why we're in Estonia of all places."

"Same," Beatrice said, dropping her bag in the hallway. "I'd also love a drink to steady my nerves."

The young woman did look a little antsy as her eyes searched the space. She twisted a box braid around her finger, a habit Celeste had noticed on the jet.

"The bar is in the living room," Lawrence said. Beatrice and Santiago followed him down the hall, leaving her with Magnus.

"What do you think?" he asked, gesturing to the home around them.

"Even though I shouldn't be, I'm a little surprised. This isn't exactly a safe house. The grungy flat in Prague? That was a safe house."

"This feels like a retirement plan," he said with a sad smile. "If such a thing is possible for our line of work."

Was he talking about Doris or them? One night, five years ago, he wanted her to run away with him. Where, she didn't know. But she couldn't fathom giving up her life under Dr. Grant's direction. Not when she'd helped Celeste get to where she was. Not when there was more to gain...

"How are you feeling about this?"

"Ready," Magnus said with a grin.

She nodded. "Yeah, you look it. Not trying to cut and run yet, so that's good."

He chuckled as he gave her a brisk pat on the back. "Now, there's my bitchy CeCe. I was beginning to wonder where she was."

She scowled and gave him the finger in response as she followed him down the hall toward the others. Even though she tried to insult him, Celeste had to admit the obvious: she had quit their crew, too. Despite her loyalty to Doris, she couldn't find it within her to continue without Magnus. It made her sick. "There's the arrogant prick we know and love."

"Love?" he said in mock dismay. "I'm flattered."

On second thought, maybe she'd bunk with Beatrice during this trip.

In the living room, Santiago was fixing drinks and Lawrence had already found himself a seat on the large white sectional. "Would you pour me one of those, Santi?"

"Everyone needs a little liquid courage this evening?" he asked, handing a glass to Beatrice, who waited nearby. He whispered something in her ear that made her roll her eyes, but she grinned anyway. Perhaps she wouldn't be bunking with Bea after all. She recognized the flirty smiles and stolen glances between the two and wondered how long it would take for her young associate to succumb to Santiago's charms.

"I'd like a good night's sleep before we hit the ground running," she said.

"Let's see where we'll be running to," Magnus said, ripping open the envelope. He read it through until a frown creased his brow. "Huh…"

"How bad is it?" she asked.

Magnus's eyes flickered to her before glancing back at the letter. "She describes seeking help from old lovers…"

Celeste pursed her lips and averted her eyes. "Huh."

"'My darling little thieves, I couldn't have become the woman you knew without a little help from some devious people. One of which was a lover who guided my hand back when we were younger and more vain. I think I loved him once. And before I knew what to do with that love, I let him go. Sebastian is just one of many regrets in my life.

"'That's where you come in. Pass along the final message he should be expecting: The South Sea is expensive, the Akoya is classic, but the Tahitian has the character you once loved. He'll know what it means. Help him and he will help you. The network of thieves in Eastern Europe could still use a crew like you.'"

"She's talking about pearls." Magnus looked at her again. "And a man named Sebastian. It sounds like he knows we're coming?"

She nodded. "I've been reading about him. He's all up and through her diary. From what I can tell, he was the man who got her into stealing. Doris met him when she was in college, and he took her all over the world. He seems to really like jewelry."

"And where do we find this Sebastian?" Beatrice asked.

Santiago brought over a drink. "Thank you," Celeste said,

taking her first sip of gin and tonic. "And that's a good question. I have no idea."

They turned to look at Lawrence, who shrugged. "She and Sebastian had an on-again, off-again kind of thing. In the eighties, while she was cutting up over here, she and Bastian were on for a spell. But when they had a falling out, I didn't hear from him anymore."

"Does he have a last name?" Magnus asked.

"He had many aliases," Lawrence said. "We'll have to research them all, I guess."

"I haven't seen anything, but I'll continue reading." Not once in her readings had she come across a full name. Which didn't seem unusual for someone writing in her private diaries.

"Bea, you're up," Magnus said. "Find me anything on a Sebastian in Tallinn. If she's convinced he's here, we'll find something."

The young woman nodded. "I'm on it."

"Santi, check out the vehicles on the property," Celeste added. "We need to know what we're working with, and which transport could be most useful for this trip."

Magnus nodded. "And I'd like to look at your workshop, Lawrence. I miss your gadgets."

The old man stood up. "Well then, let me direct you to the basement."

The estate was impressive, but Doris's basement was a marvel. It was much larger than the first floor above them, built outward and reinforced with concrete and steel.

Once they made it downstairs and Lawrence turned on the lights, she and Magnus were in awe. The gym was spacious, filled with exercise equipment and full floor mats.

"I'll take you on back and show you the real goodies," Lawrence said, leading them farther into the basement. He stopped before a large metallic door that had another keypad. Lawrence tapped in a code and Celeste watched in amazement as the door slid open. "The code is 0548."

"Doris's birthday," she murmured.

"How did you know that?" Magnus asked.

"Her diary."

Inside was a series of rooms sectioned off by glass walls. In one room sat a few lab counters that could be found in any high school science class. Behind those, several steel cabinets were built into the wall.

"This is my workshop." Lawrence pointed to that area. "Through there is the vault and over here is the gun range if you'd like to practice."

Celeste and Magnus exchanged shocked glances. "There are guns on the property?" she asked.

"When did Doris get into guns?"

Lawrence shrugged. "She'd never used them on a job, but Doris was from the South. She was always into guns. You don't have to fool with it, but we've got a small armory just in case you're interested."

They followed him to his workshop, where he began opening cabinets and revealing all kinds of tools and gadgets they might need for a job. "What y'all might be interested in is something a little less lethal." Lawrence pulled what looked like a semi-automatic handgun from the backlit cabinet. "The ammo is a simple tranq dart, takes your attacker out in just a few seconds."

He handed the gun to Celeste, who took it only to feel the weight of it in her hands. She wasn't very experienced with firearms and didn't think she should start today. She set the piece on the counter. "I don't like it," she said.

Magnus took it up, weighed it in his palm before wrapping his fingers around it. "You might not like it, but it could prove very useful in an unknown situation."

"Let's work on understanding our situation before navigating. I doubt Estonia is the same as the US when it comes to guns. We don't need the heat."

"Let's not rule it out," Magnus pressed.

"We don't have to argue about it tonight," Lawrence said. "I'll put it away for a rainy day."

Celeste cut her gaze to Magnus, who appeared annoyed with her. She didn't care. They hadn't needed a dart gun in the past, and probably wouldn't need one now. "What else do you have?" she asked.

"Some oldies but goodies," Lawrence said, reaching beneath the lab counter. He pulled out a long, flat box that contained several pairs of contact lenses in clear cases, earpieces and tiny button devices that Celeste didn't recognize.

"What are those?" she asked, pointing to the small, round, flat disks. They looked like watch batteries.

"Tracking devices for crew members. They have a strong adhesive that will stick to the skin for a long period of time. I can keep an eye on you even if the earpieces and contact lens cameras fail."

That was something she could get on board with. Celeste picked one up between her thumb and forefinger. "Even through sweat?"

"It sticks," Lawrence assured her. He turned around, pointed out some other things in the cabinets. "We've got some glasses that toggle between regular and night vision, grappling hooks, drills, several lock-picking kits… We're pretty much set up for anything you might need. All that's left is you and the crew."

The crew.

Lawrence, who was in his twilight years of stealing. Beatrice, the newbie. Santiago, the wheels. And Magnus…the other leader in this outfit. She didn't know if she could trust him, but here he was, back in the fold.

"I'll leave y'all to it," Lawrence said, leaving the counter. "I'm going to stay in the master bedroom. I figure I earned it. You kids can sort out your lodgings while you're here."

They followed him out of the steel enclosure, locked up and walked back into the gym. Celeste put her hands on her hips and surveyed the basement settings as Lawrence disappeared up the stairs. "So…"

"So," Magnus intoned while doing his own surveying. "This is Tallinn."

"The city center was nice enough."

"Yep, yep… It's a nice little city."

They fell into an uncomfortable silence once she ran out of pleasantries. It appeared he did, too. Finally, they met each other's gaze.

Celeste took a deep breath. "Where are you sleeping—"

"Are you sharing—"

They stopped short, Magnus chuckling while she nervously raked her fingers through her hair. "You go first."

"I was going to ask if you were sharing a room with anyone. There are three beds left for the four of us."

"Lord knows why Doris couldn't invest in twin beds," she muttered.

"I really don't want to sleep with Santi if I can help it," he said, shoving his hands in his pockets and rocking on his heels. "He's a loud snorer."

Celeste crossed her arms over her chest and narrowed her eyes. This sounded suspiciously like a request of some sort. "Are you trying to sleep with me, Mags?"

He shrugged with a smug grin on his face. "Would you like me to, Celeste?"

She rolled her eyes. "I'll bunk with Bea." The idea sounded ludicrous once he voiced it aloud. She couldn't believe she had actually considered it. No, they didn't need to muddy the waters even more than necessary. "You'll need all the rest you can get, old man."

Magnus raised a brow. "Old man? I'm only a couple years older than you."

"And I bet you're really feeling those years," she said with a grin. Okay, they were back on steady ground. Making fun of her ex-lover was always the best route to go.

"Why do I feel like you're taking another shot at my stamina?" he asked with a cocky grin. "It feels like you want me to prove something."

Fuck!

She could feel herself slipping right back into another flirtatious exchange. As large as the basement was, she suddenly felt suffocated by her own desire to make Magnus prove how virile he was… Celeste needed to get out of there.

"Sleep well," she said, starting for the stairs.

"I'll try my best."

17

May 26, 1976

Dear Diary:
Sebastian is back in my life after I told him we needed a break.
Well, perhaps a break is putting it mildly... The last time we
were together was in London. I'd said some nasty things to him,
told him I'd outgrown him. The jobs he'd wanted to pull were
pedestrian and two-bit. All jewelry, nothing of real substance. I
know I hurt him.

Tonight he appeared at a gala, looking like sin after a year.
When I saw him, I wanted the floor to open up and swallow
me whole. Hell would have been a better option than seeing that
man. However, I couldn't leave. Not after all the work it took to
hunt down a ticket for the damn event. It had taken me months
to cozy up to Manhattan's high society. Yes, working with Sebastian is a lot easier, but I need to do this for myself.

I spotted him instantly. Smooth talking an elderly widow dripping with diamonds. He was absolutely shameless as he flirted
with her. When he saw me, he actually smirked. Unfortunately,

I was so beside myself that I marched right up to him, ready to set him out. He was quicker, though. Rather than letting me make a fool of myself in the middle of the party, he took me by the arm and dragged me to a coatroom.

What I'm about to write…both baffles me and gives me great shame… We kissed amid minks, foxes and chinchillas. He whispered crass things in my ear as he touched me, making me want to forget about our break. I kissed him back, ready to lose myself to him in a coat closet. Of all places. God, I wanted him so badly. We didn't stop necking until I thought I heard a voice from outside the small space. I pushed him away and fled before he had a chance to muss my hair and makeup.

It wasn't until I revived myself with a drink that I realized he had left with my three-strand Tahitian pearl necklace. I'm so furious right now, I can barely hold this pen steady as I write. He stole it for me years ago and now he's taken it back. For what? So I can come to him? He's a child. But dammit, I really want that necklace back. I wanted to wear it for the university president's dinner… This is exactly what Sebastian wants. If I go to his penthouse, there's no guarantee I won't just fall into his bed, picking up right where we left off. Good Lord, Doris…get yourself together.

Celeste ended that journal entry with a smile on her face. If she was Dr. Grant's bestie back in the seventies, she would have sat up with her and laughed about how to get back at her boyfriend. Perhaps planned a quick heist for her necklace. On one level, Doris's story about Sebastian stealing her pearl necklace was humorous. With all Dr. Grant had stolen over the years, surely one necklace was just a drop in the bucket.

But on another, more primal level, one filled with trauma and desperate want, Celeste could see the loss of one piece of jewelry as something larger. A man like Sebastian could never quite understand. Or maybe he did, and he wanted to wield that power over Doris. She pondered the entry, wondering if this was still the kind of man they'd meet. How would he react to the news of Doris's passing? Beatrice was still searching the dark web for any presence of Sebastian in Tallinn, and Celeste had no doubt they'd find something soon.

Speaking of Beatrice, she had to slip out of the girl's bed with a spare blanket and pillow because she couldn't sleep for her life. Bea tossed and turned until she stole all the covers and turned herself into a human burrito. When Celeste angrily sat up to look at her, the young woman's long-discarded satin bonnet lay on the pillow beside her face, while she murmured in her sleep.

Celeste wasn't sure what to make of this entry; she just knew that she was now suddenly thirsty. That evening they had take-out from the only restaurant that was still open, and the burger and fries she had were too salty. She folded the corner of Doris's diary page and placed the book next to a table lamp before leaving the couch.

As she moved quietly through the first floor to the kitchen, she memorized the layout in the dark as she would museum blueprints. It was a weird little habit she'd developed from working with Doris, but it helped her feel more secure in strange places. It was a skill she wished she'd had in the Harrison Home, where the night felt so foreign and alienating.

In the dark, she found a glass and ran the tap until the water was ice-cold over her fingers. While she waited was when she heard the noise. An odd shuffling behind her that hadn't been there minutes before. A prickling awareness lifted the hairs on the backs of her arms and on her neck as she tuned her ears. Celeste held her body still, pretending that she was only getting water, and waited for the danger to approach her.

When it sounded a little too close, she whipped around and struck out with the heel of her hand. She connected with a jaw or a chin, she wasn't certain, but she heard the blow land and the person grunt in pain.

"The fuck?"

Celeste let out a sigh of relief and annoyance. It was just Magnus… "What are you doing here?"

He stumbled a couple steps back and held his face. In the dark, she couldn't tell how hard the blow landed but she knew she came at her would-be attacker with everything she had. Thank God she hadn't hit Lawrence.

"I was coming to get something to drink, you psycho."

"I thought someone had broken into the house," she whisper-hissed. "Why are you skulking around a mansion like some fucking gothic ghost?"

"I needed. A glass. Of water," he ground out. "I didn't realize I was skulking."

She heard how paranoid she must have sounded. In an unfamiliar house where she thought all the occupants were asleep, she really thought someone had crossed through the secure gate and made it through the back door. "I'm sorry," she whispered.

Magnus moved past her to retrieve his own glass. "And why are you still up?"

"I also needed something to drink," she mumbled. "Salty dinner."

"What a terrifying concept," he said dryly.

She reached up to touch his jaw. "Are you okay? Did I get you bad?"

Magnus let her fingers touch his chin before replying. "I'll live," he said. She released him when he tipped his head back to take a gulp. "What were you doing in the living room?"

"I was reading Dr. Grant's diary to make myself sleepy."

"Can't sleep with Bea?"

"Bea really shouldn't sleep with anyone," Celeste said, smiling in the dark. She finished filling her cup and felt instant relief with cold water washing over her tongue. She drank until she got her fill and set her glass on the counter. "She stole my covers and kicked me a couple times with those long legs of hers."

"So, we're both getting battered tonight," Magnus said, leaning against the counter. They were only inches away from one another and she could feel it even in the blanket of darkness.

"I'll live," she said.

"You could come to my room."

"You shouldn't make a habit of begging me to come to your room," she countered. Though a bed might be more comfortable than the couch. For however many nights they might be in Estonia.

He slid closer until all she could see was his shadowy figure before her. The scent of cedar and spice filled her nose and made her lean forward. It seemed to unlock some long-buried memories of hotter times with Magnus. That cologne could always make her unravel. Leave her undone. Panting for more.

"I would share my blankets with you," he murmured.

"Why are you so insistent on getting me into your bed?" she asked.

"Why do you insist on avoiding it?" Magnus asked. She swore she could hear that smirk. "Have you forgotten what it was like to blow off a little steam before a big job? It was helpful for both of us…"

Oh, God, she had not. In fact, they blew off steam *after* a big job as well. While she remembered, Magnus moved to her front, pinning her against the cabinet behind her. He was shirtless tonight, wearing only thin pajama bottoms that did nothing to hide the hot club between his thighs.

Celeste took a deep breath, unfortunately inhaling more of his intoxicating scent. She reached out and laid her hand against his ribs. She felt the rise and fall of each breath he took as he stood over her and grew wistful for the sexual play they'd had years ago. She never wanted to admit it, but she enjoyed running roughshod over his plans when they were in the field so that she could feel his dominance in the bedroom. Celeste loved that dynamic…when it worked.

"I'm not sleeping with you," she breathed.

"There's nothing I can do to tempt you?" he asked.

He was tempting her plenty, as it was, but he kicked it up a notch by touching her back, brushing his hands down her sides until they fell to her hips. She wore slightly more than he did, a pair of gym shorts and a baggy T-shirt.

"What do you have for me?" Celeste asked, knowing she was playing with fire. In the back of her mind, she thought of Doris and Sebastian and their *necking* in a coat closet. The overwhelming urges that her mentor must have had but tried to deny herself. If she let Magnus pleasure her, what would *he* end up taking?

Without words, his fingers dipped inside the waistband of her shorts and panties. In seconds, he found her wet, clenching pussy and slipped between her folds. She gasped as he wet his fingers and rubbed her clit with her juices. The motion was barely perceptible in the dark, but the sensations nearly halted her breath.

"You have no idea how much I've missed that gasp," he whispered as he leaned forward, trapping his hand between their pelvises. "I remember it turning into a moan, then a plea and then a desperate whimper."

She squeezed her thighs around his hand in response. If she spoke…she'd surely embarrass herself with senseless pleas. And she couldn't have that. Celeste wanted to wrench pleasure from him without giving him her words.

"Talk to me, Celeste," he quietly commanded in her ear. His finger dipped into her slick channel, slowly pumping in and out a few times before sliding back to her swollen clit.

She swiftly took him by the back of the neck and buried her face into his bare chest. Only he could pull this out of her, drawing volatile waves of pleasure. Her legs shook as she struggled to stand; her grip on his neck tightened. "You're such…a prick," she panted.

He sped up the movement of his finger while softly chuckling.

"You loved this prick. And I loved giving it to you. Over and over…and over. Until you tightened around me and screamed my name. Until you fell asleep on my chest. Until you finally knew what true peace meant."

Goddamn him. Her body betrayed her in the most wicked way. His one finger did what most men couldn't accomplish with their entire being. "Please," she whispered, hanging on the fringes of ecstasy.

"Please, what?" he asked, continuing his relentless stroking. "Would you like me to get you off now?"

Celeste nodded. "Yes."

"Good girl… I like it when you're polite."

She sucked in a sharp breath and lost it completely when he covered her mouth with his own. His rough kiss, skilled fingers and that arrogant comment completely unraveled her. Spirals of electricity curled throughout her body, radiating outward, making her weak and needy. She squeezed herself against him and whimpered his name tightly as pleasure washed over her.

"That's it," he murmured. "That's it…" His vigorous ministrations soon eased to a slow, languid stroke through her folds.

She tried not to completely collapse in his arms as every shudder racked her body, but Celeste was damn near a limp noodle after her orgasm. She held fast, though, planting both hands on his chest to create the illusion of space between them. "Okay, okay," she breathed.

He pulled his hand from her pants and licked his fingers clean. She heard him even though she couldn't see him in the dark kitchen. That simple action made her shockingly aroused all over again. "Go to bed, CeCe."

She panted as she pushed away from him.

Celeste had taken what she needed from him even though she wanted to keep punishing him for something she could barely remember. She'd begged him to touch her when she wanted to keep him in the past where he belonged.

And then he dismissed her.

She stopped in the kitchen entrance and turned to his silhouette. A sliver of moonlight filtered through the window above the sink, revealing his shadowed form gripping the counter behind him. His chest was still heaving.

"We can't do this again," she said in a shaky voice.

He chuckled darkly. "I hope you sleep well."

Good God, she hated him for that.

He always knew she slept her best after a good fucking.

18

"Go ahead and put your trackers on," Lawrence said through Magnus's earpiece. He adjusted the tiny device in his ear canal, trying to reacquaint himself with the annoying tickle. He pulled the small bug from his breast pocket and peeled it open to reveal its adhesive side.

"Do I need to activate it or anything?" he asked, sticking it on the left side of his chest.

"No, it starts working once you pull the plastic off. Celeste? Still waiting on yours to show up."

They sat in the back of Santiago's newly acquired BMW, waiting to be dropped off at the nightclub Deux Monde. As he carefully drove through the cobblestone streets of Tallinn's Old Town, Magnus and Celeste sorted themselves out and came up with tonight's plan.

Beatrice had found Sebastian's whereabouts, and the most current photo of him, through a dark web contact. The bar they were headed to was not too different from Santiago's establishment back home. A nightclub front on the top and something lawless beneath it.

Magnus watched Celeste fumble with her own small flat

disk. "Your dress is stunning, but I can tell you're having a hard time deciding where to put your tracker."

"It's a tad revealing, isn't it?" she asked, running her hands across the black fabric.

Her brown skin shined like bronze through the plunging neckline at her chest. She must have used some kind of tape to keep the panels from exposing her breasts. The strappy dress was nearly backless and the hem stretched downward to the middle of her thigh. Revealing? Perhaps... But *delicious* was a more appropriate word to describe Celeste.

"You should put it between your thighs," he said.

Her gaze flew to his face. "Really, Mags."

"Let's keep it PG, y'all. There are children on the line," Lawrence chided with mirth.

Beatrice chuckled. "I think he means for you to stick it to your inner thigh. I hope that's what you meant, Magnus."

More or less...

Celeste sighed. "Turn around."

"Nothing I haven't seen before, darling," Magnus said with a grin. "Do you need any help?"

She punched his shoulder.

"Fine, fine," he said, turning around to face his window. Behind him, he heard fabric shifting and shimmying around. He loved how she managed to act coy after being fingered last night. Oh, God, it felt wonderful being knuckle-deep inside her, pulling every shuddered gasp from her lungs. When she collapsed into his chest, breathing hard and twitching around his finger, he knew he had bested her.

The prickly teasing was just her way of deflecting.

Not that he hadn't tried his own way of deflecting. After all, it was Lawrence who advised him to turn on that *Nordic charm*.

"This is as close as I'm able to get, guys," Santiago said, pulling along a curb. Ahead of them, a steady stream of luxury cars

clogged the street where Deux Monde sat. It seemed like everyone had the same idea on a Saturday night.

"Celeste, can you add your glasses?" Beatrice asked. "I'd like
to watch if I can."

"Sure," she said, nudging his shoulder. "I'm decent."

By the time he turned around, Celeste was slipping a familiar pair of glasses on her face before fluffing her curls from her
forehead. "I'm not," he whispered.

"I can't believe I'm going to have to listen to them flirt all
night," Santiago muttered from the driver's seat. "If only my
Bonita Bea were here to keep me company…"

Beatrice, who was sitting in the same command center with
Lawrence, snorted. "Eyes on the road, my friend."

"Do you have the letter?" Celeste asked him.

Magnus patted his chest where the red envelope hid beneath
his blazer. "Yes."

"Good, follow my lead when we get inside," she said. "The
faster we see Sebastian, the quicker we find out what we need
to do for him."

He wasn't surprised by her tightened reins. Not one bit. "Yes,
ma'am…" Magnus sighed, exiting the vehicle. He walked around
the back of the car, opened her door and extended his hand.

Celeste looked up from the darkness of the backseat, her lips
twitching in amusement. "Thank you."

He pulled her from the car and carefully placed her on the
sidewalk. "I hope you haven't made a mistake choosing those
shoes. The cobblestones here are pretty bad."

"I don't like it any more than you do, but you can't wear a
dress like this without heels."

"I'm sorry to say it but I like them very much," he said, grinning at her legs.

"You kids have fun," Santiago said. "Let me know when to
return." The BMW pulled away, passing the line of cars before them.

She slipped her arm through his. "Just in case I fall on my face."

"I've got you." He led her by the arm down the sidewalk. It turned out Celeste was indeed appropriately dressed for the evening. Many women wore pencil-thin stilettos and moved with far more grace than his partner.

"Last night, I read an interesting entry in Dr. Grant's diary."

"Oh?"

"It seems that the Tahitian pearls play a big part in their relationship. He stole a necklace from her, one he'd given her years previous."

"Did she get them back?"

She grinned and shrugged. "It's hard to say."

"We've got two men on the door," Magnus murmured. "Did you want to relay the message to them?"

Celeste shook her head. "No. I'd rather get inside first."

"Get a drink, have a dance?"

"If dancing is required, you might be in trouble."

Magnus scoffed. "Celeste, you wound me. I'm light on my feet and my rhythm is impeccable."

Before she could deliver another barb to him, they arrived at the front doors, where the two security bouncers eyed them coldly. The one closest to Celeste gave a quick nod and allowed them entrance. Inside was a lush scene dripping with roaring twenties opulence. Red velvet tapestries draped the walls, dark parquet wood floors were polished and the high ceiling gleamed with gold tiling in the club's soft lighting. Plenty of dark corners to hide away with the one you wanted to seduce.

The woman on his arm had a look of determination that quickly squashed that idea. Of course, Magnus was also there on business, but Celeste was in charge this evening. And he didn't want to fight with her just yet. Tonight he was more interested in observing how she carried herself.

"The bar?" she asked, smiling up at him.

"Of course." He carefully led her toward the bar, navigating the crush of ultra-wealthy patrons surrounding them. Some looked like European playboys from central casting; others looked like Russian oligarchs. The women were elegant, aloof and shrewd.

The bar stretched the entire length of the club and was operated by four bartenders, all men, dressed in starched white dress shirts and black neckties. Magnus waved the closest one over and waited. "What would you like?"

"G&T, please."

"So polite," he whispered on the side without an earpiece. He ran his fingers down her bare arm and watched as a delicate blush flared between her breasts. He had hoped that the ambient noise of the club, chatter from the patrons and low-volume jazz could disguise his voice from the rest of the crew. "You think you can keep that sweet tongue after this?"

She looked up at him, her large brown eyes narrowing. "You're incorrigible," she whispered.

He couldn't help himself. After their interaction in the kitchen, Magnus felt himself being pulled right back into the push and pull they used to dance years back. He teased her, she snapped back with venom and he stoked her passions until they both gave up the fight. It had been an entertaining game for them right up until he wanted to keep her all to himself. This time, he wouldn't make that mistake.

The young man behind the bar took their order and set out to make two gin and tonics. "Any sign of an elderly French man of distinction in this crowd?" he asked.

"I need Celeste to do a slower scan of the room," Beatrice said through the earpiece. "I've got AI facial recognition based on our image of Sebastian."

"Good Lord, I'm impressed by the kid, CeCe," Lawrence intoned softly. "She's actually scanning faces through your camera feed."

Beatrice chuckled. "Slower, Celeste. Go back to ten o'clock."

Magnus watched her glance off to her left and stare at patrons sitting in a roped-off VIP section. "Anything?"

For a couple seconds there was silence on the radio waves. "There he is," the young woman said. "White linen suit, white hair, standing beside the seated black suit."

"I see him," Celeste replied.

When their drinks arrived, Magnus laid some euros on the bar and handed her a rocks glass. "Feel like approaching him now?"

Celeste took a sip and nodded. "I think that's best."

During the walk from the bar toward the VIP section, Magnus noted the amount of men who were pulled from their conversations to openly stare at Celeste. He wasn't surprised. As the only Black woman in the establishment, she was probably a unique sight. He kept a protective palm on the small of her back, letting his fingers brush against her soft skin. The stares were a mixture of curiosity and lust, both of which he was certain Celeste was accustomed to. Nevertheless, he stayed close enough to broadcast that she was *not* a solo woman.

They stopped before the roped-off area, in front of a large man who wore an all-black suit and regarded them with disinterest. Magnus had a feeling he was there for the young man hosting his many lady friends on the red velvet couches behind him. "I'm here for Sebastian," Celeste said in a strong, clear voice. The guard looked between her and Magnus before his eyes fell back on Celeste. He said nothing, but he did unclip the rope and step behind it before reclipping.

He strolled over to the elderly man, leaned over and whispered in his ear. The man whom they'd suspected was Sebastian glanced over at Celeste with a raised brow. Once he got a good look at her, his eyes widened. He muttered something to security and waved him away.

Magnus took this as a good sign.

The guard came back to them, unclipping and reclipping as

he went. "He will see you in twenty minutes," the man said in a thick Russian accent. "You wait in that area." He gestured to an empty VIP section near the DJ booth.

"Ah, look at that," Magnus murmured. "We're very important people."

"That works for me," Celeste said.

As soon as they unclipped their section and sat down, a waiter immediately joined them, setting down a gold champagne bucket and two flutes. "Compliments of Monsieur Fond du Lac."

"Merci," Celeste murmured as the young man popped the bottle and set it back in the ice. When he disappeared, Magnus draped an arm over the back of the velvet sofa and shifted closer to her. "I'm not drinking that," she said.

After her gin and tonic, he understood that she'd want to keep a clear head. But one of them needed to keep up appearances, so he poured himself a drink. "I'll be your cover."

"You're pretty keen on that, aren't you?" she asked with a sly smile.

These earpieces hampered how he really wanted to speak to his partner, so Magnus removed his and dropped it into his leftover gin and tonic.

"Why did you do that?" Celeste asked.

Magnus leaned next to her and whispered, "Because I'm not used to being surveilled like this and I think it's hindering our rapport."

Someone from the command must have said something to her because she replied with a tired sigh. "He's offline. Yeah, I know."

This situation reminded him of their first meeting at Victor Sanderson's penthouse. Celeste could keep all the bugs and wires she wanted, but he didn't work like this. He liked being a little rogue when the time called for it.

While she watched Sebastian, he moved closer to her until his lips were right at her ear. "We have twenty minutes to wait on the man who's going to give us our clue or heist or condolences," he said in a soft voice. "And I want to spend it alone with you."

"You can't work with an audience, Mags?" she asked lightly, crossing her legs away from him.

"I'd prefer not to," he admitted. He appreciated the added technology that Lawrence and Beatrice offered, but favored the old days when he could wind Celeste up and prime her with lust and adrenaline. "Where did you hide your tracker?"

She raked her fingers through her hair. "In a place where no one can see it," she said in a light voice.

"Between your thighs?"

She shook her head.

"Somewhere slightly higher?" he whispered.

Her crossed legs shifted, or flexed, he couldn't tell. She refused to answer his question.

He brushed his fingers down buzzed hair at the nape of her neck as he stared at her exposed décolletage. "I forgot to ask. Did you wake up refreshed this morning? Well rested?"

Celeste chuckled as she leaned forward and poured herself the glass of champagne she swore she wouldn't drink. She brought her flute to her lips and murmured, "Better than I expected."

"I'm glad I could help," he said, knowing that the crew was getting one side of a bawdy conversation. "You look exquisite tonight. Have you brought more dresses like that?"

"Yes. You told us to pack for the next month. I figured a few of these might be helpful."

The thought of her wearing another dress that drove him mad delighted the fuck out of Magnus. "Please tell me you brought the gown from Sanderson's emerald reveal. The one with the slit up the thigh. I only got to explore it for a moment before we were interrupted."

The blush she had slowly cultivated on her chest swiftly moved up her neck and settled in her brown cheeks. "I think that one is in the suitcase."

He groaned against her ear. "Wear it to bed tonight. I want to peel it off your body."

She shook her head. "I can't reward bad behavior."

He inhaled the sweet fragrance of the perfume coming from her neck. Gardenia… "You rewarded me last night. If you let me, I'll give you more than my fingers."

"I'm sure you could," she said, keeping her gaze straight ahead. She rarely drank from her glass. Sure enough, she kept speaking in low tones behind its rim, only pretending to imbibe Sebastian's gift. Celeste just needed something to busy her hands with. She tilted her head to the side and paused for a moment. "No, you're not missing anything important. Magnus is flirting heavily," she scoffed. "Is it working? Of course not."

He smiled as he kissed her bare shoulder. "Of course not." The crew couldn't see the spreading blush or the clenched thighs like he could. Those subtle signs were rewarding enough.

19

If Celeste had a watch, she would have checked it several times by now. Since they sat down, since Magnus plunked his earpiece into his glass, she had been fighting for her life, wondering when their twenty minutes was up.

His hot whispering in her ear bothered her tremendously and he knew it. She couldn't seem to cross her legs any tighter and suddenly felt very naked sitting beside him. Magnus casually touched her here and there, which normally wouldn't unsettle her... But it was his words that set her skin on fire. He'd always had a skilled tongue, in more ways than one, and his gift for dirty talk was unmatched. She just hated how she succumbed to it so easily.

"The eyes of every man in this club seem to come back to you," he continued whispering. "As you sit here on display like a Caravaggio, blazing with passion and full of dark mystery, they keep coming back to you, wondering..."

She took a deep breath through her nose and finally sipped the champagne she clutched so tightly. Magnus spun such a good yarn even she found herself curious. "What?" she asked.

Though it seemed impossible, his body slid closer and his

lips were at her temple, hot breath tickling the shell of her ear. "What is she hiding under that haughty expression? I'm the only man who knows what lies beneath your cool exterior, aren't I?"

She twisted her head to look at him, but quickly remembered that Beatrice had a camera feed in her glasses. Celeste pivoted back to Sebastian, who occasionally glanced at her as he talked with the pretty young man of the VIP section. "I don't know about all of that, Mags. You might be projecting."

He chuckled darkly, lips brushing against her earlobe. "Perhaps I am. I do enjoy wondering about what's beneath your facade. Since I've been around you, I've only sought to crack it just to see what's inside."

He had. Only last night.

Magnus had cracked her just enough to find a hot, aching woman who was ready to fall apart at his fingers. She hadn't lied when she'd admitted she'd slept well. Celeste had always slept like the dead after an orgasm from Magnus. If her mind wasn't on the man whom they were meant to glean information from, she would have been excited to go another round with her former lover tonight.

To any of the members of the crew listening to this strange one-sided conversation, it would seem like Magnus didn't care about the job ahead of them. Celeste knew better. Like her, he kept one eye on their mark and the other on her. He used to do this all the time when they were in the field. She just hadn't expected him to return to his old habits. She kept her gaze trained on Sebastian as she spoke. "If all goes well tonight…we could explore that," she murmured against her glass.

"Well, that sounds marvelous." The sigh in her ear sounded content as his warm palm slid up her thigh, settling on the edges of her hemline. "Because last night, when I went upstairs, I was as hard as iron, aching to be inside you."

Celeste pursed her lips and closed her eyes before saying, "I hope you were able to take care of that."

"You wanna hear about how I stood in a cold shower, gripping what should have been in your hands?"

"It sounds like you're volunteering that information."

The grip on her thigh tightened. "I got so fucking hot imagining what it would feel like to slip into you, to stroke you inside out. If your mouth could still work me over like it used to—"

"He's coming!" Beatrice's excited voice interrupted the flow of his dirty monologue just in time.

Jesus, what a terrible choice of words...

Sebastian was indeed swiftly approaching them. Celeste shoved Magnus away and abruptly stood. "Showtime," she muttered. He joined her on his feet, buttoning his blazer. In the blink of an eye, he was back in the game.

"Monsieur Fond du Lac, thank you for meeting with us," Magnus said.

The elderly man gave a short nod before focusing his attention on Celeste. She stared back, searching his wrinkled face for the younger man whom Doris fell in love with. He was a slender man, not too much taller than herself, and managed to wear the wrinkle-free, white linen suit with ease.

"My dear?"

"Doris Grant sent us to you with a message. 'The South Sea is expensive, the Akoya is classic, but only the Tahitian has the character you once loved.'"

Sebastian's green eyes closed for a few seconds. When he opened them again, they watered with tears. "I suspected I would receive such news," he said in a soft, reedy voice. "Come with me."

With a straight back, he turned on his heel and led them through the bustling crowd. Celeste quickly followed, surprised by how spry he was.

"I can't believe that worked," Beatrice said.

"He looked genuinely upset," Celeste whispered.

Sebastian stopped short in front of another security guard

who stood at a stairway leading downstairs. He quickly moved aside and let the three descend into a darkened stone wall basement. A door with an electronic keypad awaited them. Sebastian tapped out a code and let them enter a large office.

"Please sit down." He gestured to two chairs while he discarded his suit jacket and tossed it on a brown leather couch. "What are your names?"

She introduced herself first. "My name is Dr. Celeste St. Pierre, and Dr. Grant was my mentor."

Sebastian nodded as he undid the top button of his shirt and sat behind a long table that served as his desk. Celeste immediately recognized it as early-twentieth-century Thai teak and judged their host accordingly. Old money, world traveler... bordering on colonialist and a man very preoccupied with style.

"I'm Dr. Magnus Larsson. I worked with Dr. Grant years ago."

The old man nodded again. "You almost look like her, Dr. St. Pierre," he said, rummaging around inside the drawer before him.

She didn't know how to reply to that, so Celeste stayed quiet.

"I received this from Doris one month ago." He pulled out the same red envelope that kept appearing on this bizarre journey. "After not seeing her for thirty years, you can imagine my shock having read her letter. In it, she claimed to be writing from beyond the grave. That if I doubted her, just wait until the visit from her most gifted student, Celeste. Here you are..." He looked up with a tired expression.

"We're sorry to confirm this," she said.

Sebastian leaned back in his seat, steepling his hands before his mouth. "Do you know how we met?"

She shook her head. Strangely enough, her diaries never revealed that information. It was as if there was only life after Sebastian and she conveniently excised the life before from the record.

"I was about twenty-six when I went to Washington, D.C., on behalf of my father's shipping business." He trailed off as if transported to another time. "I had just left a meeting with my father's partner, on my way back to the hotel, when a young woman bumped into me. Believing it was an accident, I steadied us both and apologized to her. She hurried off before I could say anything more."

"But you soon realized you were missing something?" Magnus asked him.

The old man nodded, smiling at the memory. "Very quickly, actually. Doris wasn't very skilled at the Bump and Lift, so I hadn't made it to the end of the block before noticing. I turned around just in time to see her slip down an alleyway. She wore a red-and-white polka dot dress. She was too noticeable. Too easy to follow. Which is what I did."

Celeste couldn't imagine a time when Doris was a novice, but all thieves needed to start somewhere. "What happened when you caught up with her?"

"Ha! She was so indignant. Her eyes burned with anger, daring me to challenge her. Doris was so…enchanting in that moment. I fell in love with her instantly, ready to give myself, and anything else I could secure, over to her. But first I needed to teach her to steal correctly," he chuckled softly. "She had the passion, but as I said, not the skill. I assume she'd been lucky in the past, but I knew her luck would run out without proper instruction. Thus began our love affair."

"And the rest was history," Celeste murmured.

"Does anyone else think that's insanely romantic?" Beatrice breathed over the radio waves.

"I'm taking notes," Santiago replied.

Celeste smiled.

"You have come here for a purpose," Sebastian said, returning to the present.

"Yes," Magnus said. "Our letter said that we would need to help you before you could help us."

"Oui, exactement. Like my father, I am still shipping, but I work with very different clientele these days. Doris's letter alluded to a job that I might need help with. How she knew this is beyond my reasoning. But I do need the help. It is my hope that you can accept the challenge so that I can give you the information you need. Doris was rather insistent that I follow her rules. No item, no clue."

Magnus sighed. "Understood."

Sebastian looked at Celeste and she nodded. "Yes. That's what we assumed."

The elderly man leaned forward, planting his elbow on the table. "The job is simple to explain. Your execution might be a bit more complicated. The young man whom you saw me interact with is the son of a Russian oil man. He has been pestering me about a Fabergé egg that is soon on its way to the Kadriorg Museum." He shrugged. "I am a thief who tries not to get involved in geopolitical strife or family dramatics, but the boy says it is a Russian artifact that belongs in Russia. I have a feeling that he wants this egg to curry favor from a distant father. As I live in Estonia, full-time, I do not want this theft coming back to me. A freelance crew will do nicely."

"Where is the egg coming from?"

"The British. They're loaning the piece to the Estonians for a six-month exhibit. Apparently, they are not lending items to the Russians these days. This particular egg will arrive in two days." He slipped a manila folder across the table, toward Celeste. "The details of the egg's travel are in there. Once you've absconded with it, return here so that I may put it in storage for my buyer. Your payment will be intel from Doris, nothing more."

"Okay," Celeste said, taking the folder and standing up. "We'll get your egg by the end of the week."

Sebastian and Magnus stared at her, but the elderly man spoke first. "You behave just like her as well. A perfect clone of Doris…"

Celeste was caught off guard by his words, but quickly found her footing. "She taught me well," she said carefully.

"Oui, and I, her. But I left absolutely no imprint. She took what I gave her and ran far, far away before carving her own path." He shook his head with a sad smile. "I wonder if you truly knew the woman, mon petite. If you knew the shrewd and calculating woman who shaped you." He glanced at Magnus and chuckled. "Does *he* know what shaped you?"

Celeste's jaw clenched. "Excuse me?"

"I only ask because Doris and I only had conflict when I tried to talk to her about her past. She refused to acknowledge a past that shaped the woman she became. She couldn't address the hole in her heart that couldn't be filled with me or trinkets we stole together. Does your Magnus know he cannot fill a similar hole in your heart? That you will run and chase the next shiny thing that captures your gaze?"

"Monsieur Fond du Lac, that's quite enough," Magnus said, standing. "We'll find your item, but you will not insult Dr. St. Pierre in the process."

The elderly man nodded. "I see."

Celeste's voice was trapped in her throat as she glanced between the two men. "I'm sorry," she croaked. "But you're mistaken."

"I hope I am," Sebastian said. "Just know that I loved your teacher. If she had allowed me, I would have followed her to her end. Instead, I was only granted a letter."

His words rocked her, leaving her feeling confused. "Did you take her pearl necklace?" she asked, hoping to catch him off guard.

Instead of looking shamefaced, Sebastian chuckled as he stared into the distance. "It was our little game. She came to

me the night I stole it. When I gave it back, we made love…
and I was convinced she'd stay, but she ran again." He locked
eyes with her. "Where do you lost women run off to?"

Celeste St. Pierre did not know.

But she understood Doris's itch all too well. She currently
felt it in that basement office in Tallinn, Estonia, and she was
ready to leave the suffocating room. Quickly.

Without waiting on Magnus, she hurried up the stairs. "Santiago, it's time to go," she said as she climbed.

"Coming."

She pushed past the guard on the stairs and shoved her way
through the wealthy clientele who clogged the dance floor.

"Celeste," Magnus called behind her.

She ignored his voice and kept moving toward the exit. Relief didn't come until she ended up back on the cobblestone
streets. In the warm Estonian night air, she sucked in oxygen
and clutched Sebastian's manila folder to her chest.

Grief had shown up out of nowhere, ready to kick the shit out
of her. It felt like the mother she'd never met, her grandmother
and Doris arrived on that Saturday night only to hover above
her. None of them offered a sign as she hugged herself tightly.

"Are you okay?" Magnus said from behind her. His hand was
on her back once again but pressed firmly this time.

When she met his blue-eyed gaze, she shook her head.

"Oh, come here," he whispered, gathering her into his arms.
All the while, her mind played Sebastian's words in a loop.
Where do you lost women run off to?

As soon as the tears came, she felt immediate embarrassment.
But when they wouldn't stop, Celeste felt broken. For the first
time since she learned Doris had died, she wept like a motherless
child. The ache squeezed her chest until she could barely breathe.

"You're okay," Magnus murmured from the top of her head.
He pulled her closer until she was folded into him, safely guarded
from prying eyes. "I've got you, darling. I'm here."

Celeste didn't feel much else outside of his strong arms wrapped around her, his hot breath fanning across her temple. "I'm not running," she hiccuped, looking up at him.

Magnus's brow furrowed. "I know that. You're right here, Celeste, with us. And I'm with you all."

She desperately wanted to believe that, despite all the pain in her chest. The hollow feeling in her heart. Celeste held him tighter just so she could keep herself tethered to reality. If Magnus was offering a soft spot on Earth, she wanted to land there.

She needed him to catch her.

20

Even with makeup smeared on her puffy face and shivering beneath his blazer, Celeste still tried to convince them that she was ready to work on Sebastian's case file once they returned to the safe house.

"No, you're not going to do anything tonight. Tomorrow, however, is a different story." Magnus gingerly pulled the folder from her death grip and handed it over to a concerned Beatrice. "Hold on to this and see what you make of it."

"Sure," she said, staring at her friend.

"We all could use some rest," Lawrence said from his seat in the den. "I think things will make a lot more sense in the morning."

Magnus approached Celeste like the skittish prey she was. She was all exposed nerve right now, and any sudden movement seemed like it might make her bolt. He gently took her by the shoulders and spoke softly to her. "We're going upstairs so that you can go to sleep."

"I'm not sleepy," she protested, on the verge of tears.

This was certainly not the woman he had tried seducing in Deux Monde. She looked shockingly younger than her forty-one years, like a frightened girl who had lost her way. He hadn't expected Fond du Lac's observations to have rocked her so hard, but here he was, comforting a woman who was finally coming to terms with Doris's death.

"I'm putting you to bed," Magnus said with a firmer voice.

Her large brown eyes darted up to him and soon, resignation colored her expression. Her shoulders, which were at her ears, eased downward. "Okay," she whispered.

That was the permission he needed to guide her upstairs to his room. Once inside, he shut the door and led her to the four-poster bed. As he eased her to sit down, he knelt before her, prepared to unstrap the shoes from her feet.

"She's gone, Magnus." Her voice shook as she uttered the words. As if the idea had only just come to her.

He paused, fingers on the tiny buckle at her ankle. "She is," he replied, looking up at the fresh tears spilling down her cheeks.

"And I'm just like her... I ran from you."

Oh, this wouldn't do. Magnus didn't need her doubting herself at this stage of their journey. He needed her to be ready to steal a Fabergé egg, so they could be ready for whatever other wild shit Doris had waiting for them. Frankly, he'd never met this version of Celeste. In the time he knew her, she'd never been *this* vulnerable around him.

"You..." He paused, trying to find the right words. "You are your own woman, Celeste. Doris didn't mold you by herself." He lifted her foot, resting it against his thigh to unclasp her shoe. Once he slipped it off her, he moved on to the other. "You fought your way out of your situation and became the woman you are today."

"Like her," she replied. "He made it sound like it was a bad thing. Like she hadn't earned her spot in the world."

When her other shoe was off, he set them both off to the side and pulled her from the bed. "She did," he said. "And it's not a bad thing. Turn around."

She dutifully turned around so he could unzip the back of

her dress. He made quick work of the zipper at the small of her back and slipped the garment down her body. When she stood before him, in her panties, he quickly searched for a T-shirt for her to wear.

"Turn," he repeated.

Celeste turned, seemingly unaware that she was bearing her breasts to him. He slipped the baggy shirt over her head and let her shove her arms through. "Good girl. Are you ready for bed?"

"I'm not a child," she said sullenly.

He sighed, unsure of what to do. "Of course not."

She shoved past him and stormed into his bathroom. When she slammed the door behind her, Magnus collapsed onto his bed and dragged his fingers through his hair. "Goddammit, Sebastian," he muttered to the empty room. He unbuttoned his shirt and tossed it aside before sliding his pants down. In his underwear, he searched the floor for his pajama bottoms to wear.

The sound of water running in the bathroom pulled his thoughts back to Celeste. He'd gotten her in his bed, but the cost was far too high. He flipped back the covers and moved some of his pillows to her side. From what he remembered, she liked to sleep with a dozen pillows, all uniquely positioned around her body.

When Celeste returned to his room, her face was clear of makeup and her eyes looked a little less puffy. "I'm sorry," she said in a tight voice.

His heart dropped when he saw her. The exhaustion she wore in her body was evident. The way her brows pinched in the middle of her forehead as she spoke… *Oh, jeez.* "You don't have to apologize, sweetheart." When they were together, they rarely apologized to one another, so this felt odd.

She tried to give him a tremulous smile. "You don't mind sleeping with a weepy woman?"

It wasn't the evening he had hoped for, but the impulse to cross the room and gather her into his arms was still powerful. He wanted to comfort her so badly. To make her forget about her pain, if only for a moment. "You're not weepy. You're in pain."

She pursed her lips and nodded as she crawled into bed. He got in beside her and turned out the light, blanketing them in absolute darkness. In the silence, he listened for her shifting, her breathing. "Magnus?"

"Yes?"

"Could you hold me?"

He hesitated for a beat before shifting to her side of the bed. He gathered her in his arms, buried his face into her hair and breathed in. "Just rest," he whispered. "I'm here."

A minute passed before she spoke again. "Thank you, Mags."

The gratitude in her tone made him hold her closer. As she relaxed in his arms, he felt his own blood pressure dip. Apparently, this was what he needed. "Of course, my love."

"I usually like sleeping alone," she said. "But tonight, I need someone to hold me."

He suspected that, like him, she actually needed someone to hold her most nights. "I'm here."

She sniffled. "When I was a kid, I was okay with sleeping alone when I knew my Granny was just down the hall. But in Harrison Home, everything just seemed darker. The room I stayed in was too large…too cavernous. And in the black, inky night, I tried to hold myself tight so I wouldn't spin out."

This wasn't the first Magnus had heard about the Harrison Home for the Youth, but in the past, Celeste usually glossed over that period of her life. So he kept quiet, not wanting to interrupt her with questions, fearing she might stop talking.

"I was really quiet back then and the girls hated me. God, I feel like I was fighting for my life every time I woke up in that place. That was where I learned how to use my fists. I didn't want to, but those older girls were the worst." She let out a shuddered breath. "I don't know why they hated me, but I learned to shut myself off, keep my head down and stay busy."

"I'm sorry to hear that," he said.

"I'm glad that I got out when I did," she continued. "I graduated, got a job at a fancy Italian restaurant and tried to make money. I moved out of the Harrison Home a week after my eighteenth birthday."

"Where did you go?"

She sighed heavily. "I spent a couple months in a homeless shelter before I was able to move into an apartment with two other girls. I went to school full-time and took all the classes I could to make that two-year degree go by fast. Later, I had saved up enough money to get myself to Long Island."

"Where you met Doris."

She nodded. "She was incredible, Magnus. You should have seen her in the classroom. Sebastian wasn't kidding when he said she was enchanting. I'd already had an interest in art history, but she made history come alive. I was addicted to learning from her, and her, I guess."

"Dr. Grant was very charming," he admitted. "It's hard not to be drawn to the sun when it's shining right in your eyes."

"And when her light shined on you…"

Magnus knew exactly what she described. He felt it in the first seconds upon meeting Doris. She teased and flirted with everyone, making them feel like they were the most special person in her sight line.

Once her sniffling died down and her shuddering breaths had subsided, Magnus felt Celeste's body relax in his arms. He began to relax with her, the tension in his muscles fading.

"How are you feeling?" he whispered against the top of her curls.

Celeste stretched against him and yawned. "Better. Not quite as tight. Thank you."

"Good."

In the darkness, her face turned upward to meet his gaze. "If you would have told me, at the top of the night, that I would have fallen into your arms just to cry like a little bitch... I would have laughed at you."

Magnus chuckled. "And look at you now, crying like a little bitch."

Celeste punched him in the arm. Not hard, but just enough to let him know she was going to be okay. "Shut up."

"Tell me the truth. Before Sebastian interrupted us, I was very close to seducing you, wasn't I?"

"Were you really working in earnest to fuck me?"

"Of course." Jeez, he thought he had sounded pretty earnest. "I whispered so many filthy nothings in your ear. You weren't picking up on what I was putting down?"

Celeste snorted against his chest. "Filthy nothings?"

"I doubt you would accept my sweet nothings."

"Oh, God, no," she said. "I didn't know you were capable of being sweet."

That was what he suspected. Not that he had any effusive overtures to shower her with. She'd never responded to that in the past. Before they fell out, Celeste's style of intimacy ran a bit...rough and fast. "You don't know the depths of my soul," he said carefully. He'd gotten her to laugh and didn't want to upset their tenuous balance of jokes and gravity.

"I don't," she said somberly. "I hadn't expected to talk to you about Harrison Home. Maybe one day we can talk about your past."

His past...

As he closed his eyes, images of the hospital's fluorescent lights filled his mind. It occurred to Magnus that he'd dreamed of this scene quite recently. The night he'd lost his parents, his friend's mother had driven to the hospital. Uncle Anders, a man he barely knew, was on his way from a city two hours away.

In the meantime, he'd felt so alone that he'd sunk into himself. Unseen and unheard. People spoke around him in hushed tones, almost forgetting he was there.

"What was the first thing you ever stole?" he asked her.

Celeste was silent for a few seconds before replying. "A can of sour-cream-and-onion Pringles from a bodega."

"How did you feel when you took it?"

She snorted. "Hungry."

He smiled. "Understandable. The first thing I ever stole was the costume jewelry used in one of my uncle's productions. After my parents died, I was sent to live with him. He often brought me to his playhouse and let me wander backstage. I took a diamond-looking necklace that was meant for an actress, and when I took it, I felt...nothing."

"Nothing?"

"I didn't have any qualms while taking it. I simply put it in my pocket and walked off. I think I only felt a little guilty afterward when everyone was scrambling before the dress rehearsal."

"Mmm, no one suspected you?" Celeste asked.

Magnus shook his head. "No one accused, no one asked. No one really noticed that I was there..."

Celeste shifted in bed and suddenly the bedroom was bathed in a soft glow from the nightstand lamp. "Did you want to be caught?"

He met her piercing stare with a sad smile. "Maybe." He wanted someone to see him. He wanted his uncle to take him by the shoulders and chastise him. Remind him that his parents are looking down on him and that they might be disappointed in him. But that never happened. Uncle Anders didn't speak of his brother, Magnus's father. He simply did what was expected of a guardian. He fed and clothed him, helped him navigate his finances and the trust fund his parents left him.

"Your parents—"

"No," he said. "I don't want to talk about them just yet. One day, but not tonight."

Celeste opened her mouth to protest but seemed to change her mind. "Okay."

"I told you that story to explain why I'm here. I know you think I steal because I can, and that's kind of true. But when I was a boy, I wanted someone to notice me. No one seemed to for the longest time. Uncle Anders had his life that I had interrupted, and then I was to make my own life. And I did...until I met Doris."

Celeste frowned as she leaned against the headboard. "What do you mean?"

"Doris was the first person in decades who seemed to see me," Magnus chuckled mirthlessly, "rather, through me. She found me one evening and then she challenged me. I couldn't resist her."

Much like he couldn't resist Celeste.

Her eyes softened through his confession. "Thanks for telling me that."

"That's all you're getting from me tonight. I only told you that because—"

"Just shut up, Mags," she said, turning out the light. In the dark, she scooted back to his side, burrowing her body deep beneath the blankets. "Just take my thanks."

He let out a small breath and wrapped his arm around her. "Fine...you're welcome."

Magnus didn't like how uncomfortable it felt to be vulnerable to another person, but he was immediately lighter. *Someone* finally knew something about those early years of his desperate appetite. Celeste felt real hunger for those Pringles, trying her best to survive the day.

He was just hungry for someone to love him.

21

After a sound night of sleep, Celeste had come back to the fold refreshed and ready to ignore her meltdown from last night. Magnus was polite enough to regard her with a casual confidence that didn't betray how nice he was, and she appreciated him for it. It had been difficult for her to need him as much as she had.

It had also been difficult to hear about his childhood. She didn't want her image of him to change. For years, he'd been a gentleman thief without a past, charming enough to infiltrate others with his wit and cool demeanor. After being reminded that he'd had a life before their crew, a tragic one, she now saw a man checking his intactness when he thought others weren't watching.

If he could keep her secret, she'd keep his…

Best to leave it alone and move on.

Her crew had moved on as well. They currently gathered in the basement of the safe house, in Lawrence's workroom.

Santiago was dressed in another three-piece Armani suit, drinking from a small cup of espresso as he read over Sebastian's dossier. "The client is Yuri Popov, son of Oleg Popov, a despicably wealthy oil and gas oligarch," he sighed. "The object is

The Third Imperial egg. And the mark is the Victoria and Albert Museum of South Kensington."

"It arrives to the Tallinn Airport on Monday, at 2:45 p.m.," Beatrice added. "Sebastian was nice enough to give us information on the man who will be transporting the egg from London." She presented a photo of a middle-aged white man. "Walter Griffin, curator for the V&A."

"Who's the exhibit coordinator set to meet him at the airport?" Celeste asked.

"My best guess is a guy named Anton Lepp," Santiago said after checking his phone. "And that's our biggest problem. Whoever is there, we need to dispose of them and intercept Walter without the Kadriorg people knowing their egg is in the wind."

"That includes Anton, his driver and any security in their vehicle," Magnus murmured.

Beatrice frowned. "When we say dispose, we mean..."

"Incapacitate," Celeste finished. "We've never left bodies in the field."

Explaining the definition didn't seem to erase Beatrice's frown, but she nodded anyway. Knocking someone unconscious wasn't something the girl had any experience in, and Celeste would try her best to save her from that kind of conflict.

"Lawrence, do you have a knockout gas for such an occasion?" Magnus asked. "Something to handle several people in one fell swoop?"

The old man disappeared inside one of his cabinets and rifled around glass jars and bottles. "I might be able to whip up something for you," he said with a muffled voice. "I could even come up with an inhalant that's a bit safer than ether."

"Got any masks?" Celeste asked.

Lawrence came back to his lab counter with a jar. "Definitely. I need y'all to be alert."

"So, you're thinking of holding up the van before it gets to the airport," Beatrice said.

Celeste shook her head. "Yes, but it's a tight window between leaving the museum and getting to the airport. There's going to be eyes on that van the whole time. I don't need security spotting us too early."

Beatrice sighed. "The CCTV inside the van is probably going to cover—"

"Every angle," Magnus said. "The driver, passenger and the storage."

"Hey! I have the perfect trick for that," Bea said, excitedly.

Lawrence lifted a brow. "You talking about a jammer?"

"With an added loop," she continued. "If someone can plant the jamming device in the van, I can stop all the live CCTV and replace it with looped footage before our appearance. If no one is paying close attention, the loop could take you to the airport and beyond."

"Okay, young lady," Lawrence said, holding his hand up for a high five. "You and I need to find a way to put that together."

Celeste grinned as the oldest member of the crew teamed up with the youngest. Between their two brains, she figured they would be in safe hands.

"Mags, you'll handle Walter, then?"

He nodded. "I will."

"I'll drive the van," Santiago said. "And Celeste, you'll be in the back."

She nodded. "I'll let you know when I drop the gas."

"How will you know when to stop the van?" Beatrice asked. "How far away from the museum should we knock these guys out?"

"According to Sebastian's file, the transport vehicle is leaving at two," Santiago said. "Lawrence, how do you feel about tailing the van and picking us up later?"

"I can do that," the old man said with a nod.

Celeste chuckled. "Bea, why do you look so annoyed?"

The young woman probably didn't realize it, but she wore the same face that dealt with temperamental customers at the store: a furrowed brow and her mouth pulled down at the corners. She shrugged. "This plan just seems a little elementary. Like, are we doing enough? Thinking through all the different angles?"

Celeste exchanged a tiny smile with Magnus. To her, it was interesting to hear someone new call their plans *elementary*. They'd worked like that for years and it worked out most times. "This isn't unusual," she said gently. "We always know our individual parts and when we come together, the parts just somehow…"

"Work together," Magnus finished. "The important bit is always understanding the role you play. And sometimes the simplest plan tends to be more effective."

"Trust us?" Celeste asked.

Beatrice wrapped her arms around her middle and seemed to think about it. "I guess I'm gonna have to."

"Yes, because we need to trust you," Magnus reminded her.

She gave a quick nod. "Right." Turning to Lawrence, she tried to smile. "Well, Lawrence, I think it's time for us to get to work."

"Let's all meet back here at eight thirty tonight and see what changes we've made to the plan before we sign off on the final draft," Celeste said, surveying the team. When everyone agreed, the group broke up and headed their separate ways.

"Keep up, CeCe!"

Celeste pushed forward and willed her legs to pump until she could catch Magnus. Even though she had found herself winded, the liberation of running was something she'd missed. She only made time for herself to jog on the weekends.

A flat-out footrace against someone who was faster than her, who pushed her to be better, felt good. Magnus was like a sleek gazelle; his arms pumped up and down as he fled ahead of her. She was close behind, but watched in amazement as he leaped over dips in the land and zigzagged through a small group of trees. He must have remembered the terrain from the first lap.

She pushed harder as they rounded the corner of the estate, knowing how much was left to go. That was when she found her second wind. Adrenaline spiked through her body as she came upon Magnus. They had left the trees and were back in the open grass. She remembered on her first lap, there was a slight incline on the side of the estate that forced her to climb.

"I'm on your tail, Mags," she huffed as she ran alongside him.

"How's it look?" Magnus asked.

In the time it took her to look down at his ass, he pulled ahead of her.

"Fuck," she laughed. "It looks cute from back here."

She'd need to dig down to match his pace again, but once they were back in step, she kept her mouth shut and prepared to tackle the incline. She had a shorter stride than the antelope beside her. While he leaped with a deeper sprint, she scurried with shorter steps.

Near the peak, she managed to pull away from him by at least a yard. On the descent, she managed to expand the gap by another two yards. Soon, they'd round the last corner of the property, and the front door would be in her sights.

I still got it! Celeste chuckled to herself as she left Magnus in her dust.

When she met the outermost corner of the mansion, she cut through, not paying attention to how far Magnus was behind her. She just knew that she was winning.

The terrain changed from grass to the gravel of the circular driveway, just as the marble portico jutted away from the front of the house. It was only about sixty yards away.

And that was when she felt it.

It was like a snake sank its fangs in the back of her right thigh. Pain shot up the muscle of her ass, causing her to falter in her steps. "Fuck!" she shouted, as her hamstring seized up.

Magnus was right behind her when she felt the rough slap of his hand against her backside, then he passed her. "Looking good from back there," he chuckled, speeding past her.

"Fuck," she muttered, as she hobbled forward. "Oh, fuck me."

The rest of the race was a pathetic limp to the finish, only to be met by a gloating Magnus doing a corny dance near the porch. "I win!" he announced to the quiet nature scene that was Piriti. As far as Celeste knew, the rest of the crew was working on tomorrow's job.

"I forgot how much of a sore winner you are," she panted, wiping sweat out of her eyes.

"Apparently not as sore as you are," he said, finally approaching her to see how bad her injury was. "Did you stretch before you started?"

"Kinda." She grimaced. When Magnus suggested a quick run, she threw on her sneakers and didn't think too hard about pushing herself to his level.

"Where does it hurt?" he asked, forcing her to lean against him.

"My hamstring and butt," she said, sinking into his side. He reached below her legs and swooped her up into his arms. "You don't have to—"

"If you pulled a muscle, let's not aggravate it." Magnus pushed open the front double doors and carried her over the threshold. She briefly considered how embarrassing the bridal lift felt when she had two working feet but when the cold blast of central cooling hit her hot skin, she almost cried with relief.

"I'm going to see if Lawrence has any Bengay for you," Magnus said without a trace of irony.

"Hell no," she gritted out, shifting in his grasp. "This will pass. I just gotta give it a minute."

"You're going to just walk it off?" he asked, raising a skeptical brow.

"If you let me down, I can—hey, where are you taking me?"

Without much effort, he dipped her slightly to open the door to the basement. "Taking you to the gym. I saw some mats down there that might be helpful."

"What are the mats for?" she asked, reluctantly settling back into his embrace.

"You worried?"

When they reached the gym, he set her down so that she could lean against a wall. She watched as Magnus jogged to the stack of mats and dragged the top mat toward her before unfolding it. "Lie down," he directed, pointing to the floor.

She hesitated, but knew it was futile. If Magnus insisted on giving her a massage, she'd probably just have to succumb to it. Celeste slowly sank to the floor and released a tight breath. The world was much lovelier on her back. Her strained muscles were almost on their way to loosening under the cool air of the spacious room. She closed her eyes and groaned. "That feels so much better." And then she felt Magnus's strong hands squeeze her thigh muscle. "Shit," she hissed.

"It's gonna sting before it gets better, CeCe," he warned. He kneeled beside her, bending her knee toward the ceiling.

Celeste watched him lift her leg over his shoulder, stretching her hamstring. When he pushed her knee past a ninety-degree angle, toward her chest, she sucked in a harsh breath. "Is that your treatment, Dr. Larsson? Torture?"

He pulled back, giving her a little relief. "We're getting older, my dear. Past forty, getting out of bed can feel a little like torture." The corner of his mouth quirked into a smile as he gave another push. "Now, what possessed you to sprint like a madwoman when you hadn't stretched properly?"

Her breath hitched with the tighter stretch.

"Breathe through it," he murmured, leaning over her.

"I needed to blow off some steam," she sighed. "I'm nervous about tomorrow. It feels like Bea got into my head."

"We have a plan," Magnus said, kneading his knuckles into

the back of her thigh. "She's just nervous because you guys haven't worked with others."

"We haven't. *And* she's the new kid. Her confidence is a little shaky and she probably doesn't realize how helpful she's going to be," she said. "But is this a good plan? When's the last time you've hijacked a museum transport van?"

"It's technically not the first vehicle you or I have commandeered. You just don't like it because we're doing this with very little time for prep, and we're doing it for a guy you don't particularly like." As he spoke, he rubbed her muscle harder, digging into the left side of her butt.

The satisfied moan that escaped her throat sounded so loud in the quiet gym.

"Feels good?" Magnus asked with a smirk.

"Admittedly, yes. It seems you know what you're doing."

"Just giving your muscles a good post-workout stretch," he murmured as he released her leg. "Go ahead and flip over onto your belly."

She sighed as she rolled over. "Go easy on me."

Magnus scoffed. "You've never known me to be easy. I'm not about to start now."

22

"Go, go, go!" Beatrice hissed in their earpieces.

Magnus's muscles had been so tense that a sudden burst of energy propelled him out of the back passenger's side of the SUV. Lawrence shifted into the driver's seat once Celeste and Santi hopped out behind him.

Santiago had promised them at least one quiet, camera-free street along the route and this was as good as it got. As he rounded the passenger's side of the museum van, he caught a glimpse of Anton Lepp in the side-view mirror. The man's eyes were still forward, facing the red light ahead of them.

They didn't lock gazes until the crew surrounded the van. The man's pale blue eyes widened in shock as Magnus slapped an electromagnetic pulse on the passenger door.

Fwoom... The engine and the electronic locks powered down, leaving the inhabitant vulnerable. Beatrice said that it would take a quick minute for the van to come back to life. He had hoped that all her technology would cooperate in the manner she described in their final planning stages. Magnus pulled the door open just as he retrieved a small tranquilizing dart from his suit pocket.

Seeing that they were trapped on all sides, Anton didn't fight back. He raised his hands above his head and shouted, "We have nothing of value."

Magnus didn't reply but instead, yanked the man forward and jabbed the back of his neck with the tranquilizer. Anton immediately collapsed against his seat belt. Magnus unclipped him and shoved him over to the center console. Celeste was already in the back of the climate-controlled van, where sure enough, Anton was right: there wasn't anything of value. The Fabergé egg would be the first item this vehicle would see.

Celeste took Anton from under his arms and dragged him back to the rear of the van. Magnus heard her yank strips of duct tape to bind the man's hands and feet. After tranquilizing the driver, Santiago pressed Beatrice's frequency jammer to the dashboard and climbed into the van. Magnus moved the driver into Celeste's waiting arms. Once the men were in the back, Magnus also climbed in and smoothed the front of his crisp white shirt.

"All taped up?" Santiago asked, adjusting his seat and the mirror.

Another scratch from the duct tape roll before Celeste answered, "Secure and hidden under tarps." She threw a couple name tags to the front seats. "Put these on."

Magnus grabbed a KUMU-issued security badge for Anton Lepp. Thankfully, the man's image was such poor quality that nearly any blond could play him.

"Bea, how long before the van boots up?"

"Eighteen seconds. When the van starts, the jammer will replay the last twenty minutes of their drive."

Magnus scanned the neighborhood and street around them. Traffic was light to nonexistent, which really worked in their favor. Either they had worked so fast that no one saw them subdue the driver and passenger, or no one wanted the hassle of reporting a potential kidnapping in broad daylight.

"Keep an eye on the lights, mami," Santiago said, pressing

the ignition button. Beatrice, the girl wonder, also managed to hack into the traffic lights, forcing the van to slow down until they were able to catch up.

"You're good to go…now."

The van fired up just as the light turned green and Santiago turned on the main thoroughfare of Tallinn's business district. In the side-view mirror, Lawrence followed close behind in the black SUV with a replaceable license plate.

"We've got about fifteen minutes before the plane touches down," Magnus said, checking his watch.

"He's gotta get through customs to declare that egg," Celeste said. "We have plenty of time."

"She's right," Lawrence said. "You're good."

Magnus nodded to himself as he kept an eye on traffic. Everything was going well enough, and he tried not to be suspicious of it. They still needed to intercept Walter at baggage, lure him to the van and knock him out.

With nerves keeping his body tight, Magnus pressed his hands to his thighs to steady himself.

They had this under control.

The muffled cell phone coming from the unconscious Anton scared the shit out of Celeste.

"What is that?" Magnus said, whipping around in his seat.

Celeste removed the tarp from the man's body and patted his body down. When she rolled him over, the ringtone grew louder. "He's got a call."

"Don't answer that," Magnus said.

Celeste read the contact on the screen. *KUMU-direktor.* "Fuck. I think it's his boss. We have to answer it."

"And say what? Do you speak Estonian?"

No, of course not. Like a lot of Americans, Celeste had not been diligent about keeping up with a second language, including most of the Haitian Creole her Granny Jo had taught her.

"I can't speak Estonian, but maybe I can type it. Bea, can you get on a translating app and find me the phrase for 'I can't talk right now'?"

"On it!"

Celeste waited a painful amount of time for the ringing to stop. After what felt like forty rings, she declined the call herself, opened the text exchange between these two strangers. She held the phone right in front of her face so that Beatrice could see the screen. "Can you see what they're saying?" she asked.

"Uhh...lemme screenshot that," her assistant murmured. "For now, here's a generic message to send in the meantime."

"Thanks, sis."

For the next few minutes Beatrice slowly fed Celeste the spelling for the phrase "Ma pean sulle tagasi helistama. Lennujaama saabumine." When she finished typing, she pressed Send before succumbing to self-doubt. The silence that blanketed the van was heavy as she waited for a reply. Magnus was fully twisted in his seat, staring directly at the phone, willing it to churn out good news.

A loud beep punctuated the silence.

"What's it say?" he whispered.

Celeste held the phone to her glasses once more. "Bea?"

"Uhhhhh... Pole probleemi means... No problem!" she screeched.

The three crew members flinched from the sound of her voice. Celeste quickly turned the phone off and tucked it back into Anton's pocket. "We're in the clear," she sighed. "How far from the airport?"

"Seven minutes," Santiago said, checking his watch.

"Lawrence, how long does the tranq last?" Celeste asked.

"Long enough, CeCe."

She scrunched her nose at his terse voice as she rolled Anton back under the tarp. She would have been fine with dropping a gas bomb, but Santiago raised a good point: even with gas masks, precious minutes would have been wasted on waiting for the men to pass out and airing out the van. Celeste didn't really like the idea of jabbing someone with a sedative and was relieved to be in the back of the van.

"If you say so," she muttered.

Everyone fell back into a tense silence that carried them all the way to the airport. As Santiago maneuvered through the departure lanes, Celeste chewed her lip in anticipation. Nerves hadn't completely overridden her excitement. The familiar thrill of being with the old crew kept her blood rushing and heart pounding.

"We're here," Santiago said, pulling up to the curbside. "Is there a sign for him?"

Magnus looked around his seat. "Here," he said, pulling out a whiteboard with "Walter" written on it.

"When I see our man, what should I say to him?" Santiago asked.

"As little as possible," Beatrice said. They certainly didn't need any more linguistic battles for the rest of the day. "But if you feel the need to speak, stick with affirmatives like jah."

Magnus shook his head. "I'm going in."

"Smooth back your hair," Celeste said. "And straighten your tie."

He adjusted himself in the rearview mirror. "Better?"

"You look like a curator."

He turned in his seat to flash her what looked like a nervous grin. "Wish me luck."

"We're not working on luck," Celeste reminded him. "We're better than that."

Magnus rolled his eyes and turned to Santiago. "Is this a good place for you to stay?"

Santiago shrugged. "As good as any. Knock 'em dead, mano."

"I'll wait until I get him back to the van."

That was Celeste's cue to roll *her* eyes. As excited as she was, she was hardly in the mood for his dad jokes. When Magnus eventually hopped out of the van with his sign, Celeste met Santiago's gaze in the rearview mirror. "We've got this?"

He nodded. "Jah, jah."

23

The smart-dressed man who strode confidently toward Magnus dragged a small carry-on suitcase while carrying a metal suitcase that was handcuffed to his wrist. Once Walter spotted the sign meant for him, he flashed a set of white veneers and held out his free hand for a shake.

"Mr. Lepp, I presume? I was afraid I'd have to suffer another wait. This country's customs agency is a disaster." He looked around before giving an arrogant sniff. "I suppose that's the cost of doing business with the East."

Interesting…

He could tell that Walter would be an insufferable transport. As far as he knew, Anton Lepp was also a Doctor of Fine Arts but he chose not to correct the man. Estonia was a lovely country and he certainly didn't agree with Walter's snide comment. But more importantly, Magnus was relieved that the curator wasn't overly concerned with his appearance.

"It's good to meet you, Dr. Griffin," he greeted in a Swedish accent. Even if he couldn't speak Estonian, he could fall back on something that sounded European. "I trust you had a smooth flight from Heathrow?"

"Splendid," the man said, lifting his case. "The Imperial and I got on just fine."

"If I can direct you to our transport," Magnus said, gesturing toward the exit. "I'm certain you'll want to relieve yourself of the case."

Walter's gray brow furrowed slightly. "That won't be necessary. As I told your director, the Kensington V&A would prefer that I take strict security measures regarding the Imperial. It will be attached to me until we reach a proprietor's office."

Magnus smiled broadly while planning how to remove the cuff after knocking Walter out. "Yes, of course, Dr. Griffin. I was only considering your comfort, but we'll stick to protocol."

"Perfect!" the gentleman said, clapping his back roughly.

Magnus never let his smile waver as he ushered Walter through the hectic airport. He checked his watch and was satisfied with their timing. "We're nearly there," he murmured.

"Roger," Santiago said in his ear.

When Magnus spotted the van still parked where he left it, every muscle in his body tightened as he tried to appear nonchalant. He opened the door for Walter, who stood close by. "This is our driver, Serg."

Santiago gave a friendly wave. "Jah, jah."

"I'm afraid Serg only speaks Estonian," Magnus said apologetically. "I'll let you join him in the front while I sit in the rear of the van. He will take us straight to Kadriorg Palace."

"If you insist," Walter said, climbing into the front seat.

Magnus closed the door on him and carried his small suitcase to the back where Celeste waited. "Inject him now," he told her.

He heard her groan through his earpiece before a sputtering "What the devil?" from their latest guest, Walter.

By the time Magnus climbed into the back of the van, Celeste was dragging the man and his metal briefcase toward him. He quickly concealed them and assisted her dragging efforts. "You okay?" he asked her.

Celeste gritted her teeth as she pulled the man's dead weight. "Yeah, I just don't like jabbing people."

"You're just a big softy, aren't you?"

She shot him a glare. "Just help me find this damn key."

"Time to go, Santi."

"We're still on your tail," Lawrence said over the airwaves. "Off to the drop-off site?"

"Jah, jah," Santiago said, pulling into departure traffic.

"You wanna check his person or his bag?" Magnus asked her.

Celeste glanced between the sleeping man and his small suitcase. "I'll take the bag."

While Santiago drove them through the rougher side of Tallinn, where the Soviet-bloc towers remained, she reached for Walter's carry-on and unzipped it. The contents were just as organized as the man; everything was in its place, not a stray bottle of cologne or comb rolling about. It made things easier to rifle through. He packed two dress shirts, two pairs of slacks, a velvet sack for another pair of shoes and one toiletry bag.

"Found it," Magnus said.

Celeste looked over to find Walter's shirt shoved up to his chest to reveal a money belt strapped to his belly. "Good Lord, really?"

Magnus shrugged. "It's a good place to hide a key."

Once they freed the briefcase from Walter's wrist, Magnus was decent enough to re-dress the man before Celeste taped him up and shoved him next to the other unconscious men. "ETA on drop-off?"

"Six minutes," Santiago said. "When we stop, I'll wipe down the front, and you guys wipe the back."

"Roger," Celeste said.

Magnus made quick work of the briefcase. Celeste sucked in a breath when she saw The Third Imperial Egg nestled in a foam mold. Its rippled egg surface gleamed with eighteen karats of gold and sat atop a three-legged pedestal. Her hands couldn't help their slight tremble as she carefully lifted the egg from its case.

"Three sapphires set in wreaths of rose-cut diamonds," Magnus breathed as he watched her turn it over in her hands. "Open it."

Celeste bit back a grin. Giddiness overran her nervousness as she shared this moment with him. After all these years of stealing, she was still awestruck to hold history in her hands. This egg was a gift to Czar Alexander III, possibly in his Winter Palace, well before the First World War or the Russian Revolution.

When she pressed the diamond button, the top of the structure sprung open to reveal an upright white enamel watch that was covered in more gold and tiny diamonds. It was stunning.

"Can I keep it?" she whispered.

A broad smile lit up Magnus's face. "Of course, you can," he chuckled. "We'll just explain it to the oligarch's son and his goons."

She sighed as she gingerly closed the egg and laid it back in its foam mold. "There're always goons, aren't there?"

"Yes, ma'am." He closed the briefcase and flipped the latches tight. "The certification papers are in the back compartment, so we're good to go."

"Good, because we're here," Santiago announced. "Roll out, kids."

They ended up in a run-down neighborhood on the other side of the Telliskivi district. It looked a little dodgy, but they were all convinced that no one would tamper with a security van. Of course, the museum would eventually locate it once Santiago removed Beatrice's surveillance jamming device.

Magnus entrusted the case to her before flinging open the back door. Lawrence was waiting for them. "Hurry up now," he said, waving them toward him.

With the crew once again reunited in the same vehicle, Santiago was now in the driver's seat and ready to flee the scene. Celeste sat beside Beatrice, who beamed brightly.

"We did it," she said, bouncing in her seat.

Celeste squeezed her knee. "In large part to you, my dear. The hacking you did was brilliant!"

"Absolutely brilliant," Magnus agreed. "Thanks for pausing the stoplights."

"How did you do it?" Santiago asked.

"A lady never tells," Beatrice preened.

Apparently, Celeste had taught her young protégé well. When you're skilled enough to pull off a job like a magic trick, you keep the details to yourself. Always keep people wondering. Admittedly, those were the lessons Doris taught *her*.

"If there are no more errands to run, I'm heading back to the safe house," Santiago said.

"Please," Magnus said. "I want to get off the street before things heat up."

"Hear, hear," Lawrence agreed. "Let's get the hell outta Dodge."

24

After a celebratory dinner full of boisterous shouting about the job they'd pulled off, Celeste stayed in the kitchen with Lawrence, while the others excused themselves for wine in the drawing room.

"Lawrence, you did the cooking, you don't need to wash the dishes, too."

"I heard you the first four times, little lady," he said, running the water in the deep sink basin. "But if you want to help me wash up, I won't stop you."

"I'll dry?"

"That'll do just fine," he said, giving her a gentle smile.

They washed for a while, falling into a quiet rhythm. He washing, she drying. As she stacked the dishes back into a nearby cupboard, she caught Lawrence watching her. "What?"

He shook his head with the same wry smile. "You just remind me of her is all."

She flipped her towel over her shoulder and leaned against the counter. "I'm hearing that a lot lately."

"It's not a bad thing, CeCe. It's just the way you carry yourself. Strong-willed and driven. Whatever drove her, I see it in you."

Celeste lifted her chin and stared at him head-on. "What drove Doris?"

Lawrence shrugged. "Oh, it's hard to say exactly. To be the first, to have the last word, the next biggest prize? You know she hardly fenced any of the paintings she stole. She often liked keeping her treasures to herself."

"It's hella hard to fence a Caravaggio that should be hanging in Rome."

That earned her a chuckle. "But you know she could pull it off if she wanted to. And maybe that's what drives you, Celeste. The next biggest prize? You'll get it with the help of your crew, but what comes after that?"

She didn't know the answer to that question. "You make it sound like Dr. Grant's ambition was a flaw."

"I didn't say that. She was ambitious, but she was also clever. Knew when to let things go to grab other things."

Celeste felt her face burn from his words. She couldn't help but think of the Swedish diamonds she literally let go of years ago. Or was he referring to the grudge she still held against Magnus? She'd admittedly had a hard time letting that go. "Have you been talking to Magnus?" she asked with nervous laughter.

"No...but speaking of Larsson, I see some of Doris in him as well. He's a cautious man, but if the prize is worth it, he'll go after it."

"What prize is big enough to make Magnus not so cautious?"

Lawrence rolled his eyes. "You're smarter than that, Celeste. The man is fiercely loyal, but to very few things or people on this Earth. You were one of those people at one time... Perhaps you should be careful with that."

She took a deep breath as she listened. "We're just doing this one job," she said in a soft voice. "He won't really want to come back to the fold."

"He's already back, kiddo," Lawrence said, joining her to lean against the counter. Together, they stared into the grand dining room with the twelve-seat table and crystal chandelier. "I'm not telling you this to frustrate you. I'm just calling it as I see it."

"I'm not frustrated," she said. "I appreciate your observations."

"Whatever you two choose to work on after this score, I do believe you'll do well...together. I'm assuming that was Doris's grand scheme."

Her mentor had insinuated as much in her diaries. She wasn't blind to the parallels between her relationship with Magnus and Doris's relationship with Sebastian. Like those two, Celeste often wondered if she and Magnus were just different people who belonged to different worlds. One of want, one of privilege. "Did she ever talk to you about us?" Celeste asked.

He nodded. "She said that if *you* weren't careful, you would go your whole life looking for something only to find out it was him. She feared you might realize it too late." Lawrence turned to face her. "Do you know what you're looking for?"

Celeste scrunched her face up. "You think it's *Magnus*?"

"Is that a bad thing?" Lawrence asked, laughing at her.

"Bad? I don't know about that...more like complicated. He can be a jerk sometimes."

"And so can you, CeCe. Sometimes you're as stubborn as a Georgian mule and Magnus is the only one who can sort you out."

She rolled her eyes. "All right, old man. You're pushing it."

"So long as someone's pushing you," he said, checking her shoulder. "Go on and get some rest. I'll finish this up and turn in myself."

Celeste pushed herself away from the counter and caught him in a tight hug. He seemed startled, but quickly wrapped his arms around her. They stood like that, in the kitchen, in a quiet embrace, until Celeste finally spoke. "Thank you for being here, Lawrence."

"Of course."

She rubbed his shoulders before leaving him to his own devices. As Celeste made her way to the stairwell, she noticed that Beatrice was still lounging in the drawing room with a bottle of wine and her tablet.

"Where are the boys?" she asked, ducking her head into the entrance.

Beatrice didn't take her eyes off her tablet. "Mags went to bed and Santi is in the garage modifying our last getaway vehicle. I guess he's changing the license plate and all that?"

"That sounds about right."

"You doing okay?" Beatrice asked, glancing at her. "I know you said you didn't want to be a part of a crew, but I feel like we've worked really well together so far."

"Well enough to say 'I told you so'?"

Beatrice grinned. "Not yet. I'd love for you to see what I see. A weird little family that could work if you let it."

"Even Santi?"

The young woman shrugged. "I like him. He's cute and fun, but I'm not about to get involved with him. Not if he's going to get in the way of my goals."

The girl's words gave her pause. Echoes of the stubborn ambition Lawrence had just described seemed to clench Beatrice's jaw as she spoke. Celeste would never want to curb another woman's goals, but her protégé sounded so resolute, it was almost jarring.

"I'm not going to judge you, sis. Do what feels right," she said, backing away from the drawing room. She started up the stairs, two at a time, prepared to speak to Magnus about their stolen treasure in his room. She wanted to get a handle on how to approach Sebastian the next day.

She knocked on his bedroom door. "Mags? Are you still awake?" When he didn't answer, she pressed her ear to the door and listened for any movement. It was very quiet on the other side.

"I'm coming in because we need to talk about Sebastian," she said against the door. "I hope you're decent."

When she opened the door, she found the bedroom cloaked in darkness. Celeste used the light from the hallway to carefully walk toward his bedside. She was about to turn on a nightstand lamp when he walked out of his en suite bathroom.

"My dear… You wouldn't be in my bedroom trying to steal an egg, would you?"

His sudden presence scared the hell out of her once again. She shot up to full height, ready to deliver another palm strike.

Magnus moved faster this time. He sidestepped her and shielded his face. "Goddammit, Celeste, I'm not trying to frighten you," he laughed. "Why are you so hypervigilant?"

"Because you're always skulking around in the dark," she said, steadying her breath.

"Says the woman who snuck into my room."

Celeste watched him make the same steady approach as he had when they were in the kitchen, wondering if he'd try to kiss her again. This time, she found herself a little more amenable. "I announced myself."

He was right up on her, his body towering over her. "I was in the bathroom."

Celeste allowed herself to be walked backward, toward the wall beside his bed. She knew this dance; they had engaged in it after most scores in the past. And because they were in the dark, it made things more illicit, more dangerous. Perhaps they'd kiss, maybe they'd fuck, and tomorrow they could go back to antagonizing one another. Celeste rather liked the idea of being reckless for at least one night.

"And what did you want?" he asked in a low voice.

She stepped backward until her back came up against the wall. "I wanted to talk to you about Sebastian. I thought we'd come up with a plan to approach him."

Magnus put a hand on the wall and leaned over her. "There's

nothing to it. We give the egg to him, and we take his message from Doris. Now, what else would you like to talk about?"

"Straight to the point, huh?" She couldn't help but grin in the dark. He had her number. "I guess I can save time as well. You wanna have a celebratory fuck?"

"I like it when we're brief like this," he said, chuckling.

She shrugged. "You've been very insistent on sleeping with me. I figured I could be accommodating."

"You're so polite when you want to be." Magnus's hands slid down her arms until he took her hands and lifted them over her head. He held them there and leaned forward until his chest pressed against hers, and met her lips with a soft peck. As if he were testing his aim in the dark. "It's been a long time, CeCe…"

Her body hummed with excitement now that she was caught in his grip and without defenses. "Five years. Do you remember how this works?"

Instead of replying, he returned to her mouth with a new intensity. With her hands unable to touch him, she was powerless against his delightful assault. He angled his face and took hungry possession of her mouth; his tongue thrust past her lips and tangled with her own. He used his free hand to tilt her chin up, allowing her to return his kiss with the same demanding mastery.

Only when he pulled away was she able to catch her breath. "Something like that, right?" he breathed heavily.

"Mmm-hmm…"

"Mouthy in the field, but meek in bed?"

Celeste rocked her hips against him in response. "I've never been meek in bed, and you know that. But I don't mind letting you be the boss occasionally."

He dipped his head low and nipped the edge of her jaw. "Does my CeCe still like it rough?"

A thrill shot through her body. "Yes, please."

His tongue traced a path down the side of her neck; the sting of his teeth dragged against her skin. "So polite," he whispered. His breath blew hot, setting her already warm skin on fire.

Her arms still hadn't been released from his clutch, making it difficult to do anything more than wiggle closer to him. This was its own challenge because every time his tongue swiped across her pulse, her knees weakened from the pleasure. "How do we feel about ripping clothes?" he asked, pausing at her ear.

"No, thanks," she answered after catching her breath. "I only brought a limited wardrobe."

"Good to know," Magnus said. Finally, he released her wrists and stepped away from her.

Celeste was confused by the sudden release and distance. She trembled as she leaned against the wall. "Where are you going?" she asked, her voice sounding a bit too needy for her own taste.

"Not too far," Magnus said in a soothing tone. He turned on the nightstand's lamp, filling the room with a soft yellow glow. She found him sitting on the bed, dressed only in a snug black tank top and his boxer briefs. His blond hair was uncharacteristically messy, but it flopped over his brow in such a sexy way she thought she was staring at a different man. He swept an appreciating gaze down her body before returning to her face. "I'd like you to strip for me. Come here when you're finished." He leaned back on his hands and waited.

It would have been easy for him to overpower her with his body, but he was more clever than that. He knew that she liked dares, that a mind-fuck was just as delightful as his fingers. Celeste didn't normally follow orders. Every man she came up against fell prey to her strength or charm. Only Magnus understood that much about her and decided to toy with her the best way he knew. "Are you sure?" she asked.

Magnus leaned forward, resting his elbows on his knees, and clasped his hands together. "Now."

Her panties were already damp from his kiss; she didn't know how she'd be able to steady the tremor in her hands as she worked on unbuckling her belt. While she unfastened her pants, she noticed how his blue eyes darkened in the dim light and how his biceps clenched as he squeezed his hands together. She knew his tells.

So she pushed her jeans down her thighs as slowly as she could. When they hit her ankles, she shoved them off with her feet, casually casting them aside. She watched him as she touched the bottom of her T-shirt. Magnus appeared to be enthralled with her exposed thighs and waiting for the next bit of flesh to appear. Her fingers grazed her lower belly, just above her panties, as she lifted her shirt. Up and over her head went the shirt before she tossed it to the floor.

"Go on," he rasped, trying to keep his voice placid.

She smiled as she reached around her back and unhooked her bra. She shucked down her panties next. When she was completely bare, she held her hands out, gesturing "here it is." His nostrils flared as his blue eyes drifted downward. She took a step forward, but he held a hand up. "Hold on."

Celeste paused.

"Close the door first."

Jesus Christ, she forgot that she left the door open. Celeste was suddenly aware that they were not the only people in the mansion. Anyone could have walked by. She quickly walked to the door and closed it without looking into the hallway. When she turned back to Magnus, his eyes were focused on her ass.

"Come here."

She slowly approached him, fully aware of the swing of her hips and fully confident in her nudity. Based on his expression, Celeste knew that she was the sexiest woman in the world. She held on to his gaze and that knowledge as she walked to him. When she stood right between his open thighs, awaiting further instructions, Magnus looked dumbstruck. "Well?" she asked with a smirk.

He straightened up and ran a hand down his jaw. "You look magnificent, Celeste." The way his voice dipped lower, like a rumble from his belly, made her blush. He reached for her hip, his fingers curled into her skin and he pulled her closer. "Why haven't you aged?"

"Diamonds don't age," she said.

"They don't," he agreed, his eyes drifting up her body until they narrowed on her face.

"What are you going to do to me?" she asked, secretly thrilled by the hunger in his eyes. His jaw clenched before creasing with his devilish smile.

"You let me worry about that, my dear," he said in a low, gravelly voice. He yanked her close and clamped his thighs around her waist. Celeste was caught in the most satisfying trap of her life.

25

Celeste's fully nude body was too much for him to comprehend. Magnus experienced sensory overload as he took in the gentle slope of her full hips. They swayed as she approached him and stilled at his hand. The pooch of her lower belly was rounded and beautiful. And her breasts... Her breasts were as lovely as they were a few years ago. Her small deep brown nipples were slightly lower but the curve of both mounds was just as plump as he remembered. With her standing right between his thighs, he longed for a taste.

This is where he belonged; this is what felt safest. He could play the seducer if it meant she could play her role. No tears, no vulnerable confessions, just seduction. This naked Celeste was vastly different from the weeping Celeste from a couple nights ago. Tonight they could put everything aside for a moment of pleasure.

He slid his hand along her ribs and clutched a breast. He held her gaze as he squeezed gently. Only her nostrils flared as she lifted her chin to stare him down. It was hard to tell if he was truly in control when she held her chin like that. He wanted to take another nip at it to warn her. Magnus rolled her nipple between his finger and thumb just to watch her body quake under his touch. Her undoing was subtle, just a small dip of her imperious chin, but he spotted it nevertheless.

"You look like you're trying to hold on to something," he said softly.

Celeste raised a brow as she bit her bottom lip. He squeezed her nipple just a little tighter to feel her lean into him. Her hands rested on the tops of his thighs, her nails digging into his skin. "What am I holding on to?" she breathed.

"Control. You like it just as much as I do. Your knees are trembling at the thought of letting it go."

Her lips quirked. "It's been years since we were in this position," she said carefully. "I'm curious if you can actually take lead."

A challenge?

Magnus grabbed her by the back of the neck and pulled her forward until her mouth came crashing down upon his. She let out a surprised muffled sound when his tongue penetrated the barrier of her lips. His grip on her neck tightened as her tongue slid against his and a soft moan vibrated against his mouth. Her fingers squeezing into his thighs sent a jolt of pleasure straight to his dick.

While she shook in pleasure, he was tempted to lift her onto his lap and fuck her right there. But he needed to control himself and focus on one thing at a time. First, this kiss. He let the sensations of their mouths working together in harmony throttle the dizzying current racing through his body. Her hot, wet tongue swirled and danced in a hot rhythm that made his body heavy with lust. Celeste must have felt the same heaviness because she relaxed, sinking into his hard embrace. Her arms wound around his shoulders and clutched him tight in a desperate attempt to get closer.

Only when he finally released her did Magnus take a gulp of air. Her lips were wet and swollen, her eyelids hooded and heavy with desire. "I'm sorry I doubted you," she whispered.

His heart hammered foolishly as his hand fell from the back

of her neck. He was very conscious of each hitched breath she took as his hand made a slow path down her back. He trained his face to remain stern when he finally reached the curve of her ass, but her smooth, buttery skin made it difficult to not get giddy with anticipation. It was her teasing words that kept him in the moment.

When he brought a firm hand down on her backside, the crack filled the room and sent Celeste jumping. Her eyes widened as she gripped his shoulders. "Are you done doubting?" he asked.

Her lips parted just a scant and the tip of her tongue flicked to the corner of her mouth. "Yes."

"Now, to answer your previous question. What am I going to do with you?"

Celeste bit back a smile. "Yes?"

He unwrapped his legs from her waist and leaned back until his forearms rested against the bed. "I'm going to ask you to ride my face. And then I'm going to fuck you long and hard until your limbs lose strength." He struggled to keep the cool authority in his voice when he saw her eyes survey his body hungrily. "How's that sound?"

She nodded.

"I didn't hear you."

"Yes, please."

Magnus lay back against his bed and waited. "Go on, then."

Celeste waited for a beat and began her slow climb onto him, making her way up his torso and then around his shoulders. "Are you sure?" she asked, her voice breathless.

"Are you?" he asked, challenging her.

She inched forward until her pussy rested just above his face. "Yes."

Magnus took her by the ass and pulled her down on his mouth. He sought her clit first, flicking his tongue over it as fast as he could. She flexed above him, rocking her hips for better access, as her elbows buckled. Her taste, her scent…was enough to intoxicate, make him fall into an enticing abyss. He licked along her inner lips to the tiny bundle of nerves, faster and faster. He drank her in. Savoring every swipe and each taste of her wetness.

The weight on his face didn't bother him as he held her up. If it was his time to suffocate, Magnus would call it an honor to eat her pussy until her elbows collapsed from under her. Magnus continued to drink long beyond his fill, waiting patiently for her thighs to tremble, her body to shudder, her pants to fill the room. And when they did, he continued lapping and soothing her drenched folds, lingering just a while longer for her pleas for reprieve. She uttered a choked cry as she crouched lower. "Magnus," she whispered.

Instead of answering her entreaty, he caught her clit between his lips and hummed against her wet flesh, sending her into a state of desperate whimpering. But she didn't close her thighs around his head as he thought she might. She keened low and rocked her hips for another orgasm. Just like his Celeste, she was reaching for the next prize.

Arousal shot down to his dick, readying him for the plunge.

As he licked long and complex circles around her opening, her thighs trembled again, quaking on either side of his face. "Mags—" she panted. "Magnus, please." Her thighs finally closed around his face, threatening to cut off his oxygen.

He let her go, smacking her ass roughly.

Celeste yelped in surprise as she lifted away from him and crawled to the head of the bed. With her body supine against a mound of pillows, she looked like an absolute work of art. He was torn between staring at her and pouncing on her like a wildcat. "Are you satiated, my dear?"

"Almost," she panted. Her curls were plastered against her forehead in the same thin sheen of sweat that covered her body. "I'd like some more…please."

So polite.

Magnus grabbed her by the ankle and dragged her toward him. Before she could be flipped over onto her stomach, Celeste planted her free foot in the center of his chest and stopped him. He lifted a brow.

She smirked. "Sorry, habit."

He pushed her foot down and flipped her over before pushing her shoulders down and pulling her ass upward. "This dance doesn't work until you let me lead, baby."

She moaned into the comforter. "Right," she said, pushing back against his hot erection.

"Slow down," he said, reaching around her thigh to run his finger against her clit. At her hiss and jerk, he chuckled. "Does this feel good?"

She pushed and arched against his hand. The nub was full beneath his fingers, an easy button for him to press and pleasure. Soon enough, she was malleable and free to come again. "You know it does," she growled in frustration.

"You sound impatient, CeCe," he replied, pushing her thighs apart.

"I feel like you've proven your point, Mags."

He had to stop himself from laughing. "As you said, it's been a while. I need to know your body again," he said, running his fingers along the dimples of her lower back. "I want to remember how you shake under my touch. I need to know if you still moan when I stroke you here…" He left her clit and ran his fingertips in the crease between her thigh and lips. She tried to suppress a groan but failed miserably. "I see you still do."

Celeste pushed herself up onto her elbows and tried to look at him over her shoulders. He was elated to have her in this position. "Oh, my God, we're already talking too much," she said in a dry voice.

Another crack against her bottom. "What was that?" he asked.

She buried her face against her arm. "Nothing."

"Also, are you on any birth control?" he asked. "I obviously didn't bring any condoms on this trip." He meant to ask earlier, but he was a bit distracted.

"I am."

"Lovely. I was tested at the beginning of the month," he replied.

"Wonderful," she sighed impatiently.

"Is someone getting huffy?" He quite liked making her squirm like this. Even after making her come, she was greedy for more. In this position, he was in no danger of going soft on her, so he let her wait.

"Someone is getting—" She was cut short when his rough hand smacked her ass once again. "Please..." she whined.

Magnus released her long enough to scold her. "Please, what, CeCe?"

"Magnus," she whined.

"You can ask better than that," he said, pulling away once more. He hovered over her as she panted against the mattress.

Celeste's body shuddered as she let out a low moan of arousal. "Oh, God," she whispered.

His palm rubbed her smarting cheek. "He's not here, darling. What can I do for you?"

Her back arched with his words and member. "Please fuck me, Magnus."

"Since you asked so nicely," he breathed, spreading her open between his thumbs. When the thick head of his cock slid in, even he was at a loss for words. It was just as lovely as he remembered. He fit like a hand in a glove, and that simple memory made him sigh with relief. Magnus stretched and filled her as he pushed himself to the hilt.

"You feel just as good as I remember," he moaned.

She didn't answer. He pressed a hand on the small of her back and reveled in the sensation of his dick dragging slowly against her tight walls, before slamming back in.

His hand was still wrapped around her hip, rubbing her clit as he moved in and out at a delicious pace. She covered his hand with her own, guiding him in the right direction and with the right pressure. He rocked against her, controlling the speed, and brushing gently against her G-spot. Celeste squeezed her thighs together around him to intensify the sensation and groaned. He was so God. Damn. Close. "Faster," she panted.

His fingers tightened in response as his pace quickened. The friction, the desperate need and his craving were clawing through his body like she'd set fire to him.

Please, please, please…

Oh, God, please…

And then he broke.

Experiencing an orgasm with the woman he hadn't fucked in five years had made him come much harder than expected. He cried out in frustration, pleasure and relief as she pushed herself against his hips. He rode the wave until he was lost at sea, finally sinking below the surface. He swore that he might black out from the pleasure alone and return to her a mumbling fool.

Filling her to the brim as he hissed his release, Magnus gripped her hips hard with his fingertips as he doubled over against her back. "Jesus, Celeste." He left her entirely too quickly and collapsed on his side of the bed, panting with exertion. "Goddamn, woman," he sighed.

She slid her knees down, rolled over onto her back and closed her eyes. "Magnus…"

"Was that too much?" he asked as he fought to catch his breath.

"You know I hate complimenting you, but…it was perfect," she sighed. "I don't know why I didn't just let you do that a week ago."

He lifted his head and stared at her. "You're kidding, right?"

Celeste brushed her sweaty curls out of her eyes. "What?"

"You said I had a stick up my Nordic ass, called me an arrogant prick and made a pretty big show of saying we'd never have sex. I didn't lose all my memory when I woke up from an Ambien hangover."

She rolled her eyes. "We've said a lot of things to each other."

"And a lot of it you don't seem to remember."

This was probably a terrible time to get into a disagreement, while they were both naked and coming off a sex high...but Magnus finally wanted to have it out with her. Their simmering sexual tension and disdain for one another came from an unfortunate night in Stockholm and it never got addressed.

Celeste slowly drew herself up to face him in bed. "If you're insinuating that I don't remember Stockholm, you're mistaken, Mags. I can recall everything from that night."

"What about the black water? How about the minutes of CPR I gave you before you woke up sputtering? I asked you to quit the risky jobs with Doris and you said you would."

"I lied to you," Celeste admitted.

Anger swelled within his chest as they sat facing each other. "Why?" The single word came out cracked and strained.

She drew her knees to her chest, probably protecting herself from his judgment, which he could feel coming hard and swift. "That night, before the job, you threw out the idea of *just us*... Part of me wanted to imagine a life outside of Doris, a life of stealing with just you. I don't know what it was about that night, but I wanted you so much—" She cut herself off. "I couldn't trust you because you weren't Doris. I never thought I could do this without her."

Magnus's jaw clenched as he fought to control his tongue. Hearing her say that she had wanted him, that she imagined a life outside of Doris, made him sick with regret. What if he had taken the next step and told her that he'd loved her? What if he had been earnest for once in his dead, gray life?

"But I never thought you'd leave first," she continued. "I always wondered why you couldn't just stick it out. I stayed as long as I did because I wanted to make it up to her. I really wanted to make up for the Stockholm job."

"I admired her, Celeste, I really did," he sighed. "But after a while, I didn't want to work under the wild whims of Doris like you did. I didn't have the fawning devotion you had for her."

Her mouth fell open and Magnus almost regretted how he phrased that last part. "Oh."

"It wasn't just the Stockholm job. I was at the end of my rope in Tangier. The amount of work we were doing under Doris was relentless. The last year I spent with you guys, we had close to twenty jobs, each more sloppily planned than the last. *That's* the part I don't think you remember. Celeste, we were destined to fuck up Stockholm."

God, it felt good for him to tell the truth. He'd held his tongue for the sake of the dead, but Celeste's naive idea of her mentor needed critical examination. He expected a bit more pushback from her, but Magnus was surprised to see her head drop against her knees as she blew out a big sigh.

"I didn't know the woman, did I?"

Did any of them?

"I learned a lot from her," he said. "But once I thought I might lose you, that changed everything for me. I didn't want to see you hurt yourself, taking these risks with Doris."

He fell quiet long enough to let an uncomfortable silence fall over the room. When she finally spoke, he was thankful that she filled the space with humor. "I did not expect to have this conversation with you after being ate out and dicked down."

Magnus laughed despite the mood. "It's a conversation five years in the making, Celeste."

"I forgive you for dropping the package and I apologize for dropping myself into the river…and lying to you about joining you. Maybe I should have joined you?"

Magnus reached over and pulled her ankle until her body

was revealed to him again. "Come here, love. Let me hold you before you run off again."

She scooted closer to him so that he could spoon her. "I'm not the runner you and Sebastian think I am."

"I forgive you for not trusting me, and I'm sorry I couldn't catch you when you were falling."

"Forgiven," Celeste said, snuggling against him. "I don't know what's coming for us next, but will you catch me now?"

"I'm here, Celeste."

He meant it. So long as Magnus was with this crew, on their own terms, he'd catch his partner the next time she fell.

26

"You've got to be fucking kidding me."

"I know you're fucking lying…"

Celeste and Magnus glanced over the contents of Sebastian's red envelope after giving up the egg. They were back in the basement of his nightclub, dressed a lot more casually since the last time they met him. Since the KUMU robbery was already in the local news, threatening to spread globally, they were only there to make an exchange and get the fuck out of the country.

If there was a time to be furious with the dead Dr. Doris Grant, that time was now. After reconciling with Magnus over the past, it was difficult to read the next letter from her.

But she read it again just to make sure she wasn't going fucking insane.

"'My dear little thieves… I never took up golf, but I'm well aware of mulligans, and how helpful they are. This hunt is about correcting my mistakes and saying goodbye to the right people. I pushed you all to your limits and I witnessed your destruction at my hands. For that I am truly sorry. Return to Sweden for atonement and I guarantee you will find more help than I could give you. Whatever you remember about Stockholm, try to let go of it. A barman and a princess are going to show you the way…'" Celeste trailed off, stunned as fuck.

"What is this?" Magnus asked with more anger than she expected.

Sebastian, who had long stored The Third Imperial Egg, sat at his desk and shrugged his narrow shoulders. "That's Doris. She loved the games."

"I'm actually sick of hearing that," Celeste admitted, her voice climbing with anxiety. "I don't want to go back to Stockholm. Not for those Freya's jewels."

"And what does she mean, a princess is going to show us the way? *Princess Astrid?*" He threw up his hands and started stalking the office. "This is fucking ridiculous."

"Did you know about this?" Celeste asked, shaking the letter at Sebastian, who watched them with curiosity.

The older gentleman shook his head. "I was not aware of the contents of that letter. I was only asked to give it to you upon your delivery. I've done what was asked of me."

Celeste collapsed in a nearby chair and sighed. After they lost the jewels, she studied the Swedish news for years. She kept a Google alert on the case, she followed Princess Astrid and she watched Interpol for any updates. Nothing. She'd seen nothing about the jewels until a Good Samaritan found the box washed up on the banks of Söderström. Last summer.

"It's fascinating, though," Sebastian started with an impish grin. "For Doris to put all this together before perishing… You must admit, it's quite impressive."

Magnus stopped short and scrubbed his face with his hands. "Yes. Admittedly, it's impressive," he groaned. "I imagine she had to time everything perfectly for us to get to this point."

"She had to have faith that we'd all play our part," Sebastian continued. "She trusted you. Not many thieves work with that particular attribute."

"This was the point, wasn't it?" she murmured, staring at the letter. "Dr. Grant put this whole thing together based on these Swedish jewels. Some fucking tourist found the box and she just...I don't know, got to planning?"

She and Magnus locked eyes when she voiced her realization. "I saw the news last summer and I—" He shook his head. "I just got this sick feeling..."

"And we're supposed to meet with Princess Astrid about this?" Beatrice asked in their earpieces. "How are we going to do that?"

Good question. Astrid had not fared well in this whole debacle. In her research, she understood that her family and the Swedish press regularly maligned her after the jewels went missing. Tabloids hounded the young woman, reporting on her party-girl ways and her real estate heir American boyfriend. Why on Earth did Doris think she wanted to meet with the people who ruined her public image?

"Oh, God," Magnus muttered.

"It gets worse..." Beatrice continued. "They're going on display June twenty-fourth at the Nationalmuseum."

That was *infinitely* worse.

Retrieving a Fabergé egg before it's transported to a museum was one thing; hitting the actual museum was a whole other beast that their crew hadn't managed in a very long time.

"Cheer up, mademoiselle," Sebastian said, standing from his desk. "If Doris knew you as well as I think she did, she did not make this task an impossible one. Daunting, perhaps, but not impossible. It sounds like you and your team must rise to the occasion."

Celeste took a deep breath as she clutched the letter tightly. He was right, of course. This wasn't impossible; it was just damned annoying. She looked at Magnus again, who seemed to have calmed down. "We need to leave," she said in a soft voice.

He nodded. "And we need a plan."

Sebastian chuckled. "Ahh, to be young again. What a delightful little romp you're about to embark on! It reminds me of the time I spent with Doris in Nice, back when we stole everything that wasn't nailed down... I wish I could go back."

His wistful expression moved Celeste to smile tremulously for the first time since stepping into his basement office. She had hoped some of his nostalgia would rub off on her. "You can't go back," she said. "But you could always lend a hand, I hope? Dr. Grant said that we were supposed to make friends while we're out here."

He appeared to think about her suggestion. "I'm an old man, cherie. I cannot work in the field like I once could."

"Maybe not, but if we ever needed a favor, it would be nice to call upon a neighbor. Fabergé eggs don't come cheap, you know?"

This pulled another chuckle from Sebastian. "Cunning. Just like her."

This time, instead of jumping to anger, his comparison emboldened Celeste to ask for more. "So how about it, Fond du Lac? Any resources we might need? We can count on you to bail us out?"

The old man finally relented. "Oui, you know where to find me."

"Hopefully, we won't need your help," Magnus replied. "But we'd appreciate it all the same. Celeste, it's time for us to go. Santiago will want us prepared for departure, ASAP."

"Exactamente, Mags...vamanos," Santiago said. "If we leave now, I can get us on a chartered yacht before nightfall."

"A yacht?" Beatrice said in awe.

"I have my ways, Bea Bonita. Besides, air travel might be a little risky right about now."

Celeste ignored the two as she approached Sebastian. She held out her hand for a shake. "Thank you for getting us this far."

The old man stared at her with that same wistful expression before taking her hand and softly kissing her knuckles. "Good luck on your journey, cherie."

★ ★ ★

November 4, 2003

The young Black girl who sits at the front of my classroom had a disagreement with another student today. Over Caravaggio, of all things. Celeste's defense of his criminal life in Naples seemed a little more passionate than what was necessary, but she entertained me. Her classmate was alarmed, and I fear Celeste has further alienated herself from the rest of her peers.

I know this child, though. I've seen young ones like her before: lost and pretending to belong. Wherever she came from was a whole lot harder than the incredibly white Suffolk County. She walks in with a chip on her shoulder the size of a small boulder. Even though she sits in the front row, she watches her back and her possessions with hawk eyes. She looks like she's fought someone to get here. She makes the best out of her clothes even though I see poorly sewn holes under her arms every time she raises her hand. And she raises her hand quite a bit.

She might be the smartest student I've encountered in a very long time. She's intellectually curious and hungry to learn, like the knowledge in these textbooks might actually feed her. For all I know, it might.

After a couple months of having her in my class, she's made cautious attempts to engage me after class. First, packing her books so slowly that I might strike up a conversation with her. And I always have. Not too long after that, she would stand at my podium and pepper me with questions. Where's the most exciting place you've ever been? Have you seen these paintings at the Louvre? Do you think I have what it takes to be a curator for a museum? I told her that she's destined for far greater things than being a curator.

If I had my way, I would guide this motherless child down another path. And the urge to teach her everything I know has been bothering me since I dismissed class this afternoon. Ms. St. Pierre came marching up to the front of the class champing at the bit to complain about her milquetoast classmate. I had to shut her down.

Yes, she had made salient points about the artist and his work.

No, there wasn't anything wrong with hustling to get where you needed to go.

Yes, my dear, the kids in my class are "hella white"…

Oh, Lord, her sassy little attitude tickles me sometimes. But this time, I had to give it to her straight as she walked me back to my office. I told her to keep a cooler head. Outbursts like hers would not be tolerated in my class because I expect better out of my sole Black student. And her behavior certainly wouldn't be tolerated in any of her other classes. Nor would she get the same grace from her white professors.

Because that's all the girl really needs: a little grace…and maybe a little poise. And something to keep her mask from slipping. Because no one else needs to know how hungry she is. It's odd, but I've never met someone whose hunger outpaced mine. Every time I look into her hopeful, familiar eyes, I ask myself the same question:

Could I?

Could I mold her into someone who takes what she wants? Would she be amenable under my tutelage?

Celeste's reading was interrupted by a knock at the door. She abruptly looked up at Beatrice, who stood at the threshold. She'd almost forgotten where she was while she sank into the past. After their meeting with Sebastian, the crew fled Tallinn and got to the Stockholm safe house from five years ago, ready to plan the last leg of their job. The final heist…

"Hey, what's up?"

Beatrice bounced on the balls of her feet as she combed her fingers through her braids. "I just wanted to check on you. You've been pretty quiet since we got here. Is everything okay?"

After reading the latest Doris entry, Celeste had mixed feelings about her life. And as she now stared at her own protégé, who was giddy with excitement, those feelings went to war with one another. *Could I mold her into someone who takes what she wants?*

"I'm fine. Just sorting some stuff out. How about you?"

Beatrice rushed into her room and jumped onto the bed beside her. "I'm so excited! We're going to meet an actual princess!"

Celeste managed to grin despite her mood. "Adjust your expectations with that. She might not actually want to meet us after all these years. We did rob her after all."

Beatrice rolled her eyes and gave a dismissive wave. "I'm sure she's totally over it."

According to the Swedish tabloids, that might not be the case. Astrid was now the shame of a nation. That was, in large part, their fault.

"Maybe? Now that the jewels have been recovered, some of the heat could be off her." Celeste had her doubts, though.

However, Beatrice could not be deterred. "Either way, I have a really good feeling about this meeting. I had concerns about the Tallinn job, but everything went perfectly. I've been following the news and they still have no known suspects. There's footage of the van, but they have no idea who was driving it. The police don't have any identifiable airport footage of Magnus, either. I mean, they have photo stills of his body, his general build, but he took care to obscure his face."

Celeste raised a brow. "The police?"

"I've been spying on the Estonian Police and Border Guard records for the last twenty-four hours."

She'd always been impressed by her assistant's tech genius, but this was the first time she'd seen Beatrice really flex her muscles. The girl was now doing work that she couldn't have done without bigger challenges, without an actual crew to assist her. "Thank you for looking into that, Bea. That's going to be important when the Scotland Yard and Interpol get a hold of the case."

She grinned. "I've got some friends who will help when it gets to that point."

Celeste's heart lifted upon hearing that bit of information. "Your confidence is inspiring. I hope it rubs off on Magnus and me."

Beatrice took Celeste by the shoulders and forced her to sit up straighter. "We've got this, CeCe. If anyone can pull this off, it's you."

A smile tugged at her face as she made herself nod along to the affirmations.

"Today is not like yesterday. And tomorrow is going to be amazing," Beatrice continued. "You have me this time."

Celeste actually laughed that time. "I know that's right… I've got Bea Hill in my back pocket. Tomorrow is going to be amazing."

Beatrice shrugged her shoulder. "Simple as that!"

As she looked over her assistant's shiny, happy face, Celeste wondered if she had that same shine in her eyes when Doris eventually introduced her to this world.

Could I?

Could I mold her into someone who takes what she wants?

Celeste had already formed this girl without thinking of the consequences. It felt so natural at the time when Beatrice walked into her store with a résumé, explaining her lack of experience in antique furniture. She had hired her on the spot, knowing that Beatrice would be a perfect student. When Celeste eventually had the talk with her about what really went on behind their front, she hadn't fully expected the enthusiasm and loyalty she got. But it looked a lot like her expression now.

Celeste needed to protect that.

27

After a shopping trip throughout the city, Magnus returned to the safe house with a bag of goodies to help him with his project. Every crew member had a different bag of specialized tools, Magnus included. Wherever he went, he brought a full jeweler's kit—pliers, small hand torch, drills and various materials to create or repair pieces. In this case, he was more interested in re-creating.

He'd taken up residence in the dining room, spreading his supplies out on the table. He placed his laptop next to his mess of stuff, frequently glancing at the screen as he copied Queen Freya's jewelry set. He studied the dimensions of each piece handcrafted by Johan Jensen. Two diamonds-and-pearl-drop earrings, one delicate diamond-and-pearl crown and one necklace with the same combination, plus a large sapphire in the middle.

Jensen's particular style of Nordic modesty made his presentation of jewels dressed down and, in many cases, stark. This was the case for Queen Freya's tiara and earrings, but the necklace was truly the star of the show. His years of creating pieces for the Swedish royal family were short-lived after dying in a workshop fire. Before his death, he made this particular jewel set for Queen Freya in 1936. It passed down over the years until it reached Astrid in the late aughts.

Reproducing each piece would be challenging, but the work would give Magnus time to sit with his thoughts. He thought back earlier to this morning. Ever since they arrived in Stockholm, he'd been on edge. So much nervous energy vibrated throughout his body, he needed to get out and stretch his legs. He walked around the city until he arrived at the entrance of Nationalmuseum. He paused for a moment before going inside, but he wanted to get a closer look at the place they would have to rob. Security was not as lax as it had been years previous. There were two beefy-looking men on the door, and two more men on both stairways leading to the second floor. They appeared to watch the large groups of tourists that milled around the first floor.

Flashy signs for the new Freya exhibit pointed him upstairs, so Magnus joined the masses up the stairway closest to the museum's sculpture garden. He walked slowly through the Turn of the Century Gallery before getting to the smaller Treasury Room. A few people puttered around the exhibit, but no one seemed to notice the newer case filled with Queen Freya's jewels. Magnus planted himself in front of the glass display, staring at the pieces that had slipped through his fingers so many years ago.

That was when the thought struck him like lightning as he stood there: *I could make this.*

He didn't steal Uncle Anders's props or take up geology as an area of study for nothing. When he was a kid, he hid the fake diamond necklace, pulling it out occasionally to study its construction. His interest in what glittered quickly became a fascination with all things rocks and minerals. Magnus could do this. If he got to work today, he might make enough progress to include reproductions in their plans.

"What are you working on?" The voice behind him barely

shook him out of his reverie and hours-long concentration. When he finally looked up from his work, he realized it had grown dark outside and his hitched shoulders were now sore. With his magnifying glasses still wrapped around his head, Celeste appeared much closer and more distorted than she really was.

Magnus pushed the visor up and turned off the tiny light at his temple. "What did you say?"

Her attention was on his work at the dining room table. "Oh, my God, Mags… Are those the earrings?"

He stretched his stiff neck and yawned. "Yeah, those are the easiest pieces. The tiara is probably going to give me the most trouble, but I think I could knock that out tomorrow if I keep at the necklace tonight. The construction is simple enough, but I keep wondering about its weight. Platinum is always gonna have some heft." He ran his fingers over the necklace. "I'm especially proud of the blue spinel. I managed to shave it down to the same size and circle cut of her sapphire. Pretty good dupe, huh?"

"You've been working on this all day?" Celeste stared at him. "They're amazing…"

"I saw the exhibition this morning on my walk," Magnus said. "You like them?"

She seemed to catch herself and immediately shrugged. "I mean, it's pretty good," she said. "If it's something you're willing to Bait and Switch, they might not notice for a couple weeks."

That sounded more like Celeste. He gave her a smile as he took her hand. She allowed herself to be pulled by him until she ended up between his knees. "It's okay if you're impressed," he murmured, pulling her onto his thigh.

She settled onto his lap and began to touch his tools. She dug her hand into a large bag of cubic zirconia gems and pulled out a fistful just to let them trickle through her fingers. "So, this is what's in your tool kit," she said softly. "I've never seen you work like this."

"This is how I settle my mind," he said, resting his chin atop her shoulder. It felt nice having her in his grasp. It also felt good revealing this part of himself. He wasn't just a man who cased joints; he could create things, too.

She nodded. "I get it."

"What do you do to settle your racing thoughts?" he asked.

Celeste picked up his soldering tool and examined it. "Plan for the job."

"Mmm." That explained a lot. She never rested. She never stopped reaching for the next assignment. "I think you need a hobby, CeCe."

"Maybe you're right," she said, turning toward him.

They were suddenly very close now. Her dark brown eyes peering into his as he looked her over. Celeste's short curls fell over her forehead, and he wanted to brush them away and cradle the back of her buzzed head. "What can I do for you, Dr. St. Pierre?"

Her full lips turned upward into a smile. "I was hoping you'd sit in on a call with me and the mysterious barman from Dr. Grant's letter."

Magnus sat up straighter in his chair and instinctively pulled her closer. "You found a contact?"

"Beatrice found him the same way she found Sebastian. I was going to contact him, but I wanted you to listen in. I'm hoping we can meet with him tomorrow." She wrapped her arm around his shoulders and leaned against his chest.

Goddamn… He enjoyed this too much.

The quiet intimacy of being in her embrace, being close enough to peek down her tank top and see the goose bumps at the tops of her breasts. She smelled like fresh soap and that fruity shampoo he was quickly getting used to. The coconut and mango mixed with her natural scent created a constant Pavlov's dog reaction whenever she was near. "Get the barman on the phone," he said, nuzzling her shoulder.

"Are you able to pay attention?"

"Barely," he said, pressing a kiss on her soft skin.

Celeste chuckled as she pulled her cell phone from her pocket. She dialed and they waited while the line rang several times. "You'll let me take the lead?"

He huffed. "Of course."

"Hej?" said a deep rumbling voice over the speakerphone.

Celeste cleared her throat. "Hello, are you a barman who might know a princess?"

Magnus lifted his head and gave her a look. "Really?" he mouthed.

She shrugged and rolled her eyes.

The pause on the line made him feel like her greeting was a mistake, but the man eventually replied. "And who is asking about the barman and princess?"

"Dr. Doris Grant," she said.

"Ahh… Are you the student?"

Celeste exchanged a look with Magnus. "I am," she said cautiously.

"We meet tomorrow. 9:00 a.m. Yes?"

"Okay…where?"

"We'll be at the Mead Bar in Gamla Stan," the man said in a gruff tone before hanging up.

Magnus was indeed familiar with the location in Old Town, not too far from the harbor. He sat back in his chair. "That's the plan for tomorrow, then."

"9:00 a.m., though?" Celeste scoffed. "That's so fucking early."

He couldn't help but laugh. "You're in Sweden now, my dear. The thieves meet early here."

28

Magnus went to bed after finishing Freya's necklace and fell asleep as soon as his head hit the pillow. At some point in the night, he woke up from another nightmare. The images were scrambled visions of his parents driving through the mountains, snow blowing the windows white. Since he wasn't in the car before the accident, he didn't know what his parents said or how they looked. They had evolved into faceless ghosts who didn't speak. He managed to wake up before the inevitable happened.

Even after yesterday's exploration, being back in his home city just did not feel good. The last time he'd been to Stockholm, it was disastrous. Before that, he'd visited occasionally to get through the airport and straight on a train to see his uncle Anders in Örebro. Today, as he moved through Gamla Stan with Celeste, he felt like a ghost in a place that had moved on without him. The buildings and cobblestone streets were the same, with the exception of a few new businesses, but he was the interloper who didn't belong.

Celeste, a tourist in her own right, didn't appear to fare any better. She was mostly silent when she came downstairs from her bedroom. He'd stayed downstairs on a pullout couch, wishing he had taken his Ambien on the trip. They were pleasant to one another, reviewed where they would meet the princess and got prepared separately. He also wished that he had joined her the night before. Magnus had an unreasonable desire to be held that he kept to himself because that was what this place did to him. Stockholm closed him off from the others in a way he couldn't explain.

As beautiful and stately as the city appeared, old ghosts still lay just beneath its surface. The same feeling of dread he had, remembering how his parents never returned from their sky trip, weighed him down as they walked past the families and lovers flocking around them.

"You look like you've got a lot on your mind," Celeste said, interrupting his thoughts.

"I'm good," he lied.

Celeste cast a scrutinizing eye at him before speaking. "How do you feel about this meeting?"

Magnus shrugged. "Pretty good," he lied again.

She scoffed. "Bullshit."

It wouldn't do any good to make her shoulder his anxieties. This was his city. He knew the layout, the language and the customs. Magnus needed to project the confidence that he didn't quite have, and if it meant lying his way to success, he'd have to keep it up.

"We're going to meet them, get some information and make a plan," he said. "Same with Sebastian. It's not that hard."

She raised a sharp eyebrow and shook her head but fell silent as they approached the meeting place. A little unassuming mead bar where the lights were low and the space was cramped. At 9:00 a.m., there were no patrons sitting at the tables or bar. It felt like the perfect place to meet a princess in disguise.

Magnus opened the door for Celeste, and they were immediately greeted by a giant barrel-chested man at the bar. The man had the look of a real Viking with the sides of his head shaved and tattooed. The rest of his red hair was elaborately braided down his back. His red bushy beard was also parted and plaited down his chest. Magnus cautiously stepped in front of Celeste and reached the bar first.

"Hello. Hur mår du?"

The man remained in the same stance, large, beefy, tattooed arms crossed over his round belly, as he stared between Magnus and Celeste. He gave a slight nod and deep grunt.

Okay...he'd try a different approach. "Vi är här för att träffa en kvinna."

One of his piercing green eyes crinkled at the corner as he cracked a lopsided smile. "You can just speak English," he finally said in a gravelly voice.

The request immediately put Magnus on his back foot. Had his Swedish truly suffered after all these years? "Fine. We're here to meet a woman," he repeated in English. "It appears we might be early."

"Friends of Doris, then?" the giant asked.

"We are," Magnus replied cautiously.

"I'm Aksel," he said, extending a meaty hand toward him. "I'm sorry to hear of her passing, but delighted to hear from her in such an...unorthodox manner."

"Thank you."

Aksel turned to Celeste and greeted her with the same hefty shake. Her hand completely disappeared into his as she held on. "Nice to meet you," she breathed, tipping her head back just to look up at him. "How did you know Dr. Grant?"

"We met in a bar I owned in Copenhagen. I'm Danish, by the way," he said to Magnus. "I'm sure your Swedish is fine. I just get tired of speaking it sometimes."

"Gotcha," Magnus said, feeling strangely relieved.

"Anyway, I came recommended to Doris for a job she was seeing after in the early 2000s. I had only worked with her a couple times, but I quite liked her. I was sad to get a letter from her last year, but I understood she had a plan and that I needed to deliver it to your guest."

"Fascinating," Celeste intoned. "So, she's already aware of what Doris wanted?"

"Yes, and she is waiting on you downstairs," he said, hitching his thumb behind the bar.

They followed him down a narrow wooden stairwell into a darkened basement. Aksel crouched his impossibly large body to fit, but he moved faster than they did. Midway down the stairs, Celeste's hand reached for his shoulder to guide her. "It looks like everyone does their dirty business in bar basements these days," she murmured.

"It's the only way that she felt safe talking to you," Aksel replied. "The Swedish paparazzi aren't as rabid as the ones in Britain or the US, but they like to keep an eye on her."

Magnus felt guilty about that but decided to make his apologies to the princess herself.

When they arrived in a spacious cellar where casks of mead were stored, Aksel straightened up and gestured to the lone woman sitting at the head of an eight-person table. "Did anyone follow you?" she asked immediately upon seeing them.

"No," they answered in unison.

Princess Astrid was dressed in a simple white T-shirt, but a blond wig, baseball cap and sunglasses sat on the table before her. Her dark hair was wound tightly into a bun at the base of her neck and her brown eyes narrowed in annoyance as she stared at them.

"Take a seat," she said in a terse tone.

They did as they were told, with Aksel sitting directly to her right. Magnus and Celeste sat beside one another to her left. "Thank you for meeting us like this—" Magnus started.

"Stop there," she said, cutting him off. "We don't need to go through pleasantries. Let's just get to business so that you may finally leave me alone."

Magnus was stunned silent.

Princess Astrid slapped a red envelope on the table and sat back in her chair. "Not too long after my jewels were found, it was big enough news for Aksel to deliver that to me. Someone named Doris Grant apologized to me on your behalf. I don't know the woman outside of this letter. I have never met her, but I hear she's dead now?"

Magnus almost didn't know how to respond. This was the first person they'd run up against who didn't sound saddened by Dr. Grant's passing, and he didn't like the young woman's tone at all. "She is."

"Fine," the princess said, crossing her arms over her chest. "She expressed remorse for your little group's actions, and while I appreciate her words, the damage has already been done."

"What exactly does the letter say?" Magnus tried.

"It says that she is sorry, and she is about to die. Apparently, she had read about the scandal surrounding the jewels after they were lost and wanted to make things right."

"Make things right?" Celeste asked with a frown. "What exactly does that entail?"

The princess glared at them. "She wanted me to help you steal Freya's jewels again."

Magnus breathed through his nose as he listened. They had expected as much, but upon meeting Princess Astrid, he could see that the task was easier said than done. "I assume you have some apprehensions about the request?"

Her scowl intensified as she narrowed her eyes on Magnus. "I admit that I have not always been the best member of the Swedish royal family. Princess Clara of Spain and I have been known for our wild days in Majorca. I've spent my family's money in excess. I've gotten into a number of car accidents. And then there's the drunken parties in Gothenburg... But I tried very hard to take care of the jewels my mother lent me because they meant so much to her.

"But you took them, and were apparently not smart enough to keep them. My problems didn't stop with my parents finding out about the robbery, though. Interpol got involved with royal officials trying to collect insurance from what was assumed long gone. I was investigated for two years by this nasty little Belgian inspector before a payout could be confirmed. During that time, paparazzi followed me everywhere, my parents cut off my royal engagements and forced me into hiding. Our prime minister and the parliament also investigated me. You made me look like a fool. The shame of a nation."

Magnus cast an uncomfortable glance at Celeste. "We're sorry," he said, weakly.

Celeste didn't appear as guilty as he felt. "Why the hell would you want to work with us? Him—" she pointed to Aksel "—I get. He's Danish and probably couldn't give a fuck about the Swedish royal family. You'd probably want to help steal some jewels, right?"

To his amazement, Aksel's giant shoulder shook as deep laughter rumbled in his chest. He shook his head while covering his face. "I should not laugh, but—" a braying guffaw escaped him "—but, she's right, Princess... I don't care for your family at all."

"Once we leave here, will Interpol be waiting for us?" Celeste demanded. "What's your deal?"

Magnus was just as curious. He just wished she had used more tact in the moment.

Astrid sighed dramatically. "I'm not going to be the one who turns you in," she replied. "In fact, I might even help you."

"Why?" Magnus asked.

"Because now that the jewels have been found, our family is once again under legal scrutiny. The Belgian inspector is an art theft claims adjuster. Since the jewels were retrieved, he has made it known that the Crown must repay millions of kroner, which is technically taxpayer money." She waved a dismissive hand. "I don't understand all of the finances of it, but he still believes I have something to do with the disappearance of the jewels and now he thinks the entire royal family is involved in some kind of fraud scheme."

While he didn't follow the royals, he could easily understand how Swedish citizens might find the whole affair off-putting, as it ran opposed to their idea of Lagom. Neither the jewels nor the exorbitant amount of money were meant to be openly discussed and could call into question the necessity of a monarchy these days.

"How would helping us help you?" Celeste pressed.

Princess Astrid raised a perfect brow and smiled for the first time. "If you must know, I have a plan of my own. I'm ready to leave Sweden to be with my longtime boyfriend in America. But my parents, the press, these *people*…are so fucking critical of every minor detail in my life. Living abroad, getting married to a commoner, will just be more parts of my life to be dissected. Your theft would be a nice distraction from my problems. If the world finds out Freya's jewels can go missing under the tight security of the Nationalmuseum, maybe *I'm* not the fuckup. Maybe everyone will finally leave me alone."

Magnus scrubbed his hands down his face as he listened to the girl's royal decree. "We're supposed to trust you because you want to get back at your parents and a relentless inspector? If we're going to work together, we need something better than revenge."

She shrugged. "I don't know what else I can tell you. Revenge feels like a good enough reason for me. If you want to steal the jewels on your own, you are more than welcome to try."

"Hold on now," Celeste said. "We're not about turning away free help. Did you have anything in mind?"

The princess waited a beat before pointing a carefully manicured nail at Celeste. "I like you. No one talks to me like you do. It's like you don't care about protocol."

Magnus pursed his lips to keep from smiling. What the princess didn't realize was that Celeste could out-act all of them. She just didn't feel like the princess was worth the charm.

"You're sitting with a couple of thieves in a bar basement," Celeste said with a sweet smile. "I'm not sure how much protocol is needed."

"Please explain how we're going to pull this off," Magnus said.

"The royal family is working with the government and Nationalmuseum to hold a special gala. Some kind of nationalistic gift to the citizens to celebrate Sweden or something," she said with a scoff. "Scholars, museum donors and wealthy Swedes will be in attendance. I will be there, too, against my parents' wishes. They don't want my name or face to be associated with such a joyous occasion, but that will be the only way to get you two in as my guests."

"That takes care of our entrance," Magnus said. "Anything else?"

"Once you get in, you're on your own. I plan on giving a speech before a historian talks about Freya's jewels. If you can work around that..."

"Give us the exact itinerary as soon as you have it."

"I can send that in an encrypted message," Aksel volunteered.

Magnus's mind immediately went into planning mode even while sitting with the princess. Depending on their timing, she could make an excellent diversion.

"If you want to reach me, go through Aksel," Princess Astrid said, tucking her own hair beneath the blond wig. "I'm afraid I cannot have any more direct contact with you after today. I only did this so you could see the fallout of five years ago."

"To be fair, we only steal from people who aren't hurting financially," Celeste said. "But...after speaking to you, I now see that we've hurt you in other ways. Doris isn't the only person who owes you an apology, Astrid. I'm sorry as well."

"Thank you. My driver is coming in a few minutes," she said, standing from the table. "I'll send the invitations and information to Aksel this evening. I expect to see you three days from now."

"That's not a lot of time," Magnus said.

"And yet you're *just* in time," Astrid said, walking toward the stairwell. "Just be ready for gala night."

She disappeared before either of them could ask another question, leaving Magnus in a surreal state of trying to understand what had just occurred.

"This is really happening?" he asked the table.

"Is she always like that?" Celeste asked.

Aksel gave a hearty laugh. "Yes and yes. You had better get ready because she's hell on wheels."

29

Exhaustion plagued Celeste that evening. Perhaps that was what hanging out with a princess would do. But as tired as her body was, her mind was still keyed up and thinking of all the things they'd need to prepare for in the next few days.

After the meeting with Astrid, Celeste had asked Magnus to walk her to the museum. Once inside, Celeste walked the entire building from the basement to the third floor. It had been a long time since she had covered the length of a museum and she'd forgotten how tedious it could be while moving around recreational visitors.

Of course, she stopped at Freya's jewel display and took a closer look at the pieces from all angles. The case itself was situated against the Treasury Room's wall, standing about a foot taller than Celeste. Half of the display was a solid black pedestal while the other half was a glass encasing with the locking mechanism on its backside. She could see it touching the wall through the glass, which meant that the entire case could be moved. She tapped the clear surface with her fingertip and heard the unfortunate sound of acrylic. Not actual glass, but a much more durable plexiglass. Annoying material for smash and grabs.

Each piece had its own metal stand, with the tiara standing the tallest. Both earrings sat slightly lower on either side of the star of the show, the necklace. The bright white LED light from the top of the pedestal made every diamond and the single blue sapphire glitter beautifully. Eventually, she moved away from the display and pretended to be interested in a collection of nineteenth-century thimbles. By the time she and Magnus finished their walk-through, Celeste now had a full map of the museum stored in her mind. She clocked each key-card door, the number of motion sensors in each gallery and the number of volunteer guides and security guards.

Upon returning to the Gamla Stan town house, she and Magnus filled the team in on what they learned. Lawrence, Beatrice and Santiago set out to work immediately after they realized their time constraints. Celeste tried to hang with them as long as she could, but her constant yawning made Magnus quietly demand that she get herself some rest. He had that look in his eyes that amused and aroused her. Again, it was the strange little dance they did: she was all big dick energy in the field, and he'd bring his big dick to the bedroom after a challenging day.

She had no idea if he'd join her in her bedroom, but she took a shower and got ready for bed all the same. The Stockholm safe house was a downgrade from the one in Tallinn, but it had enough space for them to work without climbing over one another, and the water pressure was fantastic. That's all she needed. The bed that she *might* share with Magnus was a full-size IKEA model with a firm mattress, which is where she sat after exiting the small bathroom, towel still wrapped around her chest.

As she applied lotion to her legs, her mind went back to Magnus sitting at the kitchen table planning with the crew. He'd occasionally rake his fingers through his blond hair as he examined the city map. He'd ask Santiago questions about the layout, and if he remembered the streets well enough. She even remembered when he'd shoved his sleeves to his elbows so he could examine the museum floor plans.

He'd looked so handsome at that moment.

Celeste vigorously rubbed lotion on her legs and wondered what he was thinking about when he'd caught her staring at him. His blue eyes narrowed on her for a second, nostrils flaring slightly as he blushed. A shiver ran through her body as he held her gaze and bit his bottom lip. Beatrice excitedly explained the closed-circuit security system of Nationalmuseum, but Magnus kept his eyes on her as she spoke. That was when he leaned down and whispered, out of earshot of their colleagues, "Get upstairs and rest. You look a little punch-drunk and horny."

Her face burned as she looked up at him. "Excuse me?" she whispered back.

He grinned and leaned even closer to her ear. "I know you heard me the first time, CeCe. If you're a good girl, I'll come up and tuck you into bed."

She sent herself upstairs and took care of her own mental health for a moment. Getting a long shower seemed to help relax her mind and put her thoughts in order. But by the time she began applying lotion, Magnus jumped back into her brain. Celeste would rather have him here rubbing her down. She squirted more lotion into her palm and worked her way up her thigh. Her mind wandered and imagined his hands instead of her own.

When she brushed a hand near her mound, she pressed her lips together and breathed through her nose. Goddamn, she hated when he was right. She was horny as hell. But dammit, she would at least be moisturized. She rubbed briskly at her hips and tummy, skipped her breasts and worked lotion down her arms instead.

Celeste glanced at the bedroom door.

Maybe she had a little time before Magnus excused himself from the group. She could get herself off quickly before they both settled down for the night. After all, their reconciliation was precarious. There was no guarantee that they'd truly fall back into bed with one another. He might come to her, he might not. But if she handled herself, she could sleep soundly instead of being distracted by Magnus.

Celeste clutched her towel to her chest as she ran to her luggage. She kept a small lipstick vibrator in her carry-on that had been helpful on many work trips. On her way back to bed, she peeked out her door. The lights were still on downstairs, and she still heard him conversing with Bea and Santiago.

With her phone and vibrator in hand, she returned to bed and turned off the nightstand light. She settled into the darkness and slowly unwrapped her towel. Her self-pleasure routine usually lasted longer, with an exhaustive scroll of adult videos before she was ready to touch herself. Instead of that, Celeste found her favorite ASMR guy who excelled at dirty talk. She put both earbuds in and pressed Play.

"I know what you came here for..." said the deep-voiced stranger. "You want me to make you wet."

Celeste was already having a hard time staying focused. This ASMR guy was talented, but he didn't compare to the real thing whispering to her while his fingers slid down her belly. Hot breath against her neck as he nuzzled the spot behind her ear. And besides, Magnus was a champ at dirty talk. She was already used to the deep rumble of his voice as he settled in between her thighs.

"But first, you'll have to be a good girl and beg me."

Celeste closed her eyes and pressed the quiet vibrator to her clitoris and waited for something to happen. She was wet and frustrated, but she wasn't going to come without a little encouragement. While the man talked in her ear, she began imagining Magnus's body. The way his muscles flexed as he drove into her, how the cords of his forearms stood out while his fists were planted on either side of her head.

The images danced in her mind as Celeste slid her vibrator up and down. The memory of Magnus was enough for her to get close to her goal. She was barely listening to the ASMR guy now. As her fingers skated across the tips of her breasts, her breathing slowed down and she could finally relax.

She was so relaxed that she didn't hear Magnus enter the room.

Above the gentle buzz of her vibrator and the wicked voice of her ASMR guy, she didn't notice him until he bumped against the bed. Her eyes flew open as she slammed her thighs shut and ripped her earbuds away. "Jesus fucking Christ!" she gasped.

He was a dark silhouette standing at the foot of the bed. "I swear I'm not trying to make this a habit," he said with humor in his voice.

Celeste quickly wrapped her towel around her chest and felt relieved that he couldn't see how red her face was. "No, I think you really love sneaking up on me," she said.

"You don't have to stop," he said, walking around the bed.

Her heart hammered in her chest as she watched him sit down and felt the bed dip under his weight. "What?" she whispered.

"I don't want to interrupt you," he said as he took off his shoes. "You looked like you were getting somewhere."

"I didn't think you were going to come," Celeste said in a rush before cringing in the darkness.

Magnus settled against the pillows on his side of the bed and chuckled darkly. "Don't ever doubt my ability to come...to you."

The same shiver she felt at the kitchen table shot through her belly as she clutched her towel tightly. "You're not obligated to," she began, nervously licking her lips. "Besides, we're on a job right now and we probably don't need the added distraction."

"I don't know why you're suddenly coy now, like we've never had sex while working," he said, shifting in bed. In the darkness, she could faintly see his blond hair flop over his brow. "I remember a certain Philly trip where we got into some mischief."

Her grip on the towel relaxed. He was right. Their job in

Philly hadn't even been an outlier. She didn't know why she threw that flimsy excuse out there. "I guess," she said in a weak voice.

"It was a lovely trip." His voice dipped to a lower octave that curled her toes tighter than her ASMR guy. "And something like that is bound to happen again if you're interested."

"I just thought we should be professional," she breathed.

"We've already done the ole Ball and Chain," he teased. "We can just pretend to be married if you like."

Celeste scoffed at the suggestion.

"If my wife would like to continue touching herself, she's more than welcome," he continued. "She should know that her husband is here if needed."

Her breath came out in a jerky gasp. Magnus and his mouth were going to get them into trouble. Maybe he didn't mind being distracted, but she needed to focus on the prize. "I think I'll be fine."

"You'll never get to sleep without it," he said, shifting again. He was on his back now, his hands tucked behind his head. "Trust me. If I had an itch right before going to sleep, I wouldn't get a wink before scratching it."

Celeste sighed. She hated it when he was right.

"How can I help?"

It was silly for her to pretend that she didn't want him. He was offering to help her, and now she wanted to be prim about her desires. Surely she was too grown for that. "I sometimes listen to this audio recording of a man talking."

"Mmm. What's he saying?"

She frowned in the darkness. "It's silly."

"Tell me."

"He tells me when and where I can touch myself."

Magnus went quiet.

In the stillness of her bedroom, she wondered if she had spoken too candidly. He may have clammed up on her, but his body was speaking to her in other, more subtle, ways. His socked foot, the one closest to her, ran along the duvet. She could hear him take a deep breath before exhaling. "I can hear him breathing in my ear while he directs me," she continued.

"Can you?" His foot slid back to join the other one. She heard the bed creak as he adjusted himself. "What does he sound like?"

"I usually like his voice," Celeste whispered. "He has a deep… register. But I think you might be deeper."

"Mmm."

At one time, she had gotten pretty good at figuring out his grunts. This one made note of his curiosity and begged her to continue. So she did. "To be honest…husband, I've gotten used to your voice. I was trying to imagine it before you walked in."

"Mmm."

Satisfied grunt.

"Maybe I could take over for him," he suggested in a husky voice. "Just for tonight?"

They lay side by side, a foot of space separated them, but his words stroked her skin, sending goose bumps down her arms. He shocked her no end with those scintillating words. "I'd like that," she said through a shaky breath.

"Undo your towel."

Celeste wasted no time to think. The cool air kissed her breasts and tightened her nipples.

"Who would you like me to be?" he asked.

She couldn't believe that he needed to ask such a question. Celeste didn't want anyone but him. "Just yourself, please."

"So polite," he murmured. The unmistakable sound of a belt clatter filled the room.

Celeste's chest rose and fell in anticipation as she heard his zipper follow. Whenever he made note of her politeness, it meant that he was gearing up to be filthy. She expected the response like one of Pavlov's dogs. "Go on, husband."

"You were wet for me downstairs, weren't you?"

She inhaled sharply. "What makes you think that?"

"I could see it in your eyes," he murmured. "I can tell you need…something when your eyes get dark and out of focus. It wasn't just exhaustion."

She didn't answer.

"A dark blush starts at your chest, Celeste. It goes up your neck and hits your cheeks. And before I know it, your pupils dilate. It's always been that way."

"Has it?" she whispered.

"You touched the tip of your tongue to the corner of your lips when you stood up and left us. Like you were asking me to follow you."

The rumble of his voice vibrated through her body, reminding her to take up her small toy and put it to work. Celeste felt around the bed until she found the lipstick and flicked it on.

"When you came back here, you took a shower. Why didn't you touch yourself then?"

She clutched the vibrator in her left hand and thought. "I just wanted to get clean."

"So you could get dirty later?"

Her grin widened. "Maybe."

"You can't touch your clit yet," he said. She could almost hear him smiling as he dictated. "No, my dear wife. You must wait."

She didn't mind the wait.

"You didn't think about touching yourself in the shower…" He tsked before he chuckled. "Not even while your body was slippery and sudsy? Your hands didn't run along the curve of your hips? Your fingers didn't pinch your nipples for some kind of relief? Weren't you aching, my love?"

She had been aching.

"I know what I would have done," he continued. "I know what I *have* done. I was in a shower with you years ago and I didn't miss the opportunity to touch you every place I could. My hands palmed your ass as I slid into you."

Celeste fought the impulse to moan as she listened. She didn't want to miss one word of what he would have done—what he *had* done—to her wet body. "I waited," she whispered as she ran the vibrator along her breasts. When she touched the tip to her stiff nipple, she inhaled again and pressed her lips closed. Her eyes fell shut against the darkness and listened to his voice intently.

"You waited," he said with a sigh. "Even after you dried off. But you're still in your towel, wife. Did you decide you needed a release while moisturizing? While you slid your hands up your thighs?"

Her exhale sounded like a moan, and she didn't care. They were doing this. And the added touch of calling her *wife* seemed to rev her engine even harder. "I wanted to touch myself," she confirmed. "While I was moisturizing."

"I thought so," he said. "You can move the vibrator a bit lower if you squeeze your breasts for me."

She did, and spread her legs, awaiting further instructions. The tension and worry in her body unfurled like a warm jelly, flooding her body and sending calm in its wake.

"You thought you could hurry up and get yourself off before I got up here, didn't you? You didn't anticipate that I was the only arousal you needed. That's why I came in here to find you frustrated and desperate for release, isn't it?"

She nodded, not knowing if he could see her.

"You can go lower."

Celeste ran the vibrator across her belly until it settled on top of her mound. She drew a shaky breath as she rubbed her thigh with her other hand. "What would you have done, husband?"

"What I've done before, wife. I'm sure you imagined it while you touched yourself. Me licking you while you shook and thrashed above me... You love it when I use my tongue. Is it your favorite?"

"Yes," she moaned.

"But my hands do well in a pinch," he conceded. "I made you squirm in the kitchen, in Tallinn, right? But then again, it's probably my dick that truly makes you fall asleep."

"Please…"

"So polite," he sighed. The bed shifted under his weight. Even with her eyes closed, she knew that he had gripped himself in his fist and was stroking himself. "Lower."

Celeste drew her knees up and pushed the toy to its destination. The sensation almost brought her to tears, setting every nerve ending in her body on fire.

"You'll get yourself off for now, darling. But you'll want me to get you to sleep. You'll want me to fill you deep and hard until you come."

She did.

Every softly spoken taunt he issued was true.

"Because one is never enough for you," he said through gritted teeth. The rhythmic sound of flesh smacking flesh came from his side of the bed, and it kept pace with her breathing, her own stroking. The toy slipped along the wet folds of her pussy as she struggled to hear more of his words. "You always need one more prize, Celeste. Do you want me to give it to you? Do you want me to keep stoking that fire inside of you?"

"Yes," she said, squeezing her eyes shut, reaching for it.

"Inside of you is where I belong, Celeste. I don't need much more than that and I don't know if I'll ever get my fill of you."

Those were the words.

Strangely, *that* was the confession that sent Celeste over the edge and into oblivion. Her hips rose from the bed as she came, and a tidal wave of pleasure swept through her body. In the darkness, it was just him. She and Magnus floated in a vacuum of darkness and no sound. And instead of scaring her, it gave Celeste hope. All he needed was her. She hadn't heard such a declaration in years and wanted to hold on to it with both hands.

Celeste gave a shuddered breath before she could speak. "I want you." Good God, she wanted him in every way, in every position and damn near every night.

She didn't have to ask him twice, because Magnus loomed before her, at the ready. "But do you need me, wife?"

He hovered above her with both hands on either side of her head. He caged her in the old familiar way that made her feel safe. His erection pressed against her belly, reminding her that the next adventure was just around the bend. Magnus was right; she couldn't help but reach for the next available prize. But God help her, she couldn't possibly admit that she *needed* him. "Please fuck me," she whispered instead.

He exhaled against her cheek. "So fucking polite," he murmured.

30

Magnus reached his hand to the other side of the bed, expecting to touch Celeste's whisper-soft skin, but only felt air. The space she was supposed to fill was empty and cold. When he opened his eyes, he was disappointed to find her gone. He lifted his head to survey the bedroom, glancing at the bedside clock. 11:00 a.m. He had woken up entirely too late and was a little irritated that Celeste hadn't given him a nudge before leaving.

His head flopped back against his pillow as he remembered the night before. He may have said some regrettable things. Not the dirty talk that curled Celeste's toes, but the part where he asked if she needed him. To imply that he needed anything of her made him cringe. Sometimes, he accidentally veered away from playful seduction to something more serious without thinking. Today he wished he had done more thinking. He wished he had kept his placid mask up.

Her plaintive plea of "please fuck me" felt like an avoidance to his ridiculous question. Why on Earth had he asked it? He had survived quite well without needing anyone. Hell, he'd spent five years buried in his teaching and planning his own jobs without anyone. But after one night between Celeste's legs, he had returned to the same sorry sap who demanded she leave Doris and come away with him.

He pulled himself out of bed and planted his feet on the cold wooden floor to ground himself. Magnus would not ask Celeste any more silly questions related to wants, needs, loyalty or anything adjacent to…love. Fuck that. They were only together to do the job that Doris had requested from the grave. After this was all over, success or failure, Celeste wouldn't need him. They didn't have anything keeping them tethered together aside from this one assignment.

After quickly dressing, he brushed, washed his face and swished about some mouthwash before exiting her bedroom. He probably shouldn't come back. Perhaps she was right when she said they needed a bit of professional distance. Maybe it was a mistake to keep this dance going…

Magnus quickly switched gears as he headed downstairs. Raised voices caught his attention. Beatrice and Celeste sounded like they were arguing.

"I don't see why it's a problem," the young woman said.

"Bea, you've never been in the field. Now is not the time to start."

"And I think I've come up with a good plan. Plus, Santi will be with me."

Magnus headed straight for the coffee machine to pour himself a cup. Santiago stood at the counter looking on at the drama. "The ladies are scuffling?"

"Have been for the last hour," Santiago whispered out the side of his mouth. "When you two went to…bed, she and I stayed up and came up with a plan to case the joint. I think her idea might work."

"You're being a little unreasonable," Beatrice said, speaking with a mouthful of toast. "I've worked with you long enough to know how to handle myself. I've been watching you through your glasses, remember?"

Celeste paced the kitchen with her hands planted on her hips. "Be that as it may, you're too young to be out here…running around and getting into…shenanigans."

Magnus grimaced at how motherly she sounded. "Celeste, you were how old when you were in the field?"

She whipped around to glare at him. "Did I ask you?"

He raised his hands and backed away from her. "I'm just pointing out the obvious."

"Fine!" she said. "Fine, go ahead and scout the museum. It sounds like everyone agrees with her?"

Lawrence ruffled his newspaper in agreement, while Santiago and Magnus nodded silently.

"Fine," she repeated.

"Sounds good to me," Beatrice said, shrugging her shoulders. She turned to Magnus and rolled her eyes. "Just in case you missed it, Santiago and I will go the Nationalmuseum to place sensors that Lawrence developed on all the inside doors we can find—"

"And I'll also stick them on outside entrances," Santiago finished. "We can keep an eye on where people are coming and going based on how often they're tripped."

"I'm also dropping off a supply bag in the storage lockers located in the basement. If you're done with the Freya reproductions, I can take those, too."

Magnus nodded while sipping his coffee. "Just let me put the finishing touches on the tiara and you should be good to go. You up for all this, Santi?"

"I'm ready to follow Bea's expertise. I think it's time to let someone else take the lead, yeah?"

"I really don't mind," he agreed.

Celeste's burning gaze bored into the side of his face as he spoke. Yes, he was concerned about her assistant at first, but if a new person was going to join the crew, they'd need to pull their weight just like anyone else. He wasn't sure what lay at the base of Celeste's fears, but she'd have to leave them at the door. Every person counted toward completing the mission and she'd already spent an entire afternoon at the museum yesterday. They didn't need a continuous record of their comings and goings near the Freya case.

After the group came to an agreement, a flurry of activity and chaos erupted in the safe house. Celeste gave Beatrice a quick preparation for how to move in public while casing a location. Lawrence explained to Magnus and Santiago how the sensors would aid them in filling in the remaining details of a blueprint he found. Apparently, Nationalmuseum underwent some drastic remodeling in the past decade so they'd need to compare old documents to what little new information they possessed.

By the time Santiago and Beatrice were out of the house, Magnus and Celeste collapsed onto the sofa in the living room to take over the command center while Lawrence took a nap.

She sighed as she slipped a pair of headphones over her ears. "It's weird being on this side of a mission, huh?"

"Yes, we're not used to observing others," he said.

Both thieves were wearing camera glasses in the field so that he and Celeste could watch their environment. With their earpieces, they could also hear Santiago's jovial chatter while Beatrice focused on their journey. They opted to walk the distance since the museum was only across the harbor from Gamla Stan.

"How does it feel to be back in your homeland?" Celeste asked as she muted their microphones.

The question caught him completely off guard. Magnus hadn't realized such an innocent inquiry would make his body react with such anxiety. He rubbed his hand over his mouth as he stared at Santiago's monitor. "It feels fine. Bea isn't interested in Santi's overtures, is she?" he asked, changing the subject. "I think he might be barking up the wrong tree."

"She is interested, she's just letting him wear himself out," Celeste said. "Look, if you don't want to talk about your feelings regarding Sweden, just say so. I watched your face when the yacht docked in the harbor, and your face did the same thing when I asked you yesterday."

The concern on her face made him feel guilty as hell, yet he wasn't jumping to openly share the emotions that nagged at him.

"When we have free time to ourselves, it can't just be about fucking, Magnus. Sometimes we have to talk to each other."

He snorted a laugh. "I'm surprised to hear that from a woman who's more closed off than Fort Knox... What's changed since we last saw each other?"

"When we were in Tallinn, you made me feel safe enough to talk to you about Doris. God knows I didn't want to..."

He turned the idea over in his mind a few times before speaking. Sharing shit had never been a part of their relationship, and the fact that she was starting to make it that made him wonder what else their relationship could be. Perhaps not just fucking? That part was thoroughly enjoyable, but it hadn't sustained them in the past and he doubted it could now.

"My family used to live here, just outside of the city," he finally said. "I was fourteen when I lost my parents and I had to live with my uncle in Örebro. I've never really wanted to come back to Stockholm, and it seems every time I'm here, something awful happens."

Celeste propped her chin on her fist and stared at him. "It was a car accident, right? They were coming back from a ski trip."

He nodded. "I was supposed to go with them, but I thought I was growing out of those trips. I begged them to let me stay for a hockey camp."

Celeste inhaled sharply. "Oh, no..."

The idea of escaping death had always followed Magnus. It gave him the strange, contradictive habit of being reckless about his own safety but staying hypervigilant about everyone else's. "I had been staying at my friend's house when his mother broke the news to me. She said that there had been an accident on their way back from Åre. My uncle came to collect me later that night and I didn't see this city until I left for America."

As he spoke, he stared at Santiago's camera feed. Some of the views were pristine cityscapes, but most of it was Beatrice. So when he felt Celeste's warm hand on top of his, he flinched involuntarily. Neither of them had been good for a tender touch. "I'm sorry that this place has haunted you," she said softly.

"Thank you."

"Your parents are looking out for you, though. And if they could see you now, they'd be proudish."

Magnus cracked a smile. "Thanks, Celeste. I think that's probably accurate. Proud of the professor part, not so much the international jewel thief part."

"They're at the museum," she said, pointing at Beatrice's camera feed. "Microphone on?"

"Before we do," Magnus said, "tell me what's making you so nervous about Bea being in the field."

"She's a kid and I don't want her to get hurt."

"Like you've been hurt?" he countered lightly.

Celeste flicked her gaze to him long enough to roll her eyes. "Something like that."

"The best way to teach her how to be cautious is probably being cautious yourself."

"Ugh, let's go back to being emotionally closed off from one another."

"Fair enough," he chuckled. "Sex tonight?"

"Yeah, probably."

As tart as Celeste was acting, he couldn't stop grinning. He spoke about his feelings so rarely that it took her blunt force to move him out of his stoicism. It was fun to tease her, but he felt even better talking to her plainly. God, he could kiss her in that moment… "Why can't I find a woman who both frustrates and arouses me like you, wife?"

Celeste surprised him by resting her hand on his knee while

she laughed. "I often feel the same way. Does that mean we're just meant for one another?"

Fuck it. He leaned over, took her by the chin and kissed her without considering the consequences. That morning he'd wanted to avoid tangling with her like this, and now? Magnus had to recognize that they were two different people after half a decade. He found himself desperate to get to know this new woman, just as he was tempted to show her a new man.

31

"I think… I'm almost done," Beatrice said in a soft voice.

Celeste had observed her do an entire walk-through of the museum, ending with the top floor. As Beatrice pressed her final motion sensor to the door, she looked around her surroundings and let out an audible sigh. "Santi, how are you doing?"

"Not as well," he replied. "I think I have a tail."

Celeste's gaze flew to the other monitor for Santiago's camera feed while Magnus leaned forward. "What?"

"Shit, I think he's right," Magnus said. "Slowly walk away from the back door, Santi. I thought I saw a security guard in your periphery."

"You did," their getaway driver muttered.

"I'm coming downstairs," Beatrice said in a worried voice.

"No!" all three said in unison.

"You stay where you are," Celeste said.

As Santiago tried to wander off, the security guard could be heard calling after him.

"Hey, hey! You there, stop!"

"Can you make a run for it?" Magnus asked.

"Nope."

"What are you doing back here?" asked a tall blond man

dressed in a paramilitary uniform. The stern frown on his face and the gun on his hip told Celeste that there was no running away from this scene. The man's eyes roved over Santiago, who was quick with a story. Not a good one, but a story, nonetheless.

"You know, I was on my way to the park for bird-watching when I thought I spotted a mourning dove just over there."

The furrows in the guard's brow deepened as he glanced in the direction Santiago pointed. "What?"

"Jesus Christ," Celeste murmured.

"I'm afraid it just turned out to be your average pigeon. I thought I would check it out to be sure."

"Please show me your identification." Even though the man said please, it was *not* a request.

"I need ID to look at birds?"

"Sir, I suspect that you are not looking for birds. You were observed on our security behaving suspiciously."

"Huh, that's crazy. I have no idea what you're talking about…" Santiago peered closer at the man's name tag. "Sven."

"Your identification, sir."

"I don't have it on me."

Which was not too unusual for them. Either they carried fake IDs or none. As far as this man knew, Santiago was just a tourist who left his passport back at the hotel.

"Santi, you're probably going to get arrested," Magnus said into his microphone. "Do not let them know about your earpiece or your glasses."

"Fuck," Celeste muttered.

A panicked Beatrice could be seen hurrying down the stairs. "I can stop the guard."

"No, you can't," Magnus said forcefully. "Listen to Celeste and stay inside the museum. Slow down and make your way to the basement restrooms. Wait there for further instruction."

"Where are you from?" asked security guard Sven.

"I don't think that's any of your business," Santiago said. She could almost hear him smile as he said it. "Any other questions or can I be on my way?"

"If you cannot provide information on who you are and why you are touching doors behind the museum, I will have to detain you."

"I really don't remember touching the doors."

"My colleague saw you on the outdoor surveillance."

"And?" Santiago asked. "Is that a crime?"

The guard unclipped a walkie on his belt and spoke Swedish into it.

"He's notifying the police," Magnus translated.

"Don't tell them shit," Celeste said. "We're going to get you out tonight."

The frantic messages over the airwaves didn't seem to ruffle Santiago. Instead, he chuckled in Sven's face. "This is not the Swedish welcome I expected."

The guard took him by the arm and led him toward the front of the museum where they were met by another guard. These two spoke to one another in Swedish while occasionally glancing at Santiago. Sven jerked him forward, this time up the steps of Nationalmuseum.

"Where are you taking me? And why must you be so rough?"

"We are keeping you in our office until the police arrive. If you cannot tell us more information, they will take you away," said the new guard, who was also tall and blond. "We believe that you are a security threat."

"Fair enough, boys. Let's all hang out until the real cops come."

This was the tightest she'd ever seen museum security. Normally, she could spot three or four bored volunteer guides in blazers, telling people to step away from roped exhibits. "This has to be for the royal jewels," she whispered. "There's no reason for this kind of scrutiny."

Magnus nodded. "It is. Which obviously makes me nervous."

"How long should I stay in here?" Beatrice asked. She was in the downstairs bathroom now, searching all the stalls before looking directly in the mirror. She was close to tears as she spoke. "Are they really going to take him away?"

"Possibly," Celeste said. "But we're not going to lose both of you today. Just hold tight while we figure out what's happening."

"I wish I could trip the fire alarm," she huffed. "I haven't finished infiltrating the closed-circuit system yet. I should have done that before coming out here. I wasn't thinking."

"Hey, hey, your man in the field needs you to stay calm and breathe. You're not going to help him by spiraling."

She managed to take a deep breath. "He's not my man."

This made Santiago laugh, earning more suspicion from the guards who led him toward the gift shop.

Celeste buried her head in her hands and tried not to groan.

"Bea, when you feel like you've caught your breath, I'd like you to calmly leave the bathroom and walk right out of the front entrance," Magnus said.

"And go where?" she whispered, wiping her face. "I have to leave him?"

"Yes. Just go next door to the Grand Hôtel. Sit in the lobby until we get back to you."

Beatrice pulled her shoulders back and steeled herself. "Okay. I'll go. I'm so sorry, Santi," she whispered. Suddenly, the door swung open and a mother with two small children entered. Beatrice quickly washed her hands before exiting.

Magnus stood from his chair and ran to his suitcase. "Keep an eye on Santi while I meet Beatrice at the Grand. I don't want her walking back home while she's shaken up. She's not going to be able to spot a tail in her state."

As he quickly dressed in a khaki linen suit, Celeste took his seat to get a better view of Santiago's feed. "They're taking him to the security office," Celeste whispered. "How do I record this?"

"I'm up," Lawrence said from behind her, "just in time, too… Sounds like shit has hit the fan."

Celeste cut the audio. "Oh, my God, please help me, Lawrence. I need to record Santi getting detained by museum security."

"All right, kiddo, move aside."

She swiftly let him take over. Meanwhile, Santiago was looking at every possible angle of his journey to the offices. He caught the security guard swipe a key card beside the door. To his left, he spotted an open door where two more guards watched footage on about ten monitors. To his right, a preparator's office…and Lawrence was recording everything.

"Thank you, Santi," he said into the microphone.

"Mmm-hmm."

Beatrice was on the move. She was following Magnus's instructions and headed straight for the Grand Hôtel. "Good girl," she murmured.

"Okay," Lawrence said. "Santi, as far as your forgeries go, is the US your best?"

"Mmm-hmm."

"I'll find your ID and Celeste and I will get your affairs in order." Lawrence glanced over his shoulder. "Hopefully with some assistance."

"Of course." She hated that it was this early in the game, but she was going to call in the Sebastian favor if it meant getting her crew member out of jail.

Beatrice entered the lobby and quietly took a seat. "Excellent," Magnus said. "You're doing quite well, Bea. Pretend you belong there, scroll through your phone, look like a bored twentysomething."

"I'm trying," she whispered.

Magnus adjusted his cuffs through his blazer before slipping on brown leather loafers. "Good. I'll be there in about fifteen minutes."

"Glasses and tracking device before you leave," Lawrence reminded.

"Right."

"And please be careful," Celeste said in a low voice.

Magnus brushed her cheek with a hurried kiss. "I will. Keep an eye on all of us."

She nodded, touched that he had time for that fleeting affection. When she returned to Lawrence's side, she watched the monitors carefully while rubbing her thumb across her phone screen. She desperately wanted to call Sebastian, but she needed to see how security would handle Santiago. The waiting was a waking nightmare full of fear and failure.

She didn't want to fall back into the trap of believing that she could have prevented this, but it was nearly impossible. If she had just put her foot down with Beatrice, they wouldn't have left the safe house. She and Magnus could have done this reconnaissance work. She didn't doubt that Santiago could handle himself. He had suffered his fair share of jail visits. But Beatrice shouldn't have been in the position of being terrified and alone.

They couldn't go out like this. There was still so much on the line. Stockholm couldn't do this to them again.

"Just hold tight, guys. We're going to make this right."

Beatrice quietly held a thumbs-up that was visible on the monitor while Santiago, who had been left in an empty office, muttered, "Jah, jah."

32

Beatrice had done a great job of being inconspicuous because when Magnus arrived at the Grand Hôtel, it took him several minutes to locate her in their massive lobby. She hid behind a potted plant, on a settee, face down in her phone.

"She's been googling extradition laws between Sweden and the United States," Lawrence said in his ear. "Tell her we have this under control."

Magnus sat beside her on the settee. "We have this under control, Bea."

She looked up with tears swimming in her eyes. "This is all my fault."

He sighed and took off his glasses before slipping hers off her face. "Lawrence, could you give us the room and watch Santiago for a minute?"

"Muting," the old man said.

Magnus set their glasses on the small table beside them and took Beatrice's sweaty hands. "This is not your fault."

"No, because when I doubted how you guys did things, you told me that everyone knew their roles, everything just fell into place," she whispered. "Maybe I got too cocky. Maybe my role is just to be back at the command center. I thought that I could be like…" She dropped her head with a sigh.

"First of all, you're not the one who got caught. I watched you through those monitors, Bea. You covered your angles and moved with caution. You even dropped off a supply bag for us. You have enormous potential to be as good as Celeste if that's what you want. But it's going to take a few years of training to get you there."

Beatrice lifted her head. "You think?" she sniffed.

He wished he understood what drove these three women. None of them were blood related, but through Beatrice's eyes, he could clearly see the ambition of Celeste and Doris staring back at him. "I know you're much more talented than how you feel in this moment. You're going to look back on today and it won't be as devastating as you think."

She nodded. "It's just—I know how important Stockholm is to you and Celeste. I don't want to be responsible for messing that up…again."

Ahh, so there it was. "Bea, you're not responsible for the mistakes she and I made years ago."

"I know, but—"

"No," he said, firmly. "Celeste and I fucked up that night. We didn't do our due diligence to study the princess's schedule. We didn't pick the right night based on weather reports. Celeste got impatient and threw the case before I could see her. And I couldn't catch it, I got angry, took my toys and went home without trying to work things out with the crew."

Before he knew it, Beatrice released his hands and patted him on the shoulder. "I see it now."

Magnus frowned. "See what?"

"You and Celeste. I see why you two were a thing," she said with a lopsided smile. "After watching you work and bicker with each other, I know that you're basically the same person."

"I don't know if that's a good thing or a bad thing."

She shrugged. "It's only bad if you guys can't communicate based on your similarities. If you keep trying to convince yourself that you're so different from her, you'll never see her perspective on anything. Considering you two share a common goal."

He scoffed. "Which is?"

Beatrice frowned as she stared at him. "This." She gestured to the space around them. "This job is what you both want, more than anything. You're both obsessed with proving something to Doris even if she's not here. And that thing you do—calling her reckless? You saw how she worried over me this morning. You guys clearly care if we stay safe. You care about each other."

Magnus was stunned silent. Here he thought he'd rushed to the hotel to comfort a young woman, new to the game. Instead, she assured him that he still had something to learn. When he spoke, he was hesitant to reveal too much to the all-knowing Beatrice. "I don't want my partner to be hurt. I don't think you need to read into that."

Beatrice narrowed her brown eyes at him. "I'm a really smart person, Magnus. Every day, I read code far more complex than you. You're going to have to try harder."

"I see that," he said in a flat voice. "If it's all the same to you, I'd rather not talk to you about your mentor. Just like I didn't want to talk to Celeste's mentor about her."

"Fine, then," she relented. "Are you sure Santiago is going to be okay?"

He nodded. "The thing about Santiago is that he always lands on his feet. And this is not his first time in jail."

Beatrice's brow shot up.

"Oh, you didn't know?" Magnus grinned. "His charm is a bit hit or miss. It either gets him out of a jam or straight to jail. But he has so many identities, the Swedes will never find his record before we get to him."

"That makes me feel a little better, I guess."

He peered closely at her. "You really care for him, don't you?"

Beatrice blushed and gestured dismissively. "I don't want to lose a valuable member of our crew."

Magnus laughed. Talking to her was like talking to one of his students. She sat there, twisting one of her loose braids around her fingers bashfully. "Now, now, Bea... If you're forcing me to look at my life, I need you to examine your own for a minute. Do you like our getaway driver?"

She scoffed in irritation; a sound Celeste made all the time. "He's fine."

"Just fine?" he asked, teasing her. Magnus was glad her tears had disappeared, and she now appeared calm enough to take a walk with him.

He rose from the couch and took her hand. When they left the hotel and faced the bright sun, Beatrice glanced back in the direction of the museum. "He's handsome, funny and charming," she admitted. "And I don't want anything bad to happen to him."

"The worst thing that will happen to Santi is that his Armani suit will get mussed during booking."

Beatrice shot him a glare. "I'm not hearing enough concern from you, Magnus."

"Ooh, I've touched an 'I love Santi' nerve, haven't I?"

She shoulder-checked him. "I love him about as much as you love Celeste."

He had to force himself to laugh. He didn't know how she did it, but Beatrice's youthful insight always punched him in the gut. He'd just arrived to the idea that there was no other woman for him quite like Celeste, but he wasn't ready to go out on a limb and admit that he loved her. That was a bridge too far.

"I like Celeste very much," he said cautiously.

"Mmm."

"What does that mean?" he asked.

It was her turn to tease him. "Nothing. I just think you two are fooling yourselves if you think we can't see what's going on."

"Ugh, I shouldn't have asked."

"If it makes you feel better," she continued, "I haven't seen her light up with excitement around another guy since I've worked with her. She likes you very much, too."

"That information has no effect on my feelings whatsoever," he lied. "Speaking of which, when was the last guy?"

Beatrice's loud laughter startled nearby passersby as they strolled back to the safe house, and it put a smile on his face. If they ever had another job after this, he would welcome Bea into his crew with open arms.

Once you got past Aksel Lindgren's sheer size and stature, it was plain to see what kind of congenial personality he possessed. Magnus still wasn't used to being completely dwarfed by the man, though. As they stood around the dining room table coming up with plans to spring Santiago from his cell *and* rob the Nationalmuseum, he had to give up puffing his chest out to match the man beside him.

"These are your invitations to the museum gala, courtesy of Princess Astrid," he said, handing him two envelopes.

While on the phone with Sebastian, Celeste glanced at the invites and gave a quick nod. She walked to the other side of the living room to continue her conversation.

"Will you be under an alias?" Lawrence asked.

"It will be easiest to pose as a married couple," he said, catching Beatrice's tiny smile.

"That's probably for the best," she said in a singsong voice.

"Monday?" Celeste exclaimed from the next room. "That won't do at all. What if we need to get the hell out of Stockholm? I'm not leaving him."

"Uh-oh," Aksel murmured. "Problem?"

Magnus could have guessed that Sebastian was filling her

in on Swedish bureaucracy. Santiago was carted off to jail on a Friday evening, which meant getting him out before Monday could prove challenging. "With the gala being tomorrow night, we're short a man, so yeah, we might have a problem."

"Let's try to take care of one thing at a time," Lawrence said. "The event starts at 8:00 p.m. You and Celeste will be accompanying the princess, who will introduce the Swedish historian, Mats Bergen, at eight thirty."

"That will take place in the sculpture garden downstairs," Aksel said, pointing to a large room on their map. "Right in front of the café. After they've concluded the talk, partygoers will walk upstairs to the exhibit."

Celeste walked back into the dining room with a tight expression. "What does Sebastian suggest?" Magnus asked.

She put Sebastian on speakerphone and held it out for him to speak to the crew. "My suggestion is for Santiago to sit tight. I am flying into Stockholm tonight with my men, but the earliest I can negotiate with local authorities is Sunday. One of you may want to relay this information to Santi."

"On it." Beatrice was still hooked into Santiago's earpiece feed and watching everything through the camera in his glasses. She murmured something in a soft voice to their captive crew member before turning back to the group. "He says the Swedish jails are surprisingly clean and comfortable. Nothing like the Florida job? What happened in Florida?"

Magnus chuckled. "We don't have time to get into it, but he's right about the comparison."

"You are sending men here?" Aksel asked Sebastian.

"Oui. I thought I might be helpful to the cause."

"He's based in Tallinn with a lot of friends in low places." The giant nodded. "Oh."

"I don't want to insult your character, Aksel, but could we count on you to jump in as one of those friends?"

The man's face broke into a wide grin. "I would be delighted to join your crew temporarily. I have been known to create a good distraction from time to time."

Which is what they might need. "Before we can get into the particulars," Magnus said, "can anyone tell me what kind of force we might be up against...besides the assholes who held Santi up?"

"This guy," Aksel said, issuing a manila folder. "Princess Astrid's nasty little Belgian inspector."

Magnus and Celeste put their heads together and flipped through the dossier of the man who had obsessed over the royal jewels for the past five years. He was nasty all right. Hugo Vermeulen had twenty-six years of experience in the Fine Arts Theft and Recovery division of Interpol. Ten of those years were devoted to insurance fraud. And by the looks of his records, he usually got his man.

Luckily, his attention was incorrectly focused on the princess.

"What Astrid left out was that he's been completely against the unveiling from the start. He believes that the exhibit is a mistake and, at the very least, should be much shorter than the museum has planned."

"So, he's going to be there in full force," Celeste said, still holding her phone aloft. "Probably with local police."

"Perhaps," Sebastian intoned.

"Definitely," Magnus said. "And if the princess is there, he's going to keep an eagle eye on her."

"We'll need a couple distractions," Celeste said, nodding to their large friend. "That's where you and Sebastian's friends could help."

"Of course," Sebastian said.

"We're going to have to let you go, Fond du Lac," Magnus said, taking Celeste's phone. "If you find out any more about Santiago's release, please let us know."

Celeste arched a brow when he hung up. "What was that?"

"Our little crew is expanding far too quickly," he said, handing her phone back. It was bad enough they were dependent on the princess they'd wronged, but Aksel was now hanging out in the safe house. Doris should have known better than to ask Magnus to be more accepting. "I'd like to get a handle on the plan before we start including others."

"I'm very close to figuring out the building's security measures," Beatrice said. "I'd like to give you a system-wide blackout. That way, you'll have time to work before an automatic reboot kicks in."

"You think you can do that?" Magnus asked.

Lawrence chuckled. "Just you asking that is gonna fuel her flame. Watch and see, she'll get it done."

Beatrice grinned broadly. "Thank you, Lawrence."

"What's the longest you can manage a blackout?" Celeste asked.

The girl shrugged. "The longest I've ever pulled off? About ten minutes. It takes most places a while to flip the switch back on."

"Ten minutes," Magnus said with a nod.

"We've had worse."

Though he didn't like their odds, Celeste was technically correct. A job in Lisbon immediately came to mind. They had a very tight six minutes to run through a gallery, wrench Jacques-Louis David's *Oath of the Horatii* off the wall and exit before the guard made his next pass. Except back then, they had four weeks of prep and a key card that Celeste swiped from an employee.

Celeste sighed. "I hate to say it, but we probably should have brought the dart guns."

"I thought you might say that later," Lawrence said. "I broke one down and packed it in our luggage. I'll let y'all fight over who wants to use it."

"Oh, thank God," she breathed. "I really don't want to shoot anyone, but if I have to get out of a scrape, I'd like the option to knock someone out."

"Way ahead of you, kiddo. We gotta take everything into account."

Celeste studied the 2018 blueprints of the museum for a moment without speaking. Magnus could see the wheels turning in her head as she chewed her lip. When she was in the zone, there was very little that could distract her. Her dark eyes narrowed on the Treasury Room, where the royal jewels were displayed.

"What are you thinking?" he asked.

She leaned closer to the blueprints and ran her finger around the perimeter of the room. "This," she pointed, "is a ceiling grate for steel gates. They're going to lower and lock into place in the event of an emergency. If Bea can trip the alarm, that will cause enough confusion for people to scatter, leaving one of us to book it upstairs and the other to go through the employee stairwell…"

"If Bea can leave it accessible during the lockdown."

"Or I could come up from the bottom," Celeste suggested.

Magnus quickly followed her line of logic before frowning. "The basement?"

"When Bea went to the bathroom, I saw a vent over her shoulder. In the first stall, closest to the wall. I could start in the basement and—"

"I'm sorry," Aksel interrupted. "You're going to climb a ventilation shaft?"

Their guest may have found it ridiculous, but Magnus had no doubt she could pull it off. He only wondered if it was the safest option. "That should clear you from having to outrun some of the security measures. If you can secure the jewels, I could meet you at the fire stairwell at the end of The Treasury. You just have to get through this hall."

"That's the Turn of the Century gallery," Aksel pointed out.

"Right. Get to that stairwell and then get the hell out of the loading dock."

"I'll compare both routes and do a quick calculation on timing," Beatrice said while jotting notes on her tablet. "In the meantime, I think someone should book a room at the Grand."

"That's a good idea," Magnus said. "Anything goes wrong, it would give us an opportunity to have a base that's much closer than this place. I'll book a couple suites for us tonight."

"Let's take a break here," Celeste said. "When we learn of Sebastian's plans, I'll have a better idea of where to put him and his team."

"Sounds good to me," Magnus agreed.

She paused long enough to give him a tired smile. "If it weren't for today's snag, I'd say this was some of the best prep work we've done in a long time."

Magnus understood what she meant. When they worked with one mind, everything seemed to fall into place. It was a slightly more productive dance than the one they did in the bedroom. It reminded him of how the *good* years with Doris went. He returned her smile. "If we stay in sync, we could have a solid plan before we meet the princess again."

"I'd really like that." Celeste held out her pinkie finger. "Stay in sync tonight?"

Magnus gripped her finger in his and used it to pull her close until they touched foreheads. "Of course."

33

December 9, 2003

The look on my girl's face when the truth dawned on her... In the moment it took her to digest the fact that I wasn't just an art professor, I worried that I had made a mistake. That I had misjudged her. Or worse, let her down. But I had panicked for nothing. When she finally spoke up, a grin lit her face.

"I wanna do that."

Lord have mercy, she sounded so resolute. I had to fight from grinning when she nodded her head and stared at me head-on. I wish I knew the woman who raised her because she suddenly looked older in the moment. Wise to the fact that things were hard out here for a girl like her. Perhaps being an orphan will do that to a girl.

When I explained that she'd still have to continue with her education, she deflated a bit. I won't have her throw all her time and energy to an occupation that could chew her up and spit her out at a moment's notice. In her line of work, hell, any woman needed a backup plan. And I will teach her all kinds of backup plans to keep her safe. If I train her correctly, Celeste has the potential to be greater than I. When I look at her, I can tell she won't make the same careless mistakes I made. This one won't let a man hinder her abilities in the slightest…

April 19, 2017

It shouldn't come as a surprise to me that Magnus has seduced my best student. Hell, if I was twenty years younger, I'd take a run at him myself. He's slick, charming and doesn't need this job. Just like Bastian… And I can tell that Celeste is both drawn to and repulsed by him. After all, I've taught her to value her neck and the job before a man.

Sigh…but Magnus isn't just like Bastian, is he? He's cocky, for sure, but he's a lot more considerate than he lets on. He lets Celeste boss him and the team about, until he recognizes that she's barreling toward recklessness. He's the last backstop before young Celeste flings herself off a cliff for riches and wealth. Perhaps it takes an independently wealthy man to remind her that jewels aren't everything.

I also catch the way they look at each other when they think the rest of us don't notice. It's not just lust. I know they've been fooling around for a while now. No, it's more than that. Magnus watches her with a possessiveness that betrays his indifference. Celeste might give him a sharp tongue, but she stares at him with admiration.

Sometimes I'm sad when I observe them. I wonder if my time leading the group has come to an end. They've properly picked up the slack and run with it. Especially during this last trip to Paris. When those two put their heads together, they're literally one mind. I wonder if they realize how closely aligned they are? Their preparation went off without a hitch and the execution was flawless. I just sat back and watched them get the work done…and I barely contributed. Is retirement much closer than I had realized?

Maybe the kids are all right.

But what if this is the end of an era? What if they find a way to lead the group in their own image and I'm no longer needed? Perhaps that's when I'll rest. Oh, Doris, when have you actually wanted rest? Ultimately, I still love being in a game that's steadily moving out of my control. Every newly acquired piece is not just their victory; it's also mine. Who'd want to lose that because of something so silly as age? For now, I love being around Celeste, Magnus and my baby Santi. I think they make Lawrence and me feel a bit younger.

Celeste wanted to throw up.

The only thing in her stomach was this hard, bland breakfast cracker from earlier in the day and liters of water. As she paced the hotel suite that Magnus booked, she tried to steady her nerves the best she could.

But throwing up felt like it might be easier.

She finally got her answer about Doris not wanting to cede control to the crew. Everything Santiago and Magnus had said about those last jobs had now been confirmed in Dr. Grant's diary. Apparently, she had feared losing them so much that she wanted to keep them busy. Was Magnus also right about Celeste's blind devotion to Doris? Probably? Or else she would have seen Tangier and Stockholm for what they were: unorganized shit shows.

She shoved Doris's diary across the king-size bed and rolled onto her back. When she finally had a free minute to read her mentor's words, it had probably come at a bad time. There was no way she could match the confident thief Doris had observed. The girl she wrote about was a woman who now doubted every move she made. She doubted the man who was currently in the bathroom shaving. He leaned over the counter, wearing only a towel, shearing away blond fuzz that no one could see instead of consoling every anxiety that cropped up in Celeste's mind.

"Why hasn't Sebastian gotten back to us?" she asked Magnus, who wiped his face with a towel. "He said he'd be at the spot at eight thirty but didn't give any clue as to how he'd assist us. I don't like this, Magnus." She hauled herself out of bed and walked to the bathroom. "Did you hear me?"

His dark blue eyes met hers in the large mirror. "I did."

"Do you have anything to add?"

Magnus took a swipe at his jawline and washed the razor off. "I'm going to let you get all your jitters out before I interject."

For some reason this pissed her off, but it also reminded her of what Doris wrote. Cool, slick, arrogant. That was Magnus. It was Celeste's job to boss him around until he stopped her from spinning out on her own chaotic energy.

"Okay, then, you'll be happy to learn that Infinity uses The Swedish National Museum as a reference in their brochure."

"Oh, well, there you go," Magnus chuckled. "Infinity plexiglass cases are lovely boxes to put valuables in, but they certainly aren't theft-proof."

"Exactly," Celeste said, pacing the room outside the bathroom. "They've got the Abloy dead bolts, with compressed-air seals all along the case door, and locking mechanisms at the tops and bottoms of the doors. It's a slick defense, but not impossible to crack. If a thief didn't mind making a mess, the glass could be smashed after a few good strikes."

"My dear, I think you should get dressed," Magnus said, glancing at her through the mirror.

"Am I rambling?"

He nodded with a grin. "You're rambling, my love."

She sighed. When Magnus started treating her with kid gloves, she knew she was spinning like a top, threating to fling herself off a cliff, like Doris had described. Maybe once she got her gown on, she'd feel different. It usually wasn't until she put on her mask that Celeste slipped into another woman's confident skin. "I'll get dressed."

★ ★ ★

After finishing her makeup and styling her wig, Celeste finally felt a bit calmer. When she glanced into the vanity mirror and saw Magnus watching her, she realized she had transformed into another stronger woman who matched her appearance.

"You're staring," she remarked as she put her makeup away.

He sat on the edge of the bed, wearing an elegant black suit, smiling at her reflection. "I can't help it," he said. "You look enticing."

"Thank you," she said, giving her wig a final adjustment. It was a sandy-brown, wavy bob that fell to her jawline. Something easy and comfortable to move around in. "You clean up nicely as well."

"And do you buy all of your gowns with scandalously high slits on the sides or are you taking a razor to them?"

She rolled her eyes as she tucked a lock behind her ear. "It's not too scandalous." Tonight's off-the-shoulder gown was dark forest green and only revealed one thigh. The skirt was long and swished in beautiful waves as she walked.

"The wife of a geology professor probably wouldn't dress so provocatively."

Celeste sprayed a bit of perfume on her décolletage and neck. "I don't think you'd marry a woman who doesn't show out from time to time."

Magnus pulled himself off the bed and made a leisurely path toward her. "You're probably right. I don't think I would. Especially when she puts on such a delightful show."

She met his gaze in the mirror. "We have to meet the princess in an hour."

"I wear a watch."

"You have that look in your eyes."

He stood behind her and rested his hands on her shoulders. "Do I?"

The tension in her muscles instantly melted the second his

thumbs kneaded the base of her neck. "You think doing this right before a job is a good idea?"

"I think it's an excellent idea. Right now, I want to fuck you so badly I'm climbing out of my skin," he said as his hands moved up the column of her throat. "You don't expect me to work with that kind of tension."

Celeste closed her eyes and let her head loll to the side as his fingers slid along her pulse. "That kind of tension can keep you alert and on your toes." As much as she enjoyed denying him, she also wanted him. Badly.

"I work with a cutthroat thief… I'm always alert. For now, I just want to lay my sword down and pretend that I'm married to you."

Her eyes sprang open to look at him in the mirror. His eyes were locked on her face as he continued speaking in an utterly serious voice.

"You have to admit, Celeste, there's something attractive about pretending."

Her heart pounded as she grinned. "I think that's all we do, Magnus. That's a large part of our job."

"I quite like the performance of Mrs. Larsson in the emerald green gown," he said, tracing a finger down the valley of her breasts. "Here she sits, dabbing her neck with perfume while her husband fumbles with his tie. I like to imagine how she'd bat his hands away so that she can take over the job."

She tipped her head back to rest against him, luxuriating in his delicate touch. "And then pay the babysitter after we kiss the children good-night?"

"I've never envisioned having children in my fantasies. Only you."

"Fantasies? Plural?"

"Since I saw you in Victor Sanderson's party, wearing that dress, hand caught in the cookie jar, it's been difficult to get you out of my mind."

"You flatterer."

"Is it working?" he asked.

Celeste slowly stood from her stool, facing the mirror. "It is," she said to the reflection. "If we keep pretending, you can't mess up my makeup or touch my wig."

He brushed her hair out of the way and gently kissed the nape of her neck. "Your hair and makeup are safe from my hands," he murmured against her skin. He ran his hand down her hip and tugged at the slit along her thigh. "I love how efficient this dress is."

He tapped his foot between her high heels, suggesting she widen her stance. Celeste bent forward, placing her hands on the vanity's surface. "The slits help with mobility," she breathed.

"And the lack of panties?" he asked, hand between her thighs. His wide grin brightened his face and made her laugh. "Please tell me that's just a dirty little secret for your husband."

"The way your face lit up, I almost feel guilty," she said, relaxing into his touch. His fingertips, now coated in her juices, slowly slid up and down her folds. Her elbows shook as he pulled a low moan from her. "I just didn't want panty lines."

"Aww, shucks," he chuckled darkly in her ear. "You're pulling me out of the fantasy, wife."

From behind her, he used one hand to yank open his belt, while using the other to pleasure her. It clattered against the floor loudly as he worked to unzip his trousers. "Okay, then, we're supposed to go to a dinner party at your boss's house and we'll definitely be late because of your antics."

"Damn, he's never going to give me that promotion and raise."

When he entered her from the back, Celeste gasped sharply. "You work really hard, honey…"

"Pulling late hours when I could be at home fucking my beautiful wife."

"Oh, God, yes," she hissed. The angle of his thick dick and

the sweet depth of each stroke nearly stole her voice. He fucked her deliciously slow, easing out of her and teasing her pussy as he went. The sensation of feeling the fabric of his pants against her ass as he drove into her made her feel dirty in a thrilling way.

She studied his red face in the mirror, watching how he gritted his teeth every time he thrusted. His eyes were closed as he basked in his own pleasurable sensation, but once they opened and locked on her gaze, he smiled. "You're so beautiful, Celeste. You're sexy, smart, talented, and I don't know why I left you and the crew in the first place."

"Oh, God," she moaned, half listening to him. "Harder."

"I was an arrogant prick," he muttered, slamming into her faster and deeper.

"You were, and I was really stubborn," Celeste said as he pulled her up from the table. One arm wrapped around her waist and the other was like a steel bar across her breasts. From this angle, the friction between them opened up a whole new level of pleasure. Watching herself being screwed did something else to her. Her face was flush, her eyes were hooded and his hand was now squeezing her breast. Her arousal hit a fever pitch. "I didn't listen to you when you said we should have delayed the job. We should have waited."

"I shouldn't have given you an ultimatum. We could have worked it out. Together. I shouldn't have left you." He kissed her neck, nipping at her skin with his teeth before licking away the sting.

Celeste reached behind her to grasp his head, pressing him closer. "I don't want to be like Doris and Sebastian," she panted. "I just want you."

Magnus groaned in her ear. "You have no idea how happy I am to hear you say that."

How in the hell did we go from sexy role-playing to confessing long-buried feelings? Celeste was shocked by how easy the words fell from her lips and how truthful they were. As they held each other, she'd never felt closer to him. The arousal was over-whelming. "I think…" she panted. "I think I'm going to come."

"Go ahead and come, wife. I want to wring all the pleasure I can out of you."

Celeste's knees trembled as she doubled over. She caught herself on the table before her and Magnus followed her. He refused to release her and she was thankful. She wanted to feel his hot breath against her ear, feel his heart pound against her back. She wanted to be held tightly so that she wouldn't spin out into the void. She wanted to feel protected by the person who knew her best.

"Oh, fuck, oh, fuck," she chanted.

"Yes, my love. Ride it…"

She wailed as an orgasm crashed over her. *My love.*

34

Their short trip to the museum timed well with Princess Astrid's arrival. Her car pulled up just as they walked to the entrance stairs. The paparazzi snapped photos while shouting for her to walk slower and pose. Celeste and Magnus allowed her to make her entrance before following her with their invitations.

The first part of their plan started at the door, convincing a young woman who handled the guest list. While Magnus retrieved his invite from his jacket, Celeste unclasped her flat clutch and extended it to the woman. "Thank you, Dr. Jeremy Pierson. Thank you, Mrs. Linda Pierson," she said as she scrolled through her electronic tablet. Once she was satisfied with their credentials, the woman extended her hand past the threshold. "Enjoy your evening."

Magnus murmured his thanks. "Tack så mycket."

Magnus kept his eyes forward and began counting the security personnel. There was one unarmed police officer at the left stairwell. He was stone-faced and uninterested in the festivities, but alert all the same. Beside him, the Interpol agent they knew as the "nasty little Belgian inspector." He surveyed the space with a hard, cold eye. His gaze settled on the princess and seemed to stare there. Every once in a while his dark eyes would flicker to the other two guards who stood near the café. Magnus was surprised to see that they were also unarmed.

They nonchalantly pushed forward, trailing those who took time to admire the foyer and collect flutes of champagne. The double stairways leading to the second floor were roped off, so the crowd that milled around flocked to the princess near the museum's Sculpture Courtyard. "You get all of that?" Magnus murmured to Beatrice.

The young lady made a hum of affirmation. "One guard at the left stairwell, two near the café. Everyone is surprisingly unarmed. Vermeulen is staring hard at someone. The princess?"

"Exactly."

"This security is shockingly paltry," Celeste said in a low voice. "After what happened to Santiago, I really expected an entire precinct guarding the entrance."

They might be posted out of sight from the attendees. If Magnus had to guess, the museum staff probably didn't want a heavy police presence distracting from the princess and her jewels.

"They could be in the back watching this whole thing unfold," Magnus whispered.

"Drinks are up ahead and the café is serving finger food directly behind the Sculpture Courtyard… You've got a while before they open the second floor to the partygoers. Sit back and enjoy a lecture about crown jewels."

"Don't mind if I do," Magnus said, taking Celeste's arm and steering her to the nearest waiter. He plucked two flutes of bubbly and extended one to her. "Mrs. Pierson?"

"Thank you," she said with a grin.

He watched her take her first non-sip of her drink. The liquid touched her pursed lips while she admired the open space of the foyer. Magnus smiled at the small action as he sipped on his own. A little alcohol didn't bother him. In fact, it helped loosen him up.

"Would you like to take a stroll?"

"That would be lovely," he said, his eyes on the back stair-way she'd have to traverse within the hour. "I think they have some pieces near the gift shop you might like to see."

She followed behind him, squeezing his arm. "This reminds me of Sanderson's party," she whispered.

Magnus glanced down at her; the wrinkles around his eyes creased as he smiled. "I hope not too much."

"You looked very handsome that night."

"You looked perfect," he replied, rubbing small circles on her knuckles with his thumb. "I hope that's where the similari-ties end."

They stopped at two medium-size canvases from the Swedish artist Torsten Andersson. He pretended to examine them closer, but his attention was mostly on his periphery. The inspector was approaching them at a steady clip, hard and determined to speak to them.

"Act natural," he whispered to Celeste. "The Belgian is on his way."

Celeste nodded. "Yes, I enjoy the Impressionists, but I think this is a bit precious for my taste."

Magnus smiled. "You've never enjoyed the Impressionists. They're too cynical for you."

"Are you enjoying yourself this evening?" said a voice from behind them.

Magnus sucked in a breath before turning on his heel. Upon closer observation, the inspector, Hugo Vermeulen, was shorter than he thought. His face shined with an unsightly sheen of perspiration that made his overall appearance greasy. His rum-pled navy blue suit and scuffed brown shoes stuck out in a sea of pressed tuxedos. Not that the man seemed to care. He held himself with the same authoritative confidence that any man on the right side of the law would.

"Good evening," Magnus said with a smile. "I don't believe

I know you." When in doubt, fall back on what people perceived him as: an arrogant prick. He gave him a scrutinizing stare as he looked him up and down. "Staff?"

The inspector met his smile with one of his own. "You could say that." He took an uncomfortable step forward. "But it is I who should say that I do not know you, sir. You see, I have studied the guest list for the past two weeks and you...and your wife? You are quite new to the list."

Celeste sidled up to Magnus, placing her hand on his back. "We didn't know if we would attend," she said. "The princess was lovely enough to save space for us at the last minute."

Vermeulen raised a brow as his eyes cut to her. "Making it difficult to perform a background check on you, Mrs. Pierson."

"A background check?" Magnus scoffed. "For a geologist?"

"Yes...indeed. How does a geologist become acquainted with a member of the Swedish royal family? Princess Astrid, specifically?"

"She and I met in New York," Celeste jumped in. "Last year during Fashion Week. She was absolutely stunning in a pale pink Saint Laurent suit."

"Was she?"

Celeste continued with confidence. "I had to invite her for drinks after the Chuks Collins collection. I found it lovely that she appreciated his future-forward work. Are you familiar with Collins, Mr...."

"Vermeulen, Inspector Hugo Vermeulen, with Interpol." The man made no attempt to extend his hand. "And as I'm certain you can tell, I'm not familiar with the goings-on of Fashion Week. When was that?"

"Early September."

Magnus was impressed by her quick responses, but wondered if they were just a little too specific. When Hugo gave them a tight-lipped smile, his stomach fell. "*Early* September?"

Celeste didn't falter. "I believe it was."

Hugo dug his hands into his pockets and rocked on his heels. "Fascinating...considering how Princess Astrid was spending her August and September in Bangkok with friends."

Magnus pulled his shoulders back and straightened to full height. "I'm not sure what the interrogation is about, Inspector. My wife and I are here for a little history and free drinks. As a favor to Her Majesty."

The height difference didn't seem to make a difference to the dogged little man. "Perhaps I am mistaken—"

"It wouldn't be the first time," said a familiar voice at his side. Princess Astrid had joined the conversation, and two beefy private security men accompanied her. Her brown hair was swept up in a conservative bun and covered in a dainty tiara. No doubt, something from the royal collection. She wore a slinky black gown with a stylish shawl hanging loosely off her shoulders. "Inspector, surely you can find something more worth your time than harassing my guests."

The quickest flash of rage showed up on Vermeulen's face as he addressed Astrid. Although he suppressed it well enough, Magnus sensed something a little unhinged about this man. An obsessed man who hadn't found anything more worth his time in five years.

"My apologies, Your Highness," he said in a demure voice. "I was only curious about your acquaintance with these people."

"These people?" Astrid said in a shrill voice. She turned to Celeste and said in a hushed tone, "My dear Linda, I'm so sorry you had to hear that. It was never my intention that your first visit to my kingdom be so filled with suspicion and—" she cut her eyes to the inspector "—bad vibes. You must forgive him. He's Belgian."

Magnus couldn't help the undignified snort that escaped him as Hugo Vermeulen's sweaty face darkened with rage-blush. "Princess Astrid, I must insist—"

"I must insist you move on."

The man let his mask drop. "With all due respect to you and your family, I do not agree with this disgraceful display of arrogance. I do not know how you've managed this, but so long as my investigation goes unsolved, I will continue watching you."

Magnus was stunned by the man's brazenness. As were the princess's bodyguards. They took an intimidating step forward, shielding Astrid from this small man's quiet vitriol. When he realized this, he shrank back slightly.

"You are quite unpleasant, aren't you?" Magnus said with a smirk. "Interpol is definitely not sending their fun people."

Without another word, he excused himself and hurried back to the front of the museum. Celeste let out a sigh. "Is he always like that?"

Princess Astrid rolled her eyes. "For the last five years. Boys, can you give me some space?" Her two bodyguards backed away several feet so that she could speak to them privately. "Okay," she said in a quiet voice. "Are you all set up tonight?"

"We are. You know when to exit stage left?"

"I'm going to give my talk, leave the event and depending how things go for you all… I'll make a statement tomorrow." She weighed her options with both hands. "Either I'll say it's a terrible shame that our jewels were left unprotected by the man who swore to obsessively hound me for half a decade or I'm thankful that the museum's state-of-the-art security prevented another tragic loss for the kingdom of Sweden."

Celeste smiled. "Hopefully it's the former."

"Either way, it sounds like you're intentionally insulting our dear Hugo Vermeulen."

She shrugged. "You saw him. He's truly the worst. Whatever. Just make sure that I'm out of this building before you do whatever it is you're planning to do. I'm scheduled for a red-eye to Miami, and I really don't want to get held up by this huvud."

"You've got a deal," Celeste said, extending her hand. The women shook hands. "Have a good trip."

"Have a good heist."

The princess snapped her fingers and her men quickly surrounded her. As they walked off, Magnus caught a glimpse at Hugo watching them with a shrewd stare.

"So? You guys heard all of that?" he asked, addressing Lawrence and Beatrice.

"Oh, yeah," Beatrice intoned. "What is that guy's problem?"

"Celeste, be prepared to tussle with him," Lawrence warned. "You are officially on the inspector's radar."

"That's what I'm worried about," Magnus said. "He doesn't seem to like women and he seems like he's coming unglued. Maybe I should take the run."

Celeste shook her head. "I know you're fast, but I have to do this. I need you to take care of the exits and clear the way for me."

Magnus wasn't going to argue with her. Not this time and not this far into the game. "If you're confident."

She looked up at him with a broad smile. "I'm going to try to be as confident as a Swedish princess who has never done anything challenging in her life."

He laughed, thankful that she still had a sense of humor considering their circumstances. "I'll take it."

35

While the royal family may have felt the princess wasn't up for public engagements, Astrid wowed the crowd with a heartfelt speech about the jewels and what they meant to her. When she described how it felt to have them stolen, Celeste caught her glancing at Inspector Vermeulen with narrowed eyes.

When she introduced the next speaker, Celeste was surprised to see the small Belgian man step up to the podium, and not the historian. "I'd like to add to Princess Astrid's statement regarding the theft of these jewels."

The murmur rose in the small crowd as the princess returned to her private security detail. Celeste looked at Magnus's watch, wondering how this interruption would affect their timing. The princess was supposed to give a talk, take a bow and leave out the front door before things popped off.

"What is he doing?" she muttered under her breath.

"I think he wants to set the record straight," Magnus replied quietly.

"It must be known that the suspects who stole the jewelry set are still at large. This remains an open investigation." He paused, surveying the audience. "I know that saying this might not be prudent for the occasion, but justice still needs to be served to the Swedish royal family and the Swedish taxpayer."

If Celeste weren't at the Nationalmuseum to re-steal a jewelry set from five years ago, she would have thoroughly enjoyed the drama unfolding before them. Princess Astrid was fuming. She hitched her black shawl around her shoulders and shook in agitation. No, it probably wasn't prudent for this occasion, but the inspector continued.

"I'm sure the royal family is grateful that these priceless heirlooms have been returned to their rightful home. But I am afraid that this crime does come at a price...to the nation, and indeed to Europe and the arts. If any of you have any information about the case, please consider coming forward to your local police."

The entire Sculpture Garden went silent at his request.

"Jesus Christ..." Magnus muttered under his breath.

A curator who stood nearby quickly approached the podium and yanked the microphone back. "Thank you for your...words, Inspector Vermeulen," said the tall, thin man, dressed in a tuxedo. "If we could continue with the next speaker?"

The inspector kept his grip on the microphone. "I also want to add that Interpol does not support the display of this evidence."

After a bit of tug-of-war, the curator finally seized his property back. "Thank you, Inspector. Your observations have been noted."

Although it must have been difficult for him, Inspector Vermeulen was eventually forced to take a seat in the front row to listen to a talk that he didn't want to stick around for.

And neither did the princess. She muttered something in Swedish, loud enough for the back rows to hear, before storming to the exit.

"What did she say?" Celeste asked.

"Uhh...something about short asshole with sausage fingers? It's a rough translation."

"Oh, boy."

"I have to admit," Magnus whispered, "I thought your cover story was very clever on the fly. You still have it."

"And you did an excellent job of acting like a stuck-up, privileged academic. I knew you had it in you," she countered lightly, keeping a smile on her face.

"Listen up, kiddos," Lawrence interrupted. "I still don't know when Sebastian will show up, but if you're ready, I'd like to start the show."

"Right," Celeste murmured, looking at Magnus. "I'll see you on the other side?"

He nodded as he touched her knee. His hand lingered, heavy and warm against her skin, before giving a reassuring squeeze. "Be careful."

She gathered her purse and champagne flute and slowly rose from her chair, whispering apologies as she squeezed past attendees. "Excuse me, sorry, I'm so sorry..." When she exited the row, she followed the same path that the princess had taken moments earlier. Once she was near the main entrance, she faltered in front of the security guard who stood at one of the two stairways leading to the second floor.

"Excuse me?" she asked, looking high and low. "Where can I find the toilet?"

The solidly built security guard pointed past the refreshment table at the stairwell leading to the basement. "The elevator is not in operation tonight. You must take the stairs."

"Thank you," she said, placing her nearly full glass on the table. Celeste didn't walk too fast, nor did she dawdle as she disappeared from the man's view. Every move she made, she was keenly conscious of being followed by cameras.

Since the 2018 remodel, the changes to the museum basement were impressive. Not only were there coatrooms, toilets and lockers for patrons, but a spacious picnic area for large groups.

Celeste could picture busloads of schoolchildren eating bagged lunches as she wandered deeper into the cavernous space.

Her first stop was the locker room. "Help me out, Bea," she whispered.

"Number 116."

Celeste followed the numbers until she got to the correct locker. "Combination?"

"19-21-5."

She spun the dial left and right before pulling the small door open. "Thank y●u," she breathed. Celeste walked straight to the bathroom with a new supply bag. She wasn't going to dig through it until she found the appropriate toilet stall. When she did, she quickly let herself in and locked the door behind her.

After she was alone, safe from cameras and meddling inspectors, she went through the bag that Beatrice left for her. A small velvet bag of Magnus's replica jewelry, a tightly wound length of nylon rope. She raised a brow when she spotted Lawrence's tranquilizer dart gun. "Oh, boy..." she murmured to herself.

"Hey, you asked for it," Lawrence said in her earpiece. "It's just extra security. If you don't need it, don't use it."

"Let's hope I don't need it," she said as she continued through the items. "Bea, is this one of those EMF devices?"

"Slap it on the back of the plexiglass and it should disable the Abloy locking mechanism. It should be the fastest option, just be careful when you separate the case. We want to make sure that everything looks as natural as possible."

"Thank you, sis."

"Just let me know when you're at the right place. I'll cut the lights and let you get to work."

"Will do." The last few items of importance were familiar tools that she'd worked with in past jobs. A pair of nonslip socks and gloves, a roll of duct tape and two magnetic climbing handholds. She kicked her high heels off, stuffed them in her bag and slipped the socks on. She climbed the commode and stretched to feel around the vent shaft above. Four screws attached to the cover needed to be dealt with. She made quick work of them, stuck several pieces of duct tape to it and pressed the grate beside the dark opening in the wall. She shrugged into her backpack and hoisted herself up into the unknown.

"I'm in the vent," she said, pulling the grate over the opening. "I'm sticking the cover on with duct tape. I don't know how long it will last, but at least I'm hidden."

"Roger," Lawrence replied.

Celeste quickly shuffled horizontally in the darkness for a few feet before the vent bent at a ninety-degree angle. She rolled over onto her back and shimmied her upper body up the shaft and worked to stand.

It was time to use the magnetic handholds to scale the vent.

Celeste switched them on and began the labored process of sticking and unsticking her hands against the metal tunnel while her nonslip socks anchored her enough to rest her arms.

"This historian has far too many slides for this kind of audience," Magnus whispered in her ear. "But I can tell he's nearing the end. So, you might want to book it, CeCe."

She gritted her teeth as she unlocked one of her magnet handholds. When she pushed herself up, she gave a strained reply. "I hear you, Mags. I'm about halfway through this shaft. I can see the light… I'm looking forward to that blackout, Bea."

"Just remember," Bea cut in. "You've only got a matter of minutes before the officials figure out they need to run upstairs."

"Their priority should be getting these people out of the building before then," Magnus said. "By the time the lights come back on, you need to be out of the Treasury Room, CeCe."

"I know," she said, sweating under her wig. The muscles in her arms were on fire with every foot she climbed. Never did she anticipate this ventilation shaft being so fucking tall. But she was traveling to the second floor, and according to the 2018 remodel, the basement had been expanded, making her climb slightly shorter.

Thankfully, after several more minutes of upper-body strength she didn't realize she still had, Celeste was face-to-face with a second-floor vent. Her arms shook while she held herself to the grate covering, but she was securely stuck in place. As she peered through the narrow slats, her pulse quickened. "Fuck. I don't think this is the Treasury Room," she whispered.

"Okay, what do you see?" Beatrice asked.

She took a deep breath and studied the gallery in front of her. Her gaze snagged on a painting of a young woman with a cello on her lap and a lute in her hand. "Uh… I think this is a van der Helst. Maybe *The Musician*. Where does that put me?" Celeste asked, suddenly forgetting the layout of the second floor.

"It's the Dutch Golden Age… That means you're just outside of the Treasury Room. Please let me know when you want me to cut the lights."

"I'm going to kick out this vent, but I'll need to repair it with duct tape before I get inside the room. How long will I have before the steel gate comes down?"

Her protégé paused before answering. "Thirty seconds."

"Fine." Celeste took a few deep breaths. "Just give me a minute."

"CeCe…" Magnus whispered.

"Just give me a minute," she hissed. "Trust me for once."

He didn't reply.

Celeste steeled herself, wondering if she had what it took to trust *herself*. This wasn't five years ago. This was now. She was now in a ventilation shaft, wearing a beautiful ball gown, sweating like a pig. Celeste St. Pierre had the guts to pull this off. It was now or never. "Bea, cut the lights. Let's go."

36

Magnus impatiently tapped his foot in the air as he listened to the historian drone on and on about Johan Jensen's royal jewelry. This was his chance to let Celeste make decisions. This was his chance to trust her. Yet he was a mess of nerves, wondering if he could do his part to assist her. He listened to her exertions while she hauled herself up a ventilation shaft, hoping she'd have enough energy to complete the next task.

"Bea, cut the lights. Let's go."

"Okay. Wait—" Beatrice said in a panicked voice.

Magnus tensed in his chair. "What?" he whispered.

"I think we just got our distraction," Beatrice replied, now out of breath. He could hear her hurrying from one location to the next. From behind him, he could also hear the security guard's raised voices. He looked over his shoulder to find several guards who were not initially posted in the Great Hall, now running toward the entrance. "Guys, there's a car on fire near the—"

Boom!

The unexpected explosion made the gala attendees jump in their seats, while the inspector sprang from his.

"Oh, my God, a car just exploded," Beatrice said. "No one appears to be near it, but holy shit, it just exploded."

"Come away from that balcony, Bea," Lawrence snapped. "The plan is still the plan."

"Good," Celeste panted. "Because I really need y'all to cut these fucking lights."

By now, attendees were out of their chairs wondering where to move. Inspector Vermeulen was already running down the aisle and out of the Sculpture Garden. The shouts from the Great Hall grew louder as Magnus followed the excitement.

Suddenly, he found himself alone, blanketed in darkness. The only light streaming in from the museum entrance came from a massive fireball from across the street. Even from where he stood, he could smell the unmistakably acrid scent of gasoline.

He didn't have time to curse Sebastian's men for creating the most dangerous distraction because Beatrice had cut the power and gates were coming down. He could already hear Celeste frantically kicking out the grate cover. From inside the Sculpture Garden attendees finally understood something was wrong. Yelps and panicked shouts filtered out of the gallery while Magnus quietly made his way back toward the gift shop and back offices.

With Beatrice's intricate security hacking, the blackout wouldn't only hide their movements from security footage but also trigger the fire safety option in the employee exits, allowing certain doors to remain unlocked. Once the lights came back on, the doors would lock up again. Magnus had about ten minutes to get to the back exit, run through the café/gift shop storage and prop open the back security door that led to the loading dock behind the museum. After that, he'd need to get upstairs and wait for Celeste on the other side of the long hall of the Treasury Room.

Magnus skidded to a halt when he reached the gift shop door. With one last glance over his shoulder, he was certain that no one had followed him. It appeared that people were now crowding around the entrance. Many probably wondered if this was an actual emergency, while others understood it probably was, but refrained from doing anything because no one was able to confirm their fears. Unfortunately, the Swedes moved quite slowly in the face of danger.

Magnus pressed the night-vision toggle on his glasses and shoved against the employee exit. He was met with total darkness on the other side as he closed the door behind him. To his left, the stairwell; to his right, some offices; and right before him, the storage room.

His luck had held out for a little while longer as he tested the door. Unlocked. As he made his way through the unlit room, edging away from shelves and crates, he counted the seconds Celeste had before The Treasury closed off from the rest of the museum halls. About fifteen, maybe. She would make it.

She had to make it.

Magnus made it to the back door and opened it to the night air. He let out a relieved breath when he saw that the museum's rear was completely empty of pedestrians.

He went into his pockets and retrieved a small metal doorstop to prop open the back door before testing its strength. The gap between the door and the wall was just large enough to let a bit of light inside, but not noticeable from the outside. Once that was secure, Magnus ran through the storage room, back to the third part of his journey. He got through the door and jammed his tie clip right below the door hinges to keep it open for his return trip. Once he was back in the small hallway where the stairway to the second floor was, he whispered, "Gimme the time, Bea."

"Gates closed. Nine minutes, thirty seconds before auto-override," Beatrice said in a calm voice.

"You in, CeCe?" he asked.

Silence.

"Come in, CeCe. Do you copy?"

37

Once she heard the distant boom and the lights went out, it took her about fifteen seconds to kick out the grate. Another couple seconds to stick it back against the vent. And close to ten seconds to flat-out run toward the closing gate of the Treasury Room. As Celeste sprinted, her nonslip socks gripped every step and pushed her perilously closer toward danger. Toward her goal.

Ahead of her, the bottom of the gate was only two feet from the floor.

Adrenaline rushed through every nerve ending and blood vessel of her body as her arms pumped at her sides. Her only focus was what lay ahead of her, nothing else.

One.

Run...

Two.

Faster...

Three.

Now!

When Celeste drew closer to the gate and had enough momentum, she dropped to her side, slid against the polished hardwood floor, and the world slowed down. From behind her night-vision glasses, she saw the bright green line of the gate just above her. As she slid beneath the gate, Celeste angled her body so that her torso lay flat against the floor and her arms stretched wide on both sides. She held her breath until her head passed through the narrowing gap.

But it closed just as her hand made it through.

Celeste was shaken up, out of breath and sore…but she, sure as hell, made it to the other side. She couldn't help the broad smile that spread over her face as she scrambled to Freya's display.

Doing this work in the dark was going to be challenging and forced Celeste to work slower than she wanted. So she focused her gaze on the display case as she quickly pulled her tools from her backpack and found Beatrice's EMF device. After muttering a quiet prayer under her breath, she pressed it to the plexiglass and waited for the light to flicker on. When it lit up, she nearly cried with relief.

"It works," she told Beatrice. "It fucking works."

Now that localized security measures were turned off, Celeste could wrap the length of nylon rope around the entire pedestal and pull it from the wall. She yanked with both hands and managed about five inches of space between the display and the wall. "I'm going to pop the top now," she panted.

It hadn't occurred to Celeste that no one was answering her until she wedged a glass cutter in the impossibly narrow seam of the plexiglass. "Hey, anyone there?" she asked.

Silence.

Celeste frowned as she opened the acrylic case and began switching out the jewelry.

Why was no one speaking to her?

When she pushed the two real diamond-and-pearl earrings up the back of her wig, her hand brushed against her ear and her heart immediately dropped. Celeste dug her finger into her ear and felt the absence of an earpiece. When had she lost it?

Most likely in the sweaty scramble to get out of the vent, or while sliding under the gate. Somewhere in that distance, it must have fallen out of her ear.

"Fuck," she swore, sliding the diamond-and-sapphire necklace down the front of her dress. The metal and jewels scratched her skin as they settled between her breasts. Next, the tiara... Celeste hitched her flowing skirts up her thigh and carefully wrapped the delicate crown just above her knee.

She had no idea how much time she'd spent inside the Treasury Room, nor how much time until the lights would come back on. It was Beatrice who walked her through the jobs, who kept her focused on the prize. Celeste was now on her own and hated every second of it. She wanted to retrace her steps and find her earpiece but knew there wasn't time.

She had to rely on Lawrence's tracking device stuck to her thigh and the camera in her glasses. Even if she couldn't communicate with the command center, they could still see what she was seeing.

So she took a deep breath and focused on placing Magnus's reproductions under glass. With trembling hands, she hung the earrings from their metal poles, placed the tiara on the plastic stand and draped the necklace just below.

Repairing the case, shoving the pedestal back in place and removing the EMF device went faster than Celeste imagined, but a good thief always took time to wipe down surfaces and check her surroundings for leftover tools.

"CeCe?"

She nearly let out a yelp when she heard the harsh whisper in the distance behind her. She looked over her shoulder toward the darkened Turn of the Century gallery. "Mags?"

"Where the fuck is your earpiece?" His whisper-shout was loud enough to carry to her location.

Her heart floated when she recognized his annoyed voice. She grabbed her backpack and ran down the corridor. "It fell out of my ear," she said as she drew closer to him. Magnus propped the door open with half of his body, frantically waving her down. She flew into his arms and let him pull her through the doorway. In the darkness, she shoved her backpack at him. "Hold this," she said. "I need to put my shoes back on."

"According to Beatrice, we have four minutes until the lights come back on."

Celeste worked quickly to secure straps around her heels and ankles. "Did the explosion pull everyone to the entrance?"

"I think so," he muttered. "I didn't see anyone in the back."

They descended the unlit stairway until they reached the back corridor and the offices of the museum. Magnus had one hand tight on her arm, and the other on her supply bag.

"Sluta!" shouted a voice coming down the hall, opposite them. "Gå på golvet!"

A sudden beam of light flashed across them, but through the darkness. A lone security guard quickly approached, his flashlight bouncing with each step. Celeste stopped abruptly behind Magnus, bumping into him hard. The light ahead of them was nearly blinding with their night vision, but Celeste could clearly see what waited for them.

The guard was about the same large size and build as the man who detained Santiago and he was pulling a gun from his holster. Magnus tightened his grip on her as he stepped back. "Hey, we're just lost," he called out. "My wife and I got separated. I was only looking for her."

"Get on the ground!" the guard repeated in English. He was a few feet away from them, shining the flashlight in their faces.

Even while the man shouted at them, Celeste noticed that her bag had shifted from Magnus's side to his back. "Run when I say run," he said, pulling something from the backpack.

The tranquilizer gun.

Upon seeing it, Celeste's heart jumped into her throat while the guard moved himself into firing position, shouting, "Drop the weapon!"

He didn't.

Magnus shoved her into what she hoped was the storage room before pulling the trigger. She heard the soft swoosh of the dart, but the guard's firearm was much louder. Celeste screamed at the sound and turned just in time to see Magnus's body whip around from the impact.

She grabbed him by the lapels, pulled him into the storage room and slammed the door behind them. "Oh, my God, oh, my God," she cried, leaning him against the wall. "Oh, Mags, what have you done?"

He groaned. "I got him."

"Goddamn it, he got you, too!" she said, feeling around his body for the wound. When she patted his arms, her hand came away wet and warm. Upon further inspection, she felt a hole in his sleeve. One in the back of his triceps, another in the front of his biceps. "Clean through, it feels like."

"Bea says we have forty seconds of darkness left," he said, holding his arm.

Jesus, there's never enough time...

Celeste dragged him to the back door, all the while fervently praying that they could get outside before being spotted by surveillance cameras. "Hold on to me," she whispered. The door he'd propped open was still a viable exit. Celeste nudged it open and breathed the largest gulp of fresh air. Sirens blared outside, but as far as she could tell, they were in front of the museum.

Back here, the loading dock was quiet. Just beyond the property was a side street and park. If she could just get them moving in the right direction, they'd be at the Grand in no time. "How are you doing?" she asked Magnus. He stumbled over his feet while leaning heavily on her shoulder.

"Dizzy," he panted.

As frightened as she was, Celeste had to ignore her own feelings. Even though she knew he was losing blood, she pretended this was just another night of him on Ambien. She got him to the alleyway before propping him against another wall and removing his necktie. "I need to tie a tourniquet on your arm until we get to the hotel room," she said, struggling to keep her voice flat.

"That's a good idea," he said.

She tried to ignore how pale his lips had become. "Please stay awake, Magnus," she whispered as she tied his arm off.

"I will," he said earnestly. "I'm not going to leave you."

Celeste pushed down her tears as she slung his good arm over her shoulder. "Let's get you out of here, husband."

"Yes, wife."

38

He dipped in and out of consciousness several times while Celeste carried him. At one point, Magnus remembered feeling the cool breeze of the night air. Another time, he remembered Beatrice slapping him awake. But the next time he woke up, Magnus found himself inside a bathtub, getting jabbed with a needle and thread.

"Ow, Goddammit," he groused, opening his eyes to the bright lights and once-sterile tiles of a hotel bathroom. Thank God they were back at the Grand. When his eyes finally focused, they landed on the most beautiful sight: Celeste St. Pierre. Her disheveled wig tumbled over her forehead as her attention focused on the pain in his arm. Her face was red and puffy from crying, but she set her full lips in a thin grimace as she concentrated on stitching him up.

Beatrice sat on the edge of the tub near his feet, watching in horror as Celeste worked.

"Give me the gauze," Celeste said in a soft voice. He sleepily watched Beatrice retrieve a metal box from the floor. She handed over a roll of white bandages before going back to biting her thumbnail. He said nothing as Celeste lifted his arm and wound gauze around it. When she tied it off, she finally looked him in the eyes.

"Thank you," he breathed.

Her face crumpled into a sob, one that she was probably holding back as she worked. "You got hurt…"

Magnus sighed and closed his eyes. "A flesh wound," he said with a heavy breath.

Celeste bent over the tub and cried harder. "He could have killed you."

"He could have killed *you*," he countered. *Why didn't she understand that?* It was his job to protect her…he thought she knew that by now. "I love you too much for you to get hurt again, Celeste."

His blurry gaze fell on Beatrice, who was now crying at his feet.

"Why are you crying, Bea?" he asked, trying to keep his tone light. His dry chuckle quickly became a cough.

Beatrice reached into the tub and touched his leg. "I'm crying because you're alive," she hiccuped.

He closed his eyes again. "Why am I in a tub, wife?"

Celeste stroked his hair from his sweaty forehead. "Because we can't have you bleeding all over this very expensive suite. I had to sneak you through a back entrance to avoid suspicion."

"I'm sorry for bleeding," he breathed.

"No, I'm sorry," she said, cupping his cheek.

Her touch against his clammy, cold face was all he needed. Her warm fingers felt like the first mug of coffee before the start of a long teaching day. He needed her to keep touching him, petting him. When he thought her hand was leaving him, he reached up and clasped it against his chest. "Don't leave," he murmured.

"I won't," she whispered.

Beatrice looked between the two of them before standing.

"I'm going to help pack up the comms station. I assume we leave in the morning?"

"Possibly tonight. Sebastian said he'd get us out of here after he collects Santi. Get ready to move."

"Sounds good," Beatrice said as she drifted from his view.

"Sebastian?" Magnus was half listening, but what little he'd heard sounded encouraging. "Has he come for his car bombing goons?"

Celeste scrubbed a hand over her brow and nodded. "And us. He's getting Santiago out of jail now. We'll try to leave as soon as possible."

"So, we did it?" he asked, lifting his good arm to touch her. "We did what Doris asked?"

Her black-rimmed eyes met his with wariness as she stood up. Magnus watched as she pulled her skirt from the knees, past her ankles to her shins. Just above her left knee, a shiny flash of metal and diamond glittered beneath the fabric. When she revealed her entire leg, Magnus let out a startled laugh.

"We did. Five years later, but yeah," she said, trying to keep her voice steady.

He understood the tremor in her voice. He felt the same mix of excitement and fear. There would be no post-job glow that evening. Instead, Magnus was just thankful that everyone was alive.

"Jesus Christ…" he murmured.

She slipped the tiara from her leg and laid it on top of his chest. "We did it, and frankly, I don't think we should ever do it again."

He ran his fingers along the diamonds and silver frame and shook his head. "You don't mean that, CeCe. We're alive and both of us are too stupid to quit. Just give it a few months."

She sighed. "Fair… But if you don't mind, I won't return to Stockholm. I'm done with this city."

Magnus was completely on board with that. "Fair. I should get changed if we're leaving soon."

"You're not doing anything right now," Celeste said. "Except maybe go to bed. Can you get out of the tub?"

"I think so," he said as he pulled himself up. He winced at the pain shooting up his arm. "Is there anything you can give me for the pain?"

Celeste nibbled on her bottom lip. "I've got extra strength Tylenol."

"Anything in the minibar?"

"I used all the vodka on your arm."

Magnus grinned as he rested his head against the cold tile. "You're so smart."

"Can I lift you?"

"I don't want to—" He stopped himself when he saw her smile.

"Oh, shut up, Mags. I love you too much to let you crawl to bed."

She said it. She loves me.

He was probably still lightheaded from the loss of blood, but Magnus suddenly felt weightless. His heart was buoyant from her snarky admission.

39

"Huh, this is a slightly nicer yacht than the one I chartered," Santiago said, stepping on board. His bag hung heavy off his shoulder, and he still wore the same suit he was arrested in, but he looked good.

Before anyone could greet him, Beatrice screeched and nearly tackled him to the deck. Sebastian stepped away to avoid getting hit. Celeste jumped up from her seat, hoping to get a hug in, but Beatrice hung off Santi's frame like a baby sloth.

"I can't believe you're here! I'm so sorry I didn't save you!"

Santiago chuckled as he rubbed her back and kissed her cheek. "Don't worry, Bonita, you'll probably get another chance."

When Beatrice finally released him, Celeste scrubbed his buzz cut with her knuckles. "I'm glad to see you, jailbird. They treat you okay?"

"As far as jail goes, this place was decent. Luckily, Sebastian is a good actor. I have a feeling that the real US Embassy lawyers aren't nearly as threatening as he is."

"It was quite thrilling," Sebastian admitted. "I hadn't felt a rush like that since working with Doris."

Celeste held out her hand. "Thank you for coming through. We really appreciate your help."

Sebastian skipped her hand and pulled her in for a hug. "I may not have stolen anything, but you managed to make an old man feel alive again." He pulled away and peered at her. "Speaking of which, what did you think of my distraction? Très théâtral, oui?"

Celeste tried to bury her grimace under a smile. "I wish you had let us know that your diversion tactics were that explosive."

The old man managed a contrite shrug. "It was a nod to Doris. We'd done something similar during the Cold War... My apologies, mademoiselle. How is Larsson faring?"

"Magnus is below deck, sleeping off a gunshot wound."

The old man grimaced. "Merde... And the jewels?"

"Acquired."

"Excellent travail, chérie," he said, patting her on the shoulder. "I think it's more than time for us to shove off. Tallinn anyone?"

"Tallinn, please," Santiago said.

Once Sebastian and his men were on board, the captain set sail due east. Celeste and the rest of the crew descended below deck to regroup and check on Magnus, who had woken up.

"Why aren't you in bed?" Celeste demanded.

He was in the middle of changing shirts with one working arm and managed to get his face stuck in an armhole. "This is the first time Celeste St. Pierre is trying to lure me into bed."

She helped adjust his shirt, pushing it over his head. "What are you doing?" she asked, pulling it down his torso.

"I sweat through my other shirt," he hissed as she lifted his arm. "Did we get Santi?"

"I'm here, mano!"

They gathered in a common room outside the cabins, all of them breathing a sigh of relief as the gentle hum of the yacht's engine vibrated throughout the vessel.

"I think we're due for a rundown of events," Lawrence said, clapping his hands. "Some of us missed all the action."

"A damn shame, too," Santiago said from behind the bar. As

he made his drink, Celeste noted how Beatrice couldn't take her eyes off him. She smiled to Magnus, who couldn't seem to stop staring at her. "Magnus, have you ever been shot before?"

"Nope," he said, collapsing into a nearby chair. "And I don't plan on making a habit out of it."

"Was anyone ID'd?" Santiago asked.

"Not yet," Beatrice said. "The last image of Celeste is her going to the basement bathroom and then the lights went out. The security guard who Magnus knocked out may have seen your faces...but it's hard to say what he's going to remember under the influence."

Lawrence chuckled. "Poor guy is gonna wake up with a nasty hangover."

"When the inspector and curators go upstairs, they're going to find a completely locked down Treasury Room," Beatrice said with a grin. "And with all the confusion, there's no way the police have interviewed everyone who attended the gala. Collections will eventually realize they have costume jewelry, but not tonight."

"And the princess?" Santiago asked. "Will she be questioned?"

"She's long gone."

For her part, Princess Astrid left an interesting trail of social media posts detailing her evening. One TikTok video was captioned: "Get ready with me for my last royal engagement." While her makeup artist worked on her face, she shared her plans to bow out of the Swedish royal family to millions of followers. At the gala, she made an Instagram boomerang of her knocking back a glass of champagne. That caption read, "Thankful that Svenska jewels are safe again! #Freya #Boss-Girl."

The last TikTok the princess made for the night was posted while she was on a private jet. She lip-synced to a catchy pop song while showing off her left hand. A giant diamond graced her ring finger. Her massive following made the news of her engagement go viral within minutes. Celeste was impressed with the young woman's ability to be a distraction.

Santiago took a long swig of whiskey. "Did we truly get away with this?"

The rest of the crew silently looked around at one another, probably afraid to admit they'd pulled it off. In the hours after the robbery, yes, they'd made it, but a couple days from now could be different. Maybe the grate above that toilet stall would fall off. Maybe the inspector would study the footage before and after the blackout. Maybe one of the witnesses remembers a Black woman who seemed like she didn't quite belong there…

"We got the jewels," Magnus finally said.

"Hear, hear!" Lawrence said, raising a beer.

"Hear, hear."

March 30, 2023

Oh, they're going to hate this.

And there's a good chance they will hate each other.

But I have too many hopes that trump their petty squabbles. I hope that Magnus finds it in his heart to come back to the fold. I hope Celeste accepts him. I hope that Santiago desires another adventure with his friends. I feel like he's just as lonely as the other two, but he pretends to be too happy to admit it. Lastly, I pray that Lawrence has the strength to tolerate all of them.

It's strange knowing that the end is coming for me. It certainly doesn't feel like this train should be pulling into the last station, but here I am, checking my watch and gathering my bags. While it feels strange, I'm not frightened of the end. I will finally get to rest. I will see Momma and Daddy again. Cousin Willy will be waiting for me. And when we're reunited, maybe then I'll tell them about my life. It would be nice to tell someone…

I just don't want to go before I've made my peace with the crew.

I hope they know how much I love each and every one of them. I hope Celeste knows how much she's like a daughter to me. I spent so many years trying to shape and mold her, only to miss the woman she actually grew into. I don't remember telling her how proud I am of her accomplishments. It wasn't just about the paintings and jewels she stole. Celeste surpassed me in so many ways. I should have told her to be with Magnus. He's who she actually needs.

Lord, I hope she realizes that before it's too late.

I don't want her to be alone.

We all need someone. Especially near the end. I have Lawrence, my most trusted friend, but I should have worked hard for the rest. I would trade away most of my Baroque collection in the Long Island estate for another chance to see Sebastian again. If only to bump into him on the street and steal his wallet. Sometimes I dream of his pale green eyes, caught in the backdrop of a brilliant blue Mediterranean Sea. I wake up and feel a fullness in my heart. I smile and wonder how he's doing. If he still enjoys Estonia like we did in the eighties...

I can be thankful, though.

I'm happy that I lived my truth.

A Black girl from Biloxi, Mississippi, is only born with so much. The rest she picks up along the way. Some of it is luck; some of it is grit. I got both. I saw the world, loved deeply and stole so many things. The truth is, I'm quite extraordinary. I'm giggling as I write this, but it's true. I've lived an enviable life. I hope Celeste gets to live this life as well.

Celeste had tears in her eyes by the time she closed the journal. Doris's last entry, plus the end of this job, broke the dam. She sat at the foot of the bed she shared with Magnus and wept.

This time, she cried tears of relief.

She was thankful that Doris was no longer suffering. She

was glad that Doris had taught her everything she knew before leaving this Earth.

"Are you okay?" Magnus asked, standing in the cabin's doorway.

Celeste looked up and smiled. "I think so?"

She was lucky to have *him*.

"You've been crying," he said with narrowed eyes. "You rarely cry."

She shrugged. "When I do, it's for a good reason. I'm crying because I love Doris and I miss her."

Magnus pulled away from the threshold and sat beside her. "You'll cry about her from time to time, then. She was quite the woman."

"She had quite the life," Celeste said, quoting the diary entry.

"I know," he said, taking her hand. "Because she taught you. And I love you."

This was her second time hearing the words, but she believed them. Magnus, for all his faults, loved her...for all her faults.

"When did you know that you loved me?" she asked.

Magnus appeared to think about it for a moment. "While we were ring shopping." He reached down by the bed and hauled his go bag up to his lap. "When we played Ball and Chain, you made me feel something I hadn't felt in years. It scared the hell out of me."

He pulled a tiny box out of the bag and Celeste instantly recognized it. He popped it open with his thumb and presented the contents to her.

An emerald set in a ring of diamonds.

"You didn't sell this?" she exclaimed.

Magnus grinned sheepishly as he held the ring aloft. "It was hard to keep this to myself when it matched your gown perfectly last night."

"Mags, why would you keep this?" she asked in a hushed

voice while extending her hand. She stopped herself short of actually touching the small velvet box.

"I just never got around to it," he said weakly.

She shot him a deadpan look. "Really?"

He shrugged. "Truthfully, I wasn't confident in my abilities to work with you at that counter. You were right to be frustrated with me that day. We could have pulled it off. I just didn't have faith."

As she searched her memory of that day, she found the moment on the street when he looked insecure. He had evaded her with his excuses, but she felt like something was off. "But you've kept it this long?"

"As a reminder," he admitted. "To work with you, not counter."

"Is it mine?" she asked in a soft voice.

"Everything I have belongs to you, Celeste," he told her.

The tears came back in full force because the value of the ring didn't matter. It was his earnestness, his promise to her.

"I love you, Magnus." She finally held her hand out, palm down.

He grinned and shook his head. "Left hand, my love."

"Oops!" She switched hands. He started to slip it on her finger when she quickly jerked it back. "Wait, no! If you're going to do this, don't you think you should do it right? Get on one knee."

He paused, narrowed his eyes and cocked his head. "Yeah?"

"If we're no longer pretending, I want you where you belong. On your knees."

Magnus immediately slid off the bed and onto his knee. "Will you be a geology professor's wife, for real this time?"

Celeste gave a watery chuckle. "If I'm going to be married to a geologist, it must be you. I only want you."

He slipped the ring on her finger and kissed her knuckles. "You have me."

Her tears couldn't be abated. She choked back a sob as she slid off the bed to join him. She took him by the face and kissed him deeply. He took her by the waist with his good arm and drew her closer. She couldn't help but return to Doris's last diary entry and think about hope and gratitude.

She was thankful that she had him.

She'd hoped they could grow old together.

EPILOGUE

Four months later…

Beatrice leaned against the bar, staring at her mentor and Magnus. *Good Lord, they were so adorable.*

"They're going to get married, you know," Santiago whispered in her ear. "And then we'll be the only 'will-they-won't-they' couple left. Dios mío, Bonita…our sexual tension is already hitting the roof."

She turned to face him and almost bumped into his plush lips. As she slowly tore her eyes away from his mouth, Beatrice found her face growing hot. He did this to her at every turn. "I think we're just fine where we are."

Santiago chuckled darkly as he ran his hand over his closely cropped hair. She fought everything in her body to avoid his advances. She'd wanted to sleep with him in Estonia, but decided against it. Based on Celeste, she wasn't sure if it was a good idea.

Now that her mentor had come back to her one true love, Beatrice was now reconsidering.

"I know we've worked as a crew," Santiago said. "But I think these two lovebirds will be busy with being straight for a minute. In the meantime, I've got a lead on a two-man job."

Bea's ear perked up. "Really?"

"The mark is in Philly. If you're interested, I could use a techie in the field."

Electricity hummed through her body in the same way her arousal to Santiago affected her. "Yes!" she said, excitedly.

"Excellent," he said with a wicked grin. Celeste was right. He was like the devil incarnate. His mustache twitched as he stared at her lips. She desperately wanted to stroke his goatee. *Oh, God... I need to talk to Celeste.* "I have a feeling you and I will have a wonderful time," he said in her ear.

The hairs on the back of her neck lifted as his hot breath brushed against her ear. "I think I'm down."

"When I say I really didn't expect this meeting with you—" Celeste said loudly. The loud and steady thumping of techno music made it difficult to communicate. "—I mean it."

Princess Astrid shooed her bodyguard away before sitting at a small two-top table. "You and your man deserve to be haunted by me for just a little while longer," she said, slapping her purse on the table. She flicked her hair over her shoulder before taking a sip of her cocktail. "Speaking of which, where is he?"

Celeste gestured over her shoulder at Magnus, who was at the bar with Santiago and Beatrice. When she received a message from their old friend Aksel, regarding the princess, Celeste thought it would be a good idea to invite her to the bar Santiago ran in the Meatpacking District.

"How is that going?" the princess asked in a sweet voice.

"Why are you here?" Celeste asked, getting back to the topic at hand.

"I'll be honest with you," she said. "America is...different. While I now enjoy my freedom with my fiancé, I am lonely for friends. Real friends. Not the kind that know that I'm a Swedish princess."

Celeste raised a brow at this news. *The girl needed friends.* "Are you being serious?"

"I knew you lived here, and I wanted to catch up. Also, I wanted to update you on Inspector Vermeulen."

Celeste was already on top of the news. A month after the car bomb incident, Nationalmuseum released a statement that the Freya jewels had, once again, been taken. A new investigation had been opened and so far, Interpol didn't have any hard leads. Inspector Hugo Vermeulen and the museum had been roundly criticized by the press, who now turned against them in favor of the poor princess.

"My family has given up on the jewels. As far as they're concerned, Freya's jewels are lost for good. According to my siblings, my parents simply want to bury the story," she chuckled. "They've apologized to me, though. My mother wants me to have my wedding in Sweden, at the very least. I'm not sure what I'll do now that I have a whole kingdom rooting for me."

"No longer the black sheep in your family?" Celeste asked with a grin.

Astrid flipped her brown hair over her shoulder. "I'm Sweden's darling now."

Thank God… It was hard not to feel something for the girl who made such a drastic decision to change her life. Celeste was relieved that they could work together to help make that happen, and to atone for their sins. "And your fiancé? How is that going?"

A broad smile spread over her face and brightened her whole being. "I'm so happy," she breathed. "Martin makes me feel like I'm the most important woman on Earth. I wake up every morning feeling like a goddess. And I love him so much. He's smart and funny and kind. It also helps that he's wealthy… He makes me feel like I can be someone outside what I was born as. Does that make sense?"

To Celeste, it made perfect sense.

Because Magnus made her feel the same thing. When she felt a hand on her shoulder, she jumped. He was at her side. "Hello, Princess."

She rolled her eyes. "Astrid is fine, thank you."

"Förlåt, Astrid."

"Tack så mycket, Magnus."

"So, what about you two?" she asked, taking another delicate sip. "What will you do now that you've stolen my family's heirlooms?"

Celeste and Magnus looked at one another, smiling and feeling the same emotions that Astrid described between her and Martin. Magnus was back to teaching and Celeste was back to minding her store. She had a number of customers beating down her door and online orders to fulfill. They broke down every piece of the Swedish heirlooms and fenced them in several different directions. The funds were split among five crew members. Celeste gave her cut to the Harrison Home for the Youth.

"We're taking it easy," Celeste said, staring into Magnus's clear blue eyes.

He smirked as his eyes darted to her mouth. "We're trying normal for a while. We'll see how long that will carry us."

"Normal for a minute," she countered. "But after that, I think we'll probably want to get back into the fray."

Magnus leaned closer to her and whispered, "I kinda like the fray. Especially with you."

★ ★ ★ ★ ★

ACKNOWLEDGMENTS

Noah: Thank you for listening to me. Every time I leave my office to complain about the writing process, you've acknowledged that difficulty while urging me to get back to the challenge. I'm thankful that we have a similar sense of adventure and imagination. I'm thankful that you see things for what they could be and push me to do the same.

Saritza: I am incredibly lucky that I can bring all my ideas to you. Your continued excitement validates my work and makes me feel like I'm capable of pulling off ambitious jobs. The way you treat me and your other clients, advocating on our behalf, is a testament to your passion for the craft and justice in this industry. You're not just an ally, but an accomplice in changing the literary landscape.

Errin: Our relationship over the last two books hasn't only been "I write a book and you correct it." Our partnership has been far deeper than that, bordering on alchemy. Your editorial ability and imagination have driven me to look beyond plot and characters and get to the heart of a love story. Each question you've posed inspires me to find meaning in every chapter.

Thank you for taking the time and doing the labor on my behalf. Thank you for helping me turn a manuscript into a *book*.

My therapist, Kristina: It would have been nearly impossible to write about grief, let alone turn it into a rollicking adventure, without your help in healing my own grief. Talking to you about Mary and Shirley has helped me confront their passing and see these women as whole individuals, their flaws and all. Thank you for guiding me through this healing journey so that I could write about Doris and Celeste and their complicated relationship.

My cover artist, Monika Roe: Thank you for transforming my nebulous vision into the beautiful, finished product that ends up on bookshelves, far and wide. You bring excitement to my story and prepare readers for the adventure that awaits them. I appreciate the artistry you bring to the romance genre.

Readers, old and new: My beta readers who got a hold of early versions of Celeste and Magnus, thank you for giving me the feedback I needed to improve my craft. To reviewers, fans and future folks who pick up this book, thank you for taking a chance and making the investment in my work. These stories start off belonging to *me*…but eventually, they become *yours*. It excites me to know that you might request this book from your local library, you might listen to this audiobook while you're on the subway or maybe this book ends up on your nightstand, folded page corners and broken spines, thoroughly enjoyed.

Lastly, I started this book in 2019, thinking it would be my second published work. It turns out, I wasn't ready to write Celeste and Magnus's story until six books later. Even then, the project was still quite ambitious. I hated that I couldn't get it right on the first try, but I'm glad that I worked hard to get it right, eventually. I'm thankful that the people around me could see the future and believe in my abilities even while I floundered. So, I'd like to end the acknowledgment process by thanking *myself*.

Thank you, Charish, for sticking with this when it got too overwhelming. I'm extremely proud of you for not giving up on what felt too ambitious. Thank you for being reckless enough to accept a new challenge. I can't wait to see where you go next.